M000028793

"Charming. A feel-good story with a touch of humor. You'll be smiling when you finish the last page."

~ **Rachel Hauck**, *NY Times* Bestselling author

"Heartwarming and uplifting, *Her Faith Restored* by Cynthia Herron is like a down-home visit at Ida Mae's Come and Get It Diner with a slice of apple pie and cinnamon ice cream while running into old friends and meeting new ones. This trip to Ruby provides another wonderful read centered around a pair of sparring co-workers who find working together can lead to inspiring results. Highly recommended for a relaxing evening, as the Thanksgiving and Christmas season provides the perfect backdrop for a cast of characters that will work their way into your hearts and leave you satisfied yet looking forward to another installment."

~ **Tanya Agler**, author of *The Sheriff's Second Chance* and *The Single Dad's Holiday Match*

"In *Her Faith Restored* Cynthia Herron has penned a family-driven tale of sweet romance and friendship that isn't afraid to go deep in questions of faith. Softly vulnerable and willingly open, readers of Cynthia Ruchti, Karen Kingsbury and Francine Rivers will be at home in charming Ruby. Lovingly told with snappy dialogue and a small-town canvas I would love to visit, readers will find Inspirational fiction's answer to *Virgin River* and be clamoring for a Netflix adaptation of its own!"

~ **Rachel McMillan**, author of *The London Restoration* and *The Mozart Code*

"Her Faith Restored swept me away! Cynthia Herron is a Picasso of the pen. She tugged at my heartstrings with this lovely romantic tale. Her gorgeous descriptions bring the characters to life. Readers are in for a treat."

~Preslaysa Williams, author of *A Lowcountry Bride*

Her Faith Restored

The Welcome to Ruby Series

Her Faith Restored

The Welcome to Ruby Series, Book Three

By
Cynthia Herron

MBI

Her Faith Restored
Published by Mountain Brook Ink
White Salmon, WA U.S.A.

The website addresses shown in this book are not intended in any way to be or imply an endorsement on the part of Mountain Brook Ink, nor do we vouch for their content.

This story is a work of fiction. All characters and events are the product of the author's imagination. Any resemblance to any person, living or dead, is coincidental.

Scripture quotations are taken from the King James Version of the Bible. Public domain.

ISBN 9781953957-18-4

The Team: Miralee Ferrell, Alyssa Roat, Cindy Jackson
Cover Design: Indie Cover Design, Lynnette Bonner Designer

The Author is represented by and this book is published in association with the literary agency of WordServe Literary Group., Ltd, www.wordserveliterary.com.

Mountain Brook Ink is an inspirational publisher offering fiction you can believe in.
Printed in the United States of America

Dedication

For those who dream big dreams.

In memory of my beloved Daddy, my hero.

Now faith is the substance of things hoped for, the evidence of things not seen.

Hebrews 11:1 KJV

Acknowledgments

If I could step back in time and envision the Welcome to Ruby series from that vantage point, I'm sure I'd still have the same stars in my eyes and a familiar spring in my step. The dreamer, the believer, and the achiever in me would still grab life by the coattails anticipating all the goodness that was sure to come. I'd celebrate the birth of this little series with chocolate cake, sweet tea, and party streamers, and invite you along for the joy-filled ride!

Fast-forward three years to a new season and a new perspective. *Her Hope Discovered*, *His Love Revealed*, and now, *Her Faith Restored* are in readers' hands, and I'm still utterly delighted about that. There has, however, been a poignancy to this fabulous ride. Along the way, I lost loved ones—beautiful, faithful souls—who influenced my journey and shaped my writing life. I will forever be grateful, and I look forward to the day we will all meet again.

Dearest Daddy, you are forever my guy. My hero. After God, and before my husband and I married, my first love. Every word I write, every story I create, your encouragement is imprinted upon my spirit. Your words travel with me during my fictional trips. Thank you for teaching me about Jesus and everlasting life. It's because of your guidance we'll get to spend eternity together in the final chapter of the ultimate true story.

To my precious Aunt Charlene, I hold your sweet

countenance close. Your laughter, your tenacity, your heart for Jesus and His people, remain foremost in my mind. Thank you for teaching me to see others through the lens of love, rather than the eyes of judgment.

To the spirited, special woman who was my mother-in-law—Carole "Mom"—your resolve and hardiness linger in mind, assuring me that I can rise above the weight of the world because of the One who carries it.

To my family, extended family, loved ones, and friends, I'm so grateful for your continued support. I treasure you.

As always, a heartfelt thank you to my awesome agent Sarah and the WordServe Literary team for embracing this author and enhancing the journey.

And to Miralee Ferrell and the Mountain Brook Ink team—my deepest gratitude for catching my vision and helping me expand it. Thank you for giving wings to *Her Faith Restored*, book three in the Welcome to Ruby series.

Chapter One

Wrapped in Autumn's gold curtain and nestled deep within the Ozark foothills, Ruby, Missouri shone like a beacon. A close-knit community reminiscent of old ways while cognizant of new seasons, the little town glimmered in the lazy morning sunshine. The good Lord must smile on days such as this—days His timing was impeccable and His plan, perfect...even if, in our humanity, we sometimes wondered.

Why today of all days? Hadn't they maintained civility up to this point?

"He didn't mean it, Mel."

"Yes, he did." Melinda Brewer paced to the window of her office and back again. She met her friend's wide-eyed gaze with equal emotion. "Matthew Enders meant every measured word. In fact, he's been full of words since he came here six months ago."

To his credit, Enders' vocabulary rivaled Webster's. His favorite word, though, was a simple one. *Change.* When Mel considered the many changes that the new social services director had implemented at Sunset Meadows, it set her teeth on edge. She might have less clout than Enders, but she did have seniority. And as the facility's activity director she wasn't about to let him run roughshod over her plans and programs.

"If he thinks I'm going to step aside and watch him undermine everything I've accomplished in the past five years, then I have news for him. But I'll break it to him in a Christian kind of way, of course."

"Shh. He'll hear you." Her friend Sarah Dawson closed the door.

"And another thing—for him to call me 'childish' showed a complete lack of professionalism. I know the inner workings of this place like the back of my hand. That newbie doesn't know a service plan from a coffee cup."

"I believe Matt referred to it as *infantile*."

"What? Oh. Semantics." Mel waved her hand. "For him to say something like that within earshot of the residents and my fellow co-workers was rude and ego-driven."

Sarah studied her for a second and smiled. "What is it that's really bothering you, Mel?"

Hmm. Where to begin?

Mel plopped down behind her desk and kicked off her heels. It didn't take long to come up with a list. "Everything about the man bothers me. His new ideas when there's nothing wrong with my old ones. His morale-boosters. The new paint color he suggested for the activity room. The way he smirks when he thinks he's right. His choice of clothing. The truck he drives. That silly little gap between his two front teeth. The fact he could use a haircut. Should I continue?"

"No, not really. I get the picture." Sarah sat down in the chair across from her desk and leaned forward. "But let me say—not as The Meadows' office manager, but as friend to friend—from what I've observed, Matt Enders seems to be a man of integrity. He really wants to help people and most of the changes he's made have been good ones with the residents' best interests in mind. He's kind, compassionate, and easygoing. Everyone seems to like him except—"

"Me." Mel sighed. "I don't know, Sarah. I guess our personalities clash."

Her friend thought for a minute and nodded. "Could be. But you know, I think your personalities are similar. You're both go-getters, though perhaps, you're a tad more...um...spirited."

Yes, that's what her brothers said. In fact, her tenacity was what landed her the job here. She wasn't one to sit on the fence. She got things done.

"And that's always served me well. And Sunset Meadows, too, of course."

"I have to say it. Matt Enders isn't here to upset the apple cart. He's here for the same reasons you are." Sarah hesitated. "You guys may have your differences, but at the end of the day, you share similar goals. You shouldn't let a little diversity sideline your working relationship."

Mel laughed without mirth. "For heaven's sake, Sarah, in the six months Matt Enders has been here, our 'working relationship' has been strained at best."

Sarah cocked her head. "Why do you think that is?"

"Beats me." Enders grated on her nerves. She couldn't explain why.

"Well...could it be something you haven't considered?"

"Like what?"

"Like maybe you two have a thing for each other?"

Mel shot up from her chair and started to pace again. "You must be joking, Sarah."

"No. I'm not. When Andy and I first met, we couldn't stand each other. Remember?"

"But you two have been married four years!"

"Exactly. God's ways are wondrous to behold."

The knock at Mel's office door halted that train of thought. Grateful for the interruption, she ran a hand through her shoulder-length, auburn waves and slipped back into her heels. "I guess that's our cue to continue this later."

"I can't wait." Sarah rose to go. When she opened the door, she gasped. "Oh! Hello, Matt."

"Sarah." Then he directed his gaze toward Mel. "I'm sorry, Miss Brewer. I didn't realize you were in a meeting."

"Yes. Well, we're done now. Is there something you need?"

Matt Enders stepped aside to permit Sarah's graceful exit. "You could say that. Do you have a minute?"

As usual, his attire was the same—polo shirt and blue jeans—in an obvious effort to blend in around here. Casual and not too preppy. About right for the small, picturesque town of Ruby, Missouri and almost appropriate for his work place of the past several months.

His jet-black hair was neatly combed, though a little shaggy around the ears. The slight gap between his bright, white teeth wasn't as noticeable, probably due to recent orthodontic treatments. Mel hadn't meant to eavesdrop when Matt mentioned it to one of The Meadows' residents the other day.

She almost cringed when she recalled her harsh assessment of the man. Since when had she started to judge people by their appearance? It certainly wasn't a Christian thing to do, nor was it something she was proud of. It was a wonder Sarah hadn't taken her to task over it earlier.

They might not agree on various work-related issues, but it was wrong to criticize Matt's physical characteristics. If he rated *her* on a personal beauty scale, he might notice she was about ten pounds overweight and had one too many freckles.

"Come in." Mel gestured toward her inner sanctum.

"Thanks. Mind if I shut the door?"

Why? What earth-shattering piece of news merited a closed door? Was there another change he wanted to discuss? She forced her features to remain neutral.

"Easy, Miss Brewer—Melinda—I won't bite."

Said the spider to the fly.

"Be my guest." Mel brushed invisible lint from her navy slacks and slipped behind her desk as Matt closed the office door.

"Feel like you need a barrier, huh?"

"Careful, Mister Enders. You're on my turf now."

Matt Enders sighed. Not necessarily a soft, polite let's-work-this-out kind of sigh. No, it was more of an aggravated expulsion of air forced from one's lungs when he was at his wit's end.

Matt's dark brown eyes fixated on Mel's blue ones. She didn't invite him to have a seat. Hopefully, this wouldn't take long.

"It's not like me to lose my temper, especially in a public setting. I apologize if I embarrassed you—hurt your feelings—earlier."

Mel's resolve weakened, but she wasn't about to make this easy for him. Feigning nonchalance, she shuffled the papers on her desk. "Oh, Mr. Enders, you give yourself too much credit. It takes more than a grown man pitching a temper tantrum to unnerve me."

Matt stepped closer. "*Who* pitched a temper tantrum? You've sulked ever since staff meeting this morning when

I mentioned the idea of coordinating some of your weekly activities with mine."

He leaned forward, placing his palms on her desk. "Look, out of the eighty residents we have, seventy-nine turned in surveys who indicated a desire for change—for group therapy to go hand in hand with other interests. Board games, exercise, and social outings are nice, but so is discussing life and the common threads that go with the aging process." His voice softened. "If we synchronize our work, we could enhance an already great thing Sunset Meadows has going. Wouldn't you agree that sometimes a team approach is more productive than a single-handed effort?"

"I guess it depends on how you define 'team approach'."

Matt gestured with his hand. "You know—you—me—working *together* rather than apart."

"Ahh, yes. I suppose I should feel honored that you want *me* on your team. I mean, if you've got it all figured out after working here for a mere six months versus my five years then you definitely earned every bit of your degree."

His semi-attractive features registered surprise. "*Wow.* You're one tough nut to crack. Whatever got under your skin to make you so jaded?"

Mel dismissed his comment. "Is there anything else, Mr. Enders? I need to leave on time today. I have a date."

A muscle flinched in his cheek before his face turned to granite. "Poor guy. Give him my condolences."

With that he strode toward the door, opened it, and left Mel's office.

He grinned. To see pretty Melinda Brewer's mouth fall open and remain that way gave him enormous satisfaction. He'd rendered her speechless and he rather liked it.

I know, Lord. I shouldn't take pleasure in having the last word, but that woman drives me so—so—nuts! She always thinks she's right. It's either her way or the highway and she views my ideas as opposition. She thinks I'm some sort of competition, for crying-out-loud!

Nothing could be further from the truth. He and Melinda were two separate department heads with very similar goals. How had this turned into a tug-of-war match?

Matt headed to his own office two doors down and attempted to quell his frustration with the pint-sized, freckle-faced package of TNT. For whatever reason, when his and Mel's paths crossed, there was an instantaneous reaction. He didn't know why they couldn't agree. On anything.

With others, she seemed so sunny-dispositioned. In addition to scheduled activities, she mingled with the residents, joked with them, and joined them for coffee. Mel took great pains to make sure that everyone who lived there was happy, comfortable, and as active as their health and age allowed. And she demonstrated compassion and sensitivity to everyone. Everyone *but* him.

Matt didn't get it. Since moving to Ruby last spring, most folks had bent over backward in welcoming him. The Brewer family even invited him to dinner one Sunday after church. Of course, Mel hadn't liked it.

Matt plucked at the sheaf of files stacked on his desk. He remembered that day with vivid clarity. Jake and Billie

Gail Brewer's gesture of kindness meant the world to him in the wake of a new move. They were the epitome of Christian hospitality.

Their three sons, Gabe, Garrett, and Michael offered tips and pointers about life in Ruby—how *not* to wear dress shirts and ties if he wanted to fit in around here. How he should be the first customer in line on Saturday mornings at Pennies from Heaven if he wanted to sample delectable treats still warm from the oven. How *not* to leave leftovers on his plate down at the Come and Get It Diner, lest he offend the much-loved proprietress, Ida Mae Hoscutt—now, Ida Mae Farrow.

"And from now on, don't sit on the front pew at church," Gabe added. "Pastor Bill tends to spit when he gets wound up in the pulpit, and most likely, you'll be a good target. Sit about midway back and you'll be safe."

"Not from the Packards' kids though." Garrett clapped Matt on the back. "I suppose you may already know that since you bought Sam's place, but those cuties will chit-chat you to death if you let 'em. Little Faith and Hope have really come out of their shells since Sam and Charla married. They have their new mama to thank for that."

"Yeah." Mike jumped in, grinning. "But keep in mind, too, you don't want to plaster your rear end toward the back of the church either or else Erin Shaye will make cow eyes at you."

Garrett Brewer jabbed his brother. "Mike, the only one Erin has eyes for is you, and you know it."

Matt smiled, recalling the Brewer brothers' pleasant exchange. Everyone around Billie Gail's dinner table that Sunday afternoon had laughed and teased. Everyone but the youngest sibling and only sister. Melinda Brewer was reserved at best. In fact, she'd even gone home early under the guise of a headache.

"Poor lamb." Billie Gail Brewer hugged her daughter as she'd said good-bye. "You've been working too hard. All that painting and decorating at Doc Burnside's old cottage is taking its toll, I think."

"No, Mom. I'm fine. Everything's almost done. I just have the fence row out back to clear—you know, those crazy weeds and dormant vines—and Dad and the boys said they'd help me with that."

"Well, indulge your mother, Sis." Jake Brewer kissed his daughter's forehead. "It's Sunday. Go home and take an aspirin, kick back and relax. A little rest will do you good."

Melinda's ruse to get away was not lost on Matt. When her VW shot down the graveled drive, Garrett was the first to comment. "Mel sure was quiet. Must have been one booger of a headache."

"Musta been." Gabe grinned and turned toward Matt then. "Have you been giving our sister headaches?"

Matt immediately liked Mel's brothers. "I certainly hope not."

But now Matt knew. If he wasn't sure then, he was sure now.

Yep. He could almost feel the invisible bullseye eye on the center of his forehead. The one that screamed *giant migraine.*

For whatever reason, Mel Brewer disliked him. Be it her perception of his usurping her authority at Sunset Meadows or perhaps some other imaginary slight, the woman couldn't stand him. And it really was too bad, because despite the fire and ice treatment, he admired

Mel's determination and commitment. She wanted the best for residents here and didn't want the new kid on the block messing with what her view of that was.

He supposed he ought to do the Christian thing and extend some brotherly love.

Hmm...What to do?

"I've got it!" Matt snapped his fingers with the sudden revelation.

After work today, he'd buy her a bottle of aspirin and deliver it personally to her doorstep. It didn't matter whether she had a date or not. Mel would appreciate the interruption. Probably.

The absolute nerve of that man!

Mel slammed the front door to her abode so hard it almost rattled the living room window panes. Considering the amount of TLC she'd invested in this place over the past several months, it was something she would never do unless given good reason. And Matthew Enders was reason enough.

Tossing her keys on the coffee table, Mel shrugged out of her jacket and lobbed it at her comfy, new sofa. In an hour, Spencer Holms would be here and she must shift gears. Matt Enders may have ruined her day, but he was not going to ruin her evening with Spencer.

Ahh. Spencer. Dependable, predictable, good ol' Spencer. The twenty-nine-year-old science teacher she'd dated a couple of times in the past year. Mel fought the urge to yawn.

Attractive, well-mannered Spencer Holms had liked her for as long as she could remember. Like Mel, Spencer had grown up in Ruby and returned to the area after graduating college. He'd made no secret of his affection for Mel, and lately, he'd become bolder in his attempts to court her. He was a good-natured guy and eager to please. The only fly in the ointment was that Mel couldn't see herself moving past the platonic stage with a man she found so nice, yet *sooo* tedious.

Their dates were pleasant enough, though, and that was enough for now. Sharing the companionship of an attentive male at church socials and town functions was an added bonus. And besides, Mel had been frank with Spencer from the very beginning so it wasn't like she was leading him on or anything. He was a friend. Nothing more.

"I'm not ready to pursue a full-time commitment, Spencer," she'd told him after their first three dates.

"That's all right, Mel." Honesty didn't dampen his resolve. "I'll grow on you. You'll see."

Like what? A wart?

Hadn't he realized how crazy-pitiful that sounded? She doubted it. He would have had to silence the fireworks first. The ones bouncing around in his brain every time they were together. It was an awkward situation and one that required discernment. Like with Matt—only for a different reason.

The man annoyed her. He reveled in his co-workers' kudos and pats on the back. It made Mel cringe every time she heard someone say, "Good to have you on board, Enders!" and "Way to go, Matt!" when he proposed yet another cutting-edge change.

How dare he swoop into town, enter her turf, and think he could suddenly shake things up at a place she'd worked for *five years!*

Sunset Meadows was more than a senior citizen retirement complex. Like the small town of Ruby, the campus was a tight-knit community where residents were friends. It was also one of the most innovative senior housing facilities in the Ozarks, and its various programs had garnered multiple awards.

Sunset Meadows was unique. Its small-town appeal and intimate living concept made it special. Everyone—employees and residents alike—treated each other like family.

Mel poured her heart and soul into the place and wore many hats besides that of activity director, and she enjoyed it. At least she *had*. Until Matt came. Until Mister Fancy-Pants had decided to settle here and bring his fancy ideas with him.

She gave herself a mental shake and glanced around the tiny living room, her comfort zone. Far from elegant, her place held a certain cozy charm. All the furnishings were simple, yet tastefully done, with a nostalgic feel of yesteryear.

Built entirely of native stone, this historical nugget had captured Mel's heart as a child. On her walk to school each morning, she used to admire the quiet beauty that emanated from this cottage—Doc Burnside's home. One of its best features was the generous picture window where soft firelight glowed in the gloomier winter months and a Christmas tree twinkled during the holidays.

Mel dreamed the cottage would one day be hers, and when old Doc Burnside put the place up for sale, she prayed for God to open a financial door so she could purchase it.

"Tell you what, Miss Melinda," Doc drawled over coffee

and gingersnaps. "We'll draw up an owner/buyer agreement. You come up with the initial down payment, and you pay me what you can afford at the end of each month. How's that sound?"

Mel smiled, remembering.

"I...c...can't do that! That wouldn't be right. That's not fair to you, Doc."

"*Hmpf.* Fair-shmair. Let me decide what's fair, young lady. We'll make it all legal like." Doc clasped her hand and squeezed it. "In fact, I want you to have your mama and daddy take a look at the papers first. Heaven-to-Betsy, bring Jake and Billie Gail to our little closing party, too. We'll all celebrate."

Sometimes, indeed, God's ways were not our ways. Before any papers were signed last year, old Doc Burnside died peacefully in his sleep one glorious, sun-dappled afternoon. Pastor Bill found him out back leaned against an old peach tree with an opened Bible sprawled across his lap and a clump of pink peonies still clutched within a cold, frail hand.

Mel mourned the loss of such a dear soul, but she was stunned at what came next. Doc Burnside, the beloved physician with no family of his own and who'd been a fixture of Ruby forever, bequeathed Mel the cottage and the surrounding property, lock, stock, and barrel with no strings attached.

At the reading of the will, Doc's attorney grinned and handed over the keys to the place. "Tend it and treasure it as he did over the years."

Doc Burnside defined the words *Christian love.* Such a sweet memory...

Mel snapped back to the present. *Help me demonstrate that Christian love toward Matt Enders,*

Father. I don't especially like the man, but I know he's one of your children, too. Maybe we won't be friends, but help us to at least get along. And Father...thank you for all the blessings in my life...the ones I fail to remember to thank you for from time to time.

Contemplating Christian love and blessings, Mel headed toward her bedroom humming a favorite praise song.

She freshened up and changed into blue jeans and a pumpkin-colored sweater. Nothing fancy but just right for a casual dinner and a movie. She hoped Spencer hadn't dressed up because she didn't want to give the man false hope. That wouldn't do at all.

Mel ran a brush through her shoulder length hair and swiped a clear coat of lip gloss across her mouth. She was about to file a nail when three sound raps echoed from the living room. Why Doc Burnside never installed a doorbell in later years, she didn't know.

Typical. Spencer was early. His eagerness might appeal to some women, but she found his zeal trying. She didn't know why Spencer couldn't be on time for once. But at least tardiness wasn't a problem.

Resigned, Mel sighed and went to receive her date. The front door, ancient and heavy, groaned as she opened it.

"I must say, your countenance seems sunnier than earlier today."

She'd never really noticed until now how good-looking Matt Enders was. With his dark, windblown waves, coffee-colored eyes, and that cocky full smile that played upon his well-defined profile, one might even think the guy was handsome.

Personally, she'd never found that sort of casual,

rugged look appealing. Mel couldn't care less what her co-worker looked like. Though she had to admit, until this very moment his attractiveness hadn't fully registered.

"Mr. Enders?"

He grinned and held out a small orange gift bag.

"I don't understand."

"Open it. I think it's something you can use."

"Really, Mr. Enders—"

"*Matt*, please. Formalities are so boring, don't you think?"

Was he serious? He seemed to be.

"I guess we have butted heads long enough to be on a first name basis." Mel stepped aside. "Come in."

Matt strolled past, his arm inadvertently brushing hers in the process. "Beautiful. This place, I mean. It suits you."

The male, woodsy scent of him filled the room and played upon her nostrils. He was too close. *Much* too close. She stepped back in an effort to reclaim her personal space. "Yes, I think so, too. When I was a little girl, I always dreamed that one day I'd live here."

"And your dream came true."

Mel nodded. "God made it happen."

"That's the neat thing about God and dreams. He grants our hearts' desires when we least expect them."

Her face warmed. Didn't he find this awkward? They'd been at odds for months. What did he expect her to say? "Thanks for the gift, Matt. Now, if you'll excuse me, I really must—"

He held up a hand. "I know. Get ready for your date. But you must open it, Mel. You don't even know what it is yet."

Well, it wasn't ticking, so it couldn't be something that would cause her bodily harm. Plus, the sooner she opened it, the sooner he'd leave.

Okay. She'd bite. And then she'd usher him out quicker than he could blink and lock the door behind him.

With a perfunctory nod, Mel reached inside the gift bag until her fingers touched something small, round, and plastic. A bottle of some sort? She clutched the object within her palm and yanked it out. *Aspirin?*

"For the big headache I am to you."

She regretted the giggle the moment it flew past her lips, but it was beyond her control. "I don't think I've ever received a more thoughtful present."

"I suspected you'd feel that way." Matt laughed, too. "You could take two now and save the rest for our next staff meeting. Would you like me to get you a glass of water?"

"I'll pass on the water for now. But I appreciate your kindness."

Matt extended a hand. "Friends?"

Did he really expect them to shake on it? Mel stared at his outstretched palm. Her pulse galloped and her stomach churned. She wasn't raised to be unforgiving. It was un-Christian.

"Friends." The gallop became a race. When their hands connected, the warmth of his touch surprised her. His grip was tender, yet firm.

They shook, pumping the handshake twice for good measure, their palms remaining linked longer than necessary.

"Am I interrupting?'

They directed their attention to the one who stood in

the doorway. *Spencer Holms.*

For once his timing was perfect. Maybe his early arrival would send the message *I'm not ready to pursue a full-time commitment* hadn't.

Chapter Two

What did he mean 'Am I interrupting?' You bet your khaki-clad patootie you are. Matt gave Mel's hand a final squeeze and then extended his palm toward the well-dressed guy who lent new definition to the layered look.

"Matt Enders."

A flicker of recognition crossed the guy's face as he accepted Matt's proffered hand. "Ahh, so you're the one. I mean, you...work with Mel. And I, uh, recognize you from church."

Nice recovery. Matt stifled a grin. Obviously, Mel had mentioned him. He hoped it was all good.

"And you are?"

"Sorry. Spencer Holms. Mel and I see each other."

Their handshake was quick and polite. It amused him that Holms found it necessary to point out that he and Melinda were an item.

Mel cleared her throat, filling the awkward silence. "Matt was just leaving."

Holms's gaze traveled to the gift bag Mel still clutched in her hand.

"He...dropped off some aspirin."

"Aspirin?" Mr. Layered Look tugged at the neck of his beige tee shirt, somewhat visible beneath his beige dress shirt and yet another cream-colored and beige sweater.

"Hard day." Matt struggled to keep a straight face. He wondered if Holms expected an autumn blizzard or if he was always this much of a fashion statement.

"Oh?"

"Yeah. Friday staff meetings can be killers."

Holms nodded. "I see."

Relief flooded the guy's face. Relief that Matt was not his competition. Clearly, Spencer Holms had it bad for the pretty brunette who stood nearby. She, however, didn't share the same lovesick glow.

What exactly did Spencer and Mel have in common? He seemed a bit stodgy. She was a fireball. He conveyed insecurity. She exuded confidence. Holms was *beige*, but Melinda...Melinda was *beautiful*. Not in a cover-girl way, but in a classic, earthy sense.

Funny how freckles on a woman had never really appealed to him—until now. Against Mel's flawless features, they seemed perfect. Framed against thick, auburn waves that crested her shoulders, hers was an unforgettable face. Everything else was rather nice, too, Matt had to admit.

And the fact she definitely had curves in all the right places, yet chose to dress in a tasteful manner, meant modesty wasn't dead. Obviously, they shared similar principles. Holms better treat her with the respect she deserved.

Now, why should *that* cross his mind? *You're just her co-worker.*

He certainly had no dibs on Melinda Brewer. Good grief, she didn't even like him. But boy, oh, boy...when their palms connected moments ago in that truce of a handshake it sure felt like there a whole lot of potential.

Mel cleared her throat a second time, rousing Matt

from unsettling thoughts.

"Thanks for your thoughtfulness, Matt. Now, if you'll excuse us..."

"Certainly." Matt nodded. "Nice meeting you, Holms. You two have a great time."

"Good to meet you, too. We will."

Holms probably assumed Matt was out of earshot when he remarked, "He doesn't seem like such a bad guy."

It made Matt smile.

Their evening began pleasant enough. As usual, Spencer had driven to the nearby town of Sapphire. The pizza was good, the movie okay, and the conversation, light and familiar. They discussed Ruby and local news, upcoming church activities, and the fact propane had jumped a dime overnight. Then the discussion shifted. Mel listened politely as Spencer droned on about the earth's water cycle and various weather events.

Spencer reached for her hand as they drove home. "Mel, I had a wonderful time."

Wonderful? It wasn't the adjective Mel would have chosen, and she'd found it difficult to fib. Their evening together had been nice, but not wonderful.

"Chicken-bacon-ranch is my favorite kind of pizza. And the movie ended the way I hoped it would." She didn't want to hurt Spencer's feelings, but she didn't want to give him false hope about their relationship either.

As she lay in bed now, Mel wondered if she was doing just that—giving the guy false hope. Even though she'd told him she didn't want to be involved in a full-time commitment, it was clear the man still considered it a possibility. He'd reached for her hand more often tonight, and then there was that kiss business at her front door. Not Spencer's occasional peck-on-the-cheek kiss.

It began that way, but then Spencer's lips traveled from Mel's cheek toward her mouth in such a deliberate, seductive way that it made Mel's stomach lurch. They'd never kissed each other on the lips before. She wasn't a prude, but she didn't share his feelings, and he'd never pressured her for more. When she'd abruptly pulled back tonight, instead of their lips meeting, Spencer tasted air. Confusion clouded his face, then embarrassment.

"I'm sorry, Mel. You've been more than up front with me about how you feel. I guess I keep hoping..."

"Spencer, you're a good friend, but I don't think we should see—"

"Please don't say it, Mel. Just give this time. Give *us* time."

"I don't want to hurt you, Spencer, but—"

"Look." He fiddled with his key fob. "We'll go out as friends then. We can do that, can't we?"

Exasperated and eager to disappear into the sanctuary of her home, Mel nodded a slow *yes* against her better judgment. Spencer's sad eyes grew hopeful. *Oh, no.* Why had she done that?

"Super. See you at church on Sunday?"

Mel's skin prickled. He knew perfectly well she rarely missed services. Again, Spencer spun her reaction into something more, and resentment seeped into Mel's bones. Was he intentionally trying to manipulate her? She didn't want to think that, but when he leaned forward to offer a hug, Mel stepped back, indicating friendship was indeed the only thing between them. She hoped Spencer wouldn't belabor the point.

Lying in the stillness of her bedroom now, Mel watched the thin sliver of moonlight dance across her bed. It wasn't like Spencer to unsettle her so. Usually, she didn't give their time together a second thought. Their dates had always been—congenial. A friendly pastime. *Comfortable.* Perhaps, that was it. Mel had grown tired of comfortable. When had it happened?

When a tall, dark-headed stranger full of himself and his fancy ideas sauntered into town. Almost six months ago.

That Matt Enders should insinuate himself into her thoughts irritated Mel. Just not as much as it used to.

Saturday dawned sunny, bright, and full of promise. From Mel's bedroom window, a leaf blower purred in the distance. It reminded her of her own leaves out back that needed blown or raked or *something.*

Another season, no longer as new. Summer had long since exited the Ozarks and slid into autumn. Mel had been so busy renovating her beautiful cottage that she'd hardly noticed. There'd been other priorities. Things like decorating her little piece of paradise and making it her own. Additional things outdoors like pruning, trimming, and re-seeding also commanded her attention.

Disorder and busyness behind her now, the knowledge she was debt-free and living in the very place she'd loved since childhood tapped new emotions— restless ones she preferred to not yet name.

She stretched her legs and yawned, wishing she could lie there for a few moments longer. How nice it would be to roll over and soak up the early morning sunshine while contemplating the day. But duty called. Today was Sunset Meadows' fall gala, one of many annual events she'd organized and hosted for the past several years. There would be tons of fun, food, fellowship, and activities, and Mel would be in charge of most of it. Her heart leapt with excitement. She adored her job.

Many of Sunset Meadows residents had already awakened hours ago. They'd be gathered in the dining room chatting over breakfast and coffee. Later, family members would arrive for the day's events, because like other special occasions, community involvement was a given. And maybe, just maybe, this would be the year Mel could draw poor Clinton Farley out of his shell and get him to participate. Though she'd been too preoccupied at the time to think about it, she knew without a doubt that Clinton had been the only resident to pass on Matt Enders' infamous survey.

"Bunch of hogwash," he'd muttered as the surveys were handed out. And as soon as Matt's back was turned, the grouchy old codger crumpled the one-page paper and tossed it into the nearest trash can. Mel witnessed the incident and took satisfaction in it. At least someone else felt the same way she did.

She cringed at the memory. Despite her feelings toward Matt at the time, she should have at least encouraged Mr. Farley's input. But no. She'd smirked inwardly that there was at least one other person who thought Matt Enders' ideas were *hogwash*.

I'm sorry, Father. It was a petty way to behave. Matt had just grated on my last nerve that day. Maybe after our recent chat we can now be civil to each other. Please help me to be more of an encourager rather than an obstacle to those who I might have influence with. Be it Matt Enders or Clinton Farley or anyone else.

Determined, Mel shook off a stab of regret and climbed out of bed.

Matt greeted the day the same way he always did. Prayer, a short jog, and a quick breakfast.

Normally, on a Saturday, he'd spend the remainder of his free time relaxing with a favorite hobby—one he never talked about—or doing light yard work, but this Saturday morning was different. Today was The Meadows' fall gala, the biggest event since he'd been employed there. Next would be the annual Thanksgiving dinner and then a big Christmas bash for the residents and their families.

The list of activities excited him. While Matt wasn't required to attend or assist with all of them, as the newly hired social services director of Sunset Meadows, he wanted to attend as many occasions as he could. He looked forward to learning the ropes. More than that, he loved working in the field of geriatrics and this job gave him purpose.

Today he'd make a special presentation in the community room regarding new programs he hoped to implement in the future. Melinda Brewer was to be on hand, as well. *Ahh, Mel.* What a firecracker!

As he pulled onto P Highway from his graveled drive, Matt considered his pretty co-worker. A fire-and-ice kind of gal, Mel yanked his chain. Since his first day at The Meadows, Matt bore witness to her many sides. From determination to delight, annoyance to passion. Passion for her job and for doing her job splendidly. Passion for the residents. Passion for what she believed to be the right thing.

Man, oh, man. That one intrigued him. Mel certainly displayed some of that passion yesterday morning. If there had been an open spit in Mel's office then, she would have plunked Matt on it, for sure. But maybe after last night, they'd reached a new agreement. Maybe they could agree to disagree on work-related matters and be open to fresh viewpoints, in addition. He hadn't intended to undermine or usurp Mel's position at Sunset Meadows.

After his previous peace offering, Matt hoped Mel believed him. If only he'd told her what he was planning today. Yeah, that probably would've been a good idea.

They pulled into the employee parking lot at the same time. Mel sent Matt a quick nod and cut the ignition.

He smiled as he stepped down from his truck, a flashy, midnight blue affair. "So, how was the date?"

Did he really ask that? He had to be kidding.

"Isn't it a beautiful day?" She dodged his question with a question and gathered her things.

Matt nodded. "Gorgeous."

Mel's fingers trembled as she smoothed back tendrils of hair that had escaped a loosely secured up-do. She prayed he wouldn't approach her, that he'd turn and walk straight into the building without further preamble, but as providence would have it, Matt Enders strode toward her with arms extended.

"Looks like you've got quite a load there. Here, let me help."

If she'd only had her purse, tote bag, and the container of brownies, it wouldn't have been a big deal. Mel could have juggled them easily. Besides those things, however, there was the humongous basket she'd retrieved from her tiny back seat and it was stacked to the brim, almost overflowing.

As the basket tipped precariously in her arms, Mel steadied herself against her car. "No worries. I can...g...get it."

"Yes, but I'm here so now you don't have to."

His eyes were browner than yesterday, his striking features more defined in the morning light.

"Thank you."

Matt beamed. "Glad to be of service."

"Goodie bags," Mel explained, as they approached the back entrance to the building. "For visitors, today. And the residents, too, if they'd like one. I've stuffed them with magnets, notebooks, and pens, which include the facility's logo and phone number. There are also miniature packages of candy corn, mints, and gum. And a bookmark with a scripture on the front. We can do that since we're a private, Christian owned facility."

Matt paused at the door, studying her. "This is really special, Mel. Was this your idea?"

He seemed impressed. Mel's face warmed. *It's only an observation. Don't let it rattle you.* "Yes. I try to do a little extra something for all the events we have here."

"I see. You always go above and beyond. I like that about you."

A compliment? From Matt Enders? Wonders never ceased.

As they entered the building, various aromas jolted her senses—the mouthwatering scent of homemade cinnamon rolls baking in the kitchen, the sweet fragrance of newly delivered mums, last week's fresh coat of paint and the lemony whiff of just-waxed floors. Wonderful, heady smells. Atypical for many independent living facilities and retirement homes.

Matt trailed after Mel, dutifully setting the goodie basket down where she directed in her office. He grinned as she dropped her purse and tote bag on her desk.

"What?" What was so funny? Was her hair a mess? Her clothing askew? Something else the matter?

"I'm remembering...yesterday. The last time I stepped in here."

Oh, that. "You mean our chat?"

"No. I mean our confrontation."

She slid the container of brownies beside her other things. "Oh."

His nearness unnerved her. Why was that? She'd never given the tall, attractive city guy a second glance during the entire time she'd known him. Unless, of course, it was a glance of disdain. Now, here she stood with her heart racing and overcome with a nervousness she didn't understand. How absurd!

Matt held her gaze, his dark eyes a thrilling combination of intrigue and appeal. "I'm glad we're friends now. What we accomplish together will be amazing."

His voice registered a sincerity that thawed her resolve. "Yes...speaking of which, we better get moving. The gala starts at ten and there's still some preliminaries to take care of before then."

Matt saluted her, still grinning. "Sure thing. I'll check back with you later. I know we have some tasks we'll be helping each other with today."

Mel's stomach flip-flopped. The sooner he moved on,

the better. "Yes. Thanks."

Before he turned to go, Matt hesitated. "You never answered my question earlier."

"Pardon me?"

"The one about your date. How was it?"

What? She forced a response past her tongue. "Fine."

"Interesting adjective."

He strolled out of her office whistling.

Fine. Very noncommittal. Not "lousy" or "fantastic." Just *fine.*

Matt thought about it as he tidied his office. Why had he asked Mel about her date? Beating around the bush certainly wasn't his strong suit, but prying into a woman's personal life? Now, that took boldness to a new level.

Still, Mel's date continued to plague him. He needed coffee. A little liquid caffeine and he'd be good to go. That should banish any wayward thoughts he shouldn't be having in the first place.

He moved a stack of file folders to the edge of his desk, checked his e-mail, and then headed out the door toward the dining room. *Ah...the aroma of heaven.*

"Good to see you, this mornin', Mr. Enders!" Tilly Andrews, one of the kitchen staff, waved from across the room. "Special of the day is pumpkin pie spice. Stout, hot, and purty-smellin', just the way you like it."

He knew the older woman well enough to know the inference was unintentional, though the chubby-cheeked grandmother laughed even as she said it.

"Miss Tilly, you spoil us." Matt strode over to the employee's coffee bar and reached for a mug. He selected the fully loaded blend from the middle carafe and slugged back a hefty sip, promptly burning his tongue in the process. *Aw, man.*

"Now, careful, Mr. Enders. I did say it was hot, did I not?" Tilly hurried over with a Styrofoam cup loaded with ice cubes. "Here. Suck on one of these."

"Yes, ma'am. Thanks." The fact he burned his tongue with the first sip of java served as a reminder that he best re-focus. No more thoughts of his co-worker's after-hour activities. *But good night! A date with Spencer Holms?* The guy had to be about as lackluster as a shoebox. What did Mel see in him?

Okay, so he was a teacher. The guy obviously had brains. And some women might appreciate his movie star looks and his ability to color-coordinate ten shades of beige. And maybe his homegrown status was a draw. Dating a multi-generational Ruby, Missourian had to be a plus.

Still, as an outsider looking in, Matt didn't see the connection. From his vantage point, there'd been no spark between Mister Predictability and Mel. At least on Mel's part. Holms, on the other hand, lit up like the Fourth of July around Mel. It made Matt scratch his head over the curiosity of it all.

Nearby voices jarred him back to the present. One, pleasant and jovial. The other, hardened and clipped. The brief table exchange between Clinton Farley and Edwin Ramsey derailed further meanderings.

"You going to bob for apples this year, Clinton?"

Clinton regarded Edwin Ramsey, a fellow resident, with an ever-present frown. "Don't believe hell's frozen over yet. Not that I put much stock in heaven *or* hell, but you get my drift."

Edwin paused, his features softening. "Sometime, friend, I'd like to talk with you about that."

"Nope. I know you mean well, Ramsey, but it'd be best not to waste your breath about afterlife, fall galas, and the like. I'm not on this old earth to ponder junk and have fun. You live. You die. Then, your bones turn to dust. End of story. Sorry to burst your bubble."

Edwin dabbed his lips with the corner of a napkin. "With all due respect, Clinton, sorry to burst yours. You're wrong, you old sourpuss."

Good for him. Sharing the Good News with an unbeliever took guts. And *love.*

Matt stepped out of the way as old Clinton Farley rose from the table and tottered past in a huff.

"Everything okay, Mr. Farley?"

Farley did a slow U turn, aggravation evident on his tired, withered face.

"Not really, Wonder Boy. I've had it up to my eyeballs with this fall gala junk and all the other stuff around here. I didn't move to this retirement community to be sociable. I moved here because the price suited me. I couldn't care less about parties, games, or other time-busters. Three square meals a day and a place to hang my hat—that's all I signed on for when the wife up and died on me six years ago. *Humpf.*" With a rap of his cane against the shiny, tiled floor, Farley shuffled away, still muttering under his breath.

Matt's heart constricted. Hurt shadowed Farley's countenance and clung to him as he moved on. Not just a mad-at-the-Lord kind of hurt. More like a lost soul without salvation hurt.

God, show me how to help Clinton Farley... The plea

tumbled around in his brain. The prayer, brief, but heartfelt. Matt sipped his coffee, no longer hot.

"Don't let him get your knickers in a twist, Matthew." Edwin Ramsey ambled up beside him and patted his shoulder. "The Almighty's working on Clinton. That's why he's so miserable—because the Holy Spirit's speaking to his heart and Clinton's continuing to refuse Him."

"I think you're right, Edwin."

It made Matt want to pray harder. No one knew how long he had on this earth, but when someone was eighty-one, time was certainly of the essence. It convinced Matt more than ever that the new program he planned to introduce today was definitely God-directed. How could it not be? He'd exhausted other ideas.

Later, as guests filled the building, Clinton continued to dominate Matt's thoughts. With his head still in the clouds and his eyes trained on the shiny, waxed tiles, Matt proceeded down the hallway, nearly colliding with the person dashing in the opposite direction. His hands snaked out to prevent her from falling. "Oops. Sorry."

"Me, too. Mind's elsewhere, I guess."

His head bounced up at the familiar voice. "Everything all right?"

Mel's breaths came in short spurts. "I'm on my way to check on the goodie bags I set out in the front lobby. I think I made enough, but we've had such a great turn-out so far, I'm not sure if they'll last."

"Back-up plan?" Matt's hands remained on Mel's upper arms, steadying her. Or...so he told himself.

Good grief. Touching her set off alarm bells. The kind that smacked of a four-alarm fire.

He let his hands drop to his sides. Could her eyes be any bluer?

"Well, I have about fifty or so extra bags out in my car. After that, I'll requisition some pretty notepads and pens from Sarah. It'll be fine."

Her enthusiasm sparked his excitement, too. Undaunted and apparent, her zest spilled over like a Fourth of July fountain. He liked that about Mel. She was unstoppable.

"Sounds like you've got everything under control."

She gave a short laugh. "Yeah. I'd like to think so."

"See you in the community room at eleven, right?"

"Right. Your presentation. I wouldn't miss it."

Did he detect a note of condescension? No, that wasn't it. *Curiosity.* Simple curiosity about what Matt had to offer.

As people filled the building, Matt made it a point to greet them. Some visitors he didn't know, but many, like the Packard family, he did. Sam and Charla strolled along with daughters in tow, and they paused to shake Matt's hand. They often stopped by The Meadows and spent time with Sam's former father-in-law and the girls' grandpa, Edwin Ramsey.

"Good to see you, Sam. Charla." Matt shook their hands. He then leaned down and met their little daughters at eye level. "My, you girls get prettier every day."

Faith Packard giggled. "Yep. That's what Mama and Daddy say all the time."

"Uh-huh." Hope nodded in agreement. "We have new dresses." The child twirled to emphasize the fact. Then, almost as suddenly, she stopped in mid-twirl. "Hey! I smell somethin' good!"

"That would be popcorn. If you and your parents follow those signs there, you won't miss it. There's even more treats in the dining room and snack areas."

Their dad grinned as each girl grabbed a hand, ready to move on. "Guess we'd better go check it out. Thanks, Matt."

"My pleasure. Have fun, gang."

As the foursome bounced down the hall, arms entwined, Matt smiled. *What a happy family.* He really enjoyed Sam's former home—the home he'd purchased when moving to Ruby—and he and the Packards had become good friends over the past several months. In fact, he'd actually met Charla Packard first.

While he'd finished his MSW last year, Matt had worked part-time for the moving company that helped Charla relocate to this quaint, Ozarkian town. Charla Packard was Charla *Winthrop* then. She'd been a big city transplant with high hopes and even bigger dreams.

Ruby, Missouri had endeared itself to Matt, too. Once he'd returned home, he'd never been able to shake the nostalgic feel of the little town where no one knew a stranger. When he'd researched Ruby and the surrounding towns and found that Sunset Meadows had an opening for a social services director, Matt couldn't believe his luck. Or, rather, divine intervention. He'd applied for the position and had been hired one week following his initial job interview.

Other town regulars filtered into The Meadows that morning—Horace, the town deputy and his wife Hattie, Chuck and Ida Mae Farrow from the Come and Get It, Ned and Nora Brewster who owned the local market, Pastor Bill and wife Sharon from church, and a slew of others.

Outdoors, there were horseshoes, croquet, apple bobbing, and face painting for the kids. Inside, there were facility tours, quilt raffles, and craft demonstrations. The dining room boasted festive tables with an endless buffet of homemade cakes, cookies, pastries, and candies. At lunchtime, the kitchen staff would serve hot dogs and hamburgers, stew and chili. Everyone came and went as they liked, but most folks came and stayed.

A few minutes before eleven, Matt made his way down to the community room, the main gathering area for many of Sunset Meadows' frequent activities. It was a bright, spacious place with lots of comfy furniture, card tables, a big screen television, and a baby grand piano. Almost everything in the room had been donated by very generous benefactors.

Today, a podium had been erected near the far end of the room, opposite the main entrance. The director of The Meadows was concluding his opening remarks, then Matt would speak, and Mel would follow.

Matt hadn't made notes—he was a fly-by-the-seat-of-his-pants kind of guy. He already knew what he planned to say, and as Foster Pearce wound down his preliminary comments, Matt edged closer to the makeshift stage.

"...And so, dear friends," Foster closed, "you've once again blessed us with an overwhelming turn-out today. Thank you. Now, it's my immense pleasure to introduce a young man many of you already know—a man who is newer in our midst. He came to our lovely community and to our own Sunset Meadows to expand upon The Meadows' philosophy in truly making a difference. Please join me in welcoming Matthew Enders. Matt, come on up."

The crowd erupted in applause as Matt stepped up to the podium and accepted the handheld mic from his boss—a small statured, but big-hearted gentleman whose youthful exuberance belied his late forties.

"Thank you, Foster. And thanks, everyone." Matt gestured with his hand. "You've certainly made me feel welcome."

Again, the room applauded. Out of the corner of his eye, Matt noticed Mel standing beside her friend Sarah Dawson. Wearing tan slacks and a cranberry-colored sweater, Mel rocked her wardrobe choice. He'd thought so earlier and wished he'd complimented her then.

Her shoulder-length auburn hair was caught up in a loose bun and secured with a glittery band. A few dark wisps had managed to escape, framing her pretty face. She ceased clapping before the others, Matt observed, as if anticipating what he had to say. Her face registered an interesting shade of pink as Sarah whispered something in her ear.

"*A-hem.*" Matt cleared his throat and raised a palm, silencing the crowd. "As most of you know, I'm not big on formalities."

"That's good, 'cause neither are we, son!" one of the male residents boomed.

"Nope. Wrong neck of the woods for that!" someone else chimed.

Laughter rippled through the room, and Matt laughed, too. "Good. Because, after growing up in the city and then migrating to the east while I furthered my education, I finally feel like I've come home. It's awesome to settle down in a place where a man isn't judged by his big words or his head knowledge, but by his integrity and his heart."

Again, applause. The crowd's kindness tugged his heartstrings. Big cities might have paid him more, but no way could they compete with this homegrown generosity. Ruby was exactly where he was meant to land.

"I can't tell you how refreshing it is to live in a town where your neighbors are your best friends. Where camaraderie isn't a foreign concept. Where pulling together leaves no room to tear apart." Matt paused. The audience stood spellbound, with necks craned forward. Could they sense his excitement? Folks' body language seemed to indicate so. He plunged ahead. "Not only do I love this town, but working here is pretty cool, too. To earn a paycheck each week for what I do is a blessing because this is more than a job. It's my passion. And because of that passion, I want to help Sunset Meadows move forward. I'm excited about the new programs I've started here, besides others I hope to implement in the near future."

"Atta boy, Matt! Tell us more!"

Matt grinned at Hiram Ledbetter, the sixty-something fellow, who frequented The Meadows where his cousin resided.

"Well, part of running a great facility, or any organization for that matter, is discovering ways to make a good thing greater. Advancement isn't a matter of 'keeping up with the Joneses,' but rather, key in preventing stagnation. Without occasional change, there can't be growth. I'm not merely talking numbers. I'm speaking more of intrinsic transformation. To be open to change means availing ourselves to new opportunities, new possibilities. Something almost all of you—" Matt motioned toward The Meadows' residents with his hand, "are obviously in favor of as indicated by the recent surveys I distributed."

Mel's spine straightened. A subtle shift in position, perhaps, to anyone else, but because of their difficult history, noteworthy to Matt's trained eye.

He hoped his new idea would be well received. "With this in mind, I'm thrilled to tell you about an innovative program that we'll introduce in the coming weeks."

Foster Pearce nodded his approval. When Matt broached the idea with him last week and his boss offered his full support, today's confirmation came as no surprise.

"This is cutting-edge stuff, Matt. How soon can you get the ball rolling on this?"

Foster's endorsement pleased him. Not because it was his idea, but because of what this would mean to The Meadows' residents and the community. Lives would be changed, God willing.

Matt didn't consider himself an eloquent speaker, but he spoke from the heart now, the only way he knew how. "In keeping with Sunset Meadows' Christian philosophy, it's my deepest desire to focus on joy and fulfillment. Fulfillment in your daily lives, and in your relationships. One way I believe we can achieve this is to add a weekly chat session—a group meeting, but one that teams up each person with a partner, too. With a friend, there's more accountability."

Matt observed the audience's smiles and nods of approval, and his spirit soared.

With momentum building, he forged on. "I'm in the process of refining the program, but I plan to facilitate group discussions, enlist the efforts of various speakers from time to time, and tackle a variety of subjects that are of particular interest to the retirement community. But this program is open to anyone, regardless of age. You don't even have to be a resident here to participate. 'Age' is a state of mind. It shouldn't be a word that limits.

Productivity is integral to all our lives."

"Amen!" Deputy Sapp gave a thumbs-up. "That's what I call real community involvement. Say, Matt, do you have a name for this baby yet? You know, a tagline or somethin'?"

Matt grinned at the beloved local. "I'm glad you asked, Horace." He waited for a minute, letting interest percolate. "I considered our fine town—Ruby—and how, in many ways, it's like a little slice of paradise. That said, I want the program to be a conduit. A model to remind us that God has prepared something beyond Ruby—for those who accept God's free gift of salvation through His son Jesus. Many of us in this room have already accepted that gift. Still, He's molding us and shaping us, and He wants to give us the desires of our hearts in accordance with His will. That's the focus of this new effort."

Did that sound too preachy? He scanned the crowd's faces for irritation or boredom but saw only interest. Great. He hadn't lost them.

"No matter what juncture of life we're at, God wants us to realize our full potential and share His message with others. So, I've decided to name our newest program *GIFTS*. Specifically, *GIFTS: A Partnership in Growth and Love*. A simple concept, but one that communicates what this program is about."

Matt let it sink in. "When we think of a 'gift,' we think of something treasured, something special. It's given freely and we don't expect anything in return. *GIFTS*. An acronym for *God's incredible, free treasure supplied*."

The crowd, which had grown in size during Matt's presentation, clapped and cheered.

"Brilliant!" someone hollered.

"Love it!" another chimed.

"When do we start?" Edwin Ramsey wanted to know.

Foster stepped forward and leaned into Matt's microphone. "We're in the process of fine-tuning all the details, but we hope to have this off the ground by Thanksgiving next month. Matt has worked hard. He and another staff member have discussed reshuffling various programs. GIFTS will be up and running just in time for the holiday season, friends. What do you think about that?"

The applause reached a crescendo. The room pulsed with excitement as folks turned to their neighbors, and chatter grew louder. Only one pair of hands ceased in midair. Hands that fell to the sides of a now somber-faced individual.

Foster failed to notice. Instead, with abundant fanfare, he blustered, "Mel Brewer, come join us. We want to hear from you, too!"

Chapter Three

...He and another staff member have discussed reshuffling various programs.

Yes, they had. But nothing had been determined as to which programs would be "reshuffled." And this was the first time Mel had heard about *GIFTS*. Not such a clever acronym, yet another fabulous program that Matt Enders had conceived. All without so much as one word about it to her, Sunset Meadows' lowly Activities Director.

Mel's cheeks burned. Had it not crossed Matt's mind to discuss this with her? What about other activities already on her agenda? What would her role be in this endeavor?

A dozen thoughts ran through her mind. None of them complimentary. And now here she was being called to the podium by her boss to deliver what she'd thought was to be a far different speech. *Unbelievable.*

Her head spun. Mel had planned to talk about *change* and its positives. How she looked forward to working with Matt. Now, she drew a blank and bristled with irritation and something else, too. Disappointment.

She'd hoped they'd chipped through the icy barriers of the past few months. She'd hoped their handshake last night meant something. She'd hoped—

"Mel, go on..." Sarah whispered, nudging her elbow. "Everyone's waiting..."

Mel shook off the sliver of sadness that pricked her

heart. He'd played her for a fool, but she refused to act like one. If Matt Enders thought that she was some brainless sap who would happily cheer him on from the sidelines while he tromped all over her programs under the guise of a religious themed chat fest, then Mister Team Approach had another think coming.

Disappointment simmered to a slow boil. In fact, it thickened to gravy-like resentment.

"Mel..."

She shot her friend a dazzling smile. "Relax, Sarah. I'm all about rolling with the punches."

"Uh-oh," Sarah muttered as Mel moved forward. "Don't be rash..."

"Me? Rash? Of course not."

Mel strode with confidence toward the makeshift stage. Foster beamed and pumped Mel's hand when she reached the low-rise platform.

"Here she is, friends. The young woman who keeps us on our toes and we love it. Our own Miss Melinda Brewer!"

The audience whooped and hollered. Clearly, Foster thought the world of her, and he probably assumed that she and Matt had discussed GIFTS and worked out previous undercurrents.

At staff meeting yesterday, Foster praised Mel's work ethic, her compassion, and her dedication to Sunset Meadows. To demonstrate anything less than those qualities now would reflect poorly on those she cared about. Integrity and heart mattered to her, too. Both professionally and personally.

Still, the way Matt had handled GIFTS rankled her. He knew it would, and yet, he chose silence over dialogue. Well, they might have to work together, but after hours, her time was her own. Whatever they needed to discuss could be done here. At least she didn't have to see him beyond work. That wasn't being un-Christian, but rather, work-oriented and professional.

As Foster released Mel's hand, Matt offered his.

Nice show. But she'd play along.

She accepted his proffered hand, attempting to quell the resentment that threatened to take root. His grip surprised her. Gentle, yet firm. Like yesterday. His palm nearly swallowed hers, and his touch coaxed goosebumps along her arms. Why?

An attack of nerves. That's all.

Mel ended the handshake first, but not before his thumb softly caressed her hand. *Why did he do that?* Had she imagined it? She didn't think so. Matt's eyes flashed with emotion. Did he realize how awkward this must be for her? Did he regret placing her in this position?

"Well..." Mel accepted the microphone from Matt, refusing to pity him. "For a man who is glad to be in a place where he isn't defined by his 'big words' that was quite an eloquent speech, Matt. Let's give him another round of applause, folks!"

Matt's confusion shifted to understanding as the audience again extended him accolades. "So, this is how it's going to be?" he whispered.

Mel held the mic away from her mouth. "You betcha."

Yikes. If he'd been a slice of bread, he'd be toast. A charred piece, at that. Matt didn't necessarily blame Mel, though, he'd hoped for a shred of understanding. Couldn't she see how beneficial a program like GIFTS would be? That it had the potential to change lives and challenge stereotypes?

Of course, she recognized that. She also recognized

Matt's lack of communication and took it as a personal slight. He'd intended to discuss the new proposal with Mel, but for various reasons, he'd wanted to wait for better timing.

Who was he kidding? Man, he'd bungled this. While not his intention to be secretive, he realized that's how it appeared. That sweet butter-wouldn't-melt-in-her-mouth smile didn't fool him for a second.

Somehow, she made it through the next ten minutes. Mel didn't remember what she said exactly—something about looking forward to progress and new directions and how excited she was to be part of it.

Good thing she adapted easily. It removed an element of stress from the equation.

With the presentation over, Mel mingled a while with some of the residents and visitors. As they migrated toward the dining room where lunch was being served, she made her way back to her office. She couldn't escape quick enough. What started out as a fun-filled day, headed south fast. How could Matt do it? How could he support her to her face and then completely blindside her like this?

"You okay?" Sarah poked her head inside the doorway. "I guess GIFTS came as a surprise, huh?"

"Yeah. A surprise." Mel forced a smile.

"Sounds like a great addition though."

"Uh-huh. Great."

Sarah pursed her lips. Took a deep breath. And blew it out. "I'm sure Matt will come talk to you...about everything. In the meantime, how about joining me for lunch?"

How like her friend—sensible, and kind to the core.

"Sure. I just want to unwind for a sec. I'll meet you there in a bit. Grab me a bowl of chili?"

"You got it."

Alone again, Mel plopped in her chair and leaned back against the soft, supple leather, shutting her eyes. When she heard the door close, she assumed Sarah had backtracked and closed the door out of respect for her privacy.

"It must have taken a lot of energy to deliver such a heartfelt discourse."

Her eyes snapped open.

"I mean, I was touched." Matt's tone belied the grin he wore.

Him. Mel sprang from her chair like a jack-in-the-box, and a stack of papers went flying. She reached toward her desk to steady herself. "Well, that's certainly what I live for—to touch you, Matt." Flustered, she kneeled to gather the scattered forms and sheets of paper.

Matt bent to help her, their hands brushing in the process. "Oh?"

"That's not what I meant, and you know it."

"I should say not. Handholding is a pretty personal thing."

She jerked her hand back, as if scalded. Why did he suddenly think this was so amusing?

"You had multiple opportunities to discuss GIFTS with me—at staff meeting yesterday, in my office after lunch, last night, this morning, or on countless occasions prior—and you never said one word. And then, Mister Team Approach, to spring it on me right there in front of Foster, our co-workers, the residents, everyone—it was nothing short of rude and vain. Not to mention—

unprofessional, irresponsible, insensitive—"

Matt held up a hand to silence her. "*Whoa.* That's certainly not what I intended, but you're right. I did try to discuss it with you a number of other times, Mel, but our conversations usually went south so quickly that—"

"What about last night? What about that 'peace offering' you brought over? You could have told me then. It didn't end badly—we parted amicably."

Matt's face grew serious. He took her cue and stood, as she did, handing her the remaining stack of papers. "That's exactly why. I knew if I broached the matter last night, we wouldn't really have time to discuss it. You had a date with—what's-his-name—Splinter?"

Mel glared at him. "*Spencer.* But that's an excuse, and you know it. What about this morning when you helped carry my things inside?"

"You seemed pressed for time."

"Another excuse."

"Okay, Mel." Matt blew out a sigh. "But it's also the truth—at least how I saw it anyway, and..."

"And what? Please don't keep me in suspense, Matt. I'm all ears."

He paused, as if carefully choosing his words. "The tension between us has been thick for months. You'd never even smiled at me until yesterday...until last night when I dropped by. Did you know that, Mel? We've worked together for six months now and nothing—only a slight nod every now and then or a tight-lipped glance of acknowledgement. When I caught you off guard with my little present and you actually giggled—gotta admit, that was pretty cool. Then this morning, when it almost happened again, I didn't want to ruin what I'd hoped to be a fresh start between us. I didn't want to be the source of your discontent anymore. Dishonest? No. Selfish? Yeah."

"So, you thought it best to handle things this way?"

"No." His voice softened. "I'd hoped we could work through this. Look, Mel. I'm not your competition. We're both two different department heads with the same goal. That is, to continue to excel at what we do best—improving our residents' quality of life with Christ-like compassion."

Mel glanced away. Why did she unexpectedly feel like a hand-slapped child? Matt should be the one ashamed of himself.

"I really do want to work as a team, Mel. That's not some song and dance I've been handing you. I'm sorry I didn't approach this differently."

Ugh. There it was again. An apology. "Yes, well...I regret that my past behavior has seemed...unfriendly. I know we both want what's best, and you're probably right. We won't get anywhere without teamwork."

Matt extended his hand, a slow grin lifting the corners of his mouth. "That's the spirit."

The butterflies returned and fluttered in her stomach. *For heaven's sake.* This made no sense. Didn't Matt ever tire of shaking her hand?

Matt's hand tingled. Like he'd poked his fingers in an electrical outlet and couldn't let go. The perfect fit of her palm in his drew new awareness. Did she sense it, too? He'd bet his next cup of coffee she did.

Co-workers. Friends. Not friends. Friends. *Wow. Lady, you make my head spin.* He considered the absurdness of it all. Emotional whiplash wasn't his idea of fun, but he had to admit—Mel Brewer kept him on edge. In an exhilarating kind of way. The knowledge lit on his shoulders and refused to budge. In fact, it rode there the rest of the day.

As Matt tidied up his office and prepared to go home, Clinton Farley ambled past his doorway. The ill-tempered fellow hadn't taken part in anything today. He'd come to the dining room at noon for a bowl of stew and cornbread, but that was about it.

Rising from his desk, Matt jogged after Clinton. "Hey, Mr. Farley..."

Clinton turned around briefly and regarded him with a frown. Then he continued the trek toward his room.

Matt caught up to him. "Say, we missed you today."

"Did you? Did you really now?"

Clinton picked up the pace. For an elderly guy, he moved pretty good.

"Yes, we—I—really did."

"Well, I'll believe that when hell freezes over. Not that I put much regard in heaven or hell, you know."

"I'd like to talk with you about that sometime, Mr. Farley."

"Yeah, you and everyone else around here. I'll save you time and you save your breath."

Mel leaned against the door frame, stifling a yawn. Other than the bumpy speech affair, the fall gala rocked. Everyone seemed to enjoy themselves, and even though she and Matt would never see each other outside of work, perhaps they'd overcome a hurdle or two today. He knew where she stood. She knew where he was headed. Could it work? She exhaled a long, wobbly breath. Time would tell. She exited the building and headed toward her car, remembering the handshake. The one in her office. The one that left her undone—again.

Admittedly, Matt's hands were very nice—larger than her own, of course, still tanned from the summer sun with nails neatly trimmed. His calloused palms proved that he'd done more in life than push a pen.

Mel recalled the fleeting caress from earlier—the way he'd made little sideways motions with his thumb when he shook her hand at the podium today, and again, this afternoon in her office. Maybe Matt's typical greeting? No way. That was the type of thing one did when showing...affection.

Could it be? Uh-uh. Surely, she had it pegged wrong. Matt regarded her the same way she did him—as a co-worker and nothing more.

She pressed the button on her key fob, unlocking the car doors. Her basket and container were much easier to handle now that their contents were empty, and she tossed them inside the back seat along with her tote bag and purse.

"Hey, Mel! Got a minute?"

Matt smiled as he approached. She could only wonder what else he had on his mind. Hadn't they made their amends earlier? *Oh, no... not another handshake.*

Determined to avoid a replay, Mel stuffed her hands in the pockets of her jacket. "Did you need something?"

"Sorry. I know it's been a long day." He joined her at her car, securing the strap of his laptop bag over his shoulder. "Clinton Farley. I'm worried about him."

Not what Mel expected him to say, but she'd felt that way, too. "The staff's done everything to draw him out of his shell. Nothing seems to work."

"He's just so bitter. I mean, has he always been such a cynic? Has he ever taken part in any of the activities here? I've read his file, so I know the basic stuff—widower, moved to The Meadows a few years ago, no children or other family that anyone knows of."

Yes, Clinton Farley's story broke Mel's heart. During his residence at The Meadows, Clinton had made few friends, although Pastor Bill continued to stop by, despite the cold shoulder treatment. A good-hearted soul, their pastor. Never dissuaded from his calling.

Mel reached up to push a tendril of hair away from her face. "Marabel and Clinton Farley were childhood sweethearts and they were married almost sixty years." *Sixty years.* Such a long time. "They had a son early in their marriage, but he was stillborn. Clinton used to attend church with Marabel until that happened and then he stopped. I understand when Marabel died a few years ago, Clinton refused visitors and rarely left his house. Dad said he grew harsh. He's not really joined in anything here, though I keep hoping that maybe one day, he will."

She recalled countless times when she'd attempted conversation with Clinton, trying desperately to include him, but the man had rebuffed most of her efforts, as well as the other staff's and residents' endeavors to include him.

Mel prayed Clinton's heart would soften. His unbelief in anything remotely Christian seemed blatantly obvious. If he were to suddenly die today, where would he spend eternity? By his own admission, he questioned heaven's existence. Though no one really knew for sure, she doubted he had a relationship with the Lord. At least, his words and actions didn't indicate so. And when he'd thrown Matt's infamous survey in the trash...well, her own conscience bothered her now. She should have tried to talk to Clinton that day.

"I think God's working on Clinton Farley." Matt studied her. "I think you and I can help Clinton see that—if we work together, that is."

What did Matt have in mind?

"Relax. I'm not asking for the moon here. Just supper."

"Excuse me?"

"Yeah. Lunch was a long time ago, and with the way we both ran all day, I know you're probably starved like I am. Why don't we grab a bite to eat and we'll kick around a few ideas about Clinton?"

Seriously? For six months, she'd seen Matt Enders almost on a daily basis, but until recently, she'd merely tolerated him. Now, in the past few days alone, her emotions had run the gamut—everything from tolerance to thorough irritation, respect, amusement, even *like*. As in friendship *like*. She was still considering that one. And now this.

A supper invitation? To see Matt outside of work would be too intimate. If he were a female co-worker, the choice would be easy. There wasn't the same dynamic involved. As it happened, though, Mel could barely be near the guy without alarm bells sounding. He caused her heart to race at the oddest times and her cheeks to burn at the most inconvenient moments. He pushed all her buttons and she pushed back.

"Let me be blunt, Matt. After our somewhat awkward history, pardon me if I question your motives."

A flicker of something unreadable shadowed Matt's

face, but his grin never wavered. "No motives. I want to figure out a way to help Clinton Farley. And let *me* be blunt—if I wanted to ask you out on a real date I would. I wouldn't disguise it with some misconceived notion of *it's all in a day's work.*"

"Oh."

Oh? What a stupid response! Where were her quick comebacks? Her sharp tongue?

"Sorry. Didn't mean to prick your ego."

Of all the nerve!

"No need to apologize. You didn't. A date with you would never cross my mind."

His laughter echoed throughout the half-emptied parking lot. "Touché. How about it then? Supper—at my place?"

Still too intimate. Much, much too intimate. Somewhere neutral would be better. In fact, discussing this at work in an office setting would be best. To see Matt outside of The Meadows, even if it were to discuss work and ways in which they could help Clinton, would set the stage for familiarity. Mel might have to see Matt at church on Sundays since he'd recently become a member there, but other than that, she had no plans to become his buddy. A courteous, amiable working relationship was all she hoped for or wanted.

Mel pulled her hand from her jacket pocket to check the time. So much for subtlety. "Look, Matt, this day's been crazy-long. I agree that we need to find a way to help Clinton, but why don't we talk about this more on Monday? I usually block off an hour or so in the afternoons for—"

"Gotcha. Monday sounds good." Matt offered his hand

then, catching Mel completely off guard. "I'm curious though. This boundary thing. Is it just me or do you do this with everyone?"

"Excuse me?" She ignored his outstretched palm.

"You know. Boundaries. Established parameters. It's only my perception, but it seems that you have more of them with me."

Matt let his hand fall to his side.

"I...don't know what you're talking about. If you're inferring that I—"

"Intentionally keep me at a distance."

"Yes. Well, no. I'm not intentionally 'keeping you at a distance.' Look, Matt, I'm relieved that we're working through some professional issues, but anything beyond that is—"

"Off limits?"

Mel exhaled, the whoosh of air more from aggravation than necessity. "Yes. Of course."

Matt continued to grin. "I see. Including friendship? Isn't that integral to a good working relationship?"

Where was he going with this? "Yes, I want to be your friend, Matt. In a professional sense. I thought we'd already established that."

"Yes. So did I." He reached up to capture a stray tendril of her hair that had once again blown free. "That's why I want to clarify your position on the matter."

The gesture seemed too personal and it unhinged her. She stood silent as he gently tucked the loose strand behind her ear, his fingers lingering near the nape of her neck a little longer than necessary.

"I mean, this friendship thing—is it to be solely at work then? 'In a professional sense' would kind of insinuate that."

Mel fumbled with her keys and laughed. "Well, if I see you in town somewhere, I'm not going to ignore you. I'll wave or say 'hi' or *something.*"

Matt laughed then. Not a nervous kind of laugh, but a deep, hearty, very amused hoot. "Gee, that's big of you, Mel. You wouldn't want to hurt my feelings or anything."

"No, I wouldn't." She refused to smile. "I know how sensitive you are."

"All right then. See you at church tomorrow."

He stepped back and extended his hand—again.

Nope. Not just his imagination. He knew that now. Every time their palms connected, there was a definite charge. A very distinct current that could light up an entire street block.

Mel sensed it, too. And judging by the way her pretty face turned an interesting shade of crimson, it obviously unnerved her.

She snatched her hand away. "Well, I'll see you at services in the morning then."

"Yes. In the morning."

Mel nodded and turned to go. Matt couldn't keep his mirth at bay as he watched her drive away—with the hem of her jacket caught in the closed car door—the long, tan string flapping a carefree "good-bye" in the early evening breeze.

He bet Mister Layered Look never garnered the same reaction.

Her heart beat fast on the short drive home. It might be funny if her response to Matt's handshake routine didn't always have the same dreaded effect. She could have laughed at her own awkward getaway. Laughing, however, wouldn't solve things.

A half-hour later, after she'd marched into her house, her hand still tingled. Every time the man touched her, she reacted this way. *Ridiculous.* She purposely deterred her own thoughts.

Over a grilled cheese sandwich and a bowl of chicken noodle soup, Mel scanned her little dwelling. Over the past several months, she'd worked hard at restoring her home. She'd refinished the hardwood floors, applied fresh coats of paint to walls, washed windows, and updated lighting. Not wanting to downplay the original charm of the place, Mel had left many of the cottage's unique features intact. Doc Burnside would be proud.

Mel loved it here. It fueled a secret desire to maybe one day expand her efforts in the world of small business. The only thing missing was someone to share her piece of paradise with.

Where on earth did that come from? She scooted away from the table, leaving a few remnants of her meal, and tossed her paper napkin aside. Rising, she padded into the living room and plopped down on the sofa as if a physical change in location would halt her thoughts. She should have known better.

The firelight's soft glow only added to Mel's discombobulated mood, stirring musings of romance and prospects. For goodness sake, twenty-seven wasn't ancient, but suddenly, she felt so old. In college she hadn't dated much, preferring to concentrate on her studies so she could move on with her future. Now that she'd been out on her own for several years working in a fabulous job and settled in the home of her dreams, a part of her yearned for something more. Someone to share the happily-ever-after part with.

She knew someone who'd turn handsprings at the chance to fulfill that hankering, but somehow, Spencer Holms didn't fit that bill. Oh, he said all the right things, did all the right things, but that was just it. Mel couldn't see herself with "Mister Right."

Who she envisioned as her knight-in-shining-armor was someone who was more of a risk-taker and less of a stuffed shirt. Someone innovative—energetic. Someone full of life and comfortable in his own skin. Someone who didn't conform to the correct way of doing things simply because it had always been done that way. Someone who, perhaps, might be viewed as "Mister Wrong." Someone like...like...

She couldn't even say his name, much less think it. Mel glanced heavenward, letting her head sag against the back of the sofa.

Remember, you dislike change and you've only started tolerating the man. Don't go getting all dreamy-eyed because his handshake makes you feel a little weird. Like a bad case of indigestion, it'll pass.

Besides, she had more important things to think about right now. Things like Clinton Farley and his self-alienation...Spencer and his ardent pursuits...the annoying chime of her cell phone.

Mom. The ring tone drew mixed emotions. Not that she didn't love her mother, but she knew exactly how this would go. Before the fifth chime clanged, she caved and answered it.

"Hi, Mom." Why didn't she let it go to voicemail?

"Hi, lamb. I wanted to make sure you were still coming for Sunday dinner tomorrow."

"Don't I always, Mom?"

"Yes. But I know you're probably exhausted from the day's events and I wanted to double-check."

"I'm a little tired, but I'll be there. I'll bring green bean casserole. I know how Daddy loves it."

"Wonderful, darling. It'll go perfect with my beautiful rump. Besides roast, I'm making mashed potatoes and gravy, of course, corn pudding, salad, my homemade angel biscuits, and the usual assortment of fruit pies—cherry, peach, and apple. Maybe even blueberry."

"Wow, Mom. You usually only make two. Pies, I mean. Do you think we'll really need all that?"

"You bet we will. Your daddy and brothers have enormous appetites. You know that, lamb. And besides, with an extra person I don't think it'll hurt to have more."

Who had her mother invited to dinner this time? Pastor Bill? His wife, Sharon, was still in Sapphire visiting a sick relative. Lord, love him. The man could preach, but turn a pan? She doubted it.

Well, no matter. It wasn't uncommon for her parents to extend dinner invitations. Tending to others' needs were second nature to them.

Okay. So, Mel had refused his supper invitation. No biggie. They'd see each other soon enough.

Matt slugged back a gulp of sweet tea and almost choked in the process. Every time he envisioned Mel's jacket string saluting him in the breeze, he could hardly contain his laughter. What was she doing now? Grabbing a bite to eat—alone—like him? He set down the glass tumbler and fumbled with his cell phone, resisting the urge to text her. He was the last person she wanted to hear from. Then again...

Nope. He wouldn't do it. He wouldn't bother Mel anymore tonight. No sense in reheating the frying pan when the fire would still be there tomorrow.

Instead, Matt pondered the day's events and gave in to the grin that lit in his chest and worked its way up his throat and out. He speared a juicy bite of steak with his fork and popped it into his mouth, savoring the succulent smokiness. *Mmm...Bliss.* A meat and potatoes kind of guy, he could eat beef every day if it were good for him. He wondered if Mrs. Brewer sensed that when she invited him to Sunday dinner.

Chapter Four

Given the choice of Christmas every day or a sunny fall morning in the Missouri Ozarks, Mel would choose the latter every time. That's how much she loved it here. Except for her college years, she'd never lived anywhere but Ruby, and she had no desire to ever move away from her hometown. Where else could she go where everyone knew everyone—where your friends and neighbors knew when you sneezed, shopped, or had your hair done? Not many places that she could think of.

It wasn't like knowing everything about everybody was a particularly terrible thing. Just weird sometimes. People meant well. Town folk liked to look out for their own, Mom and Dad said. At least no one came and tucked her in at night. Though, given the opportunity, some good souls would absolutely do that. A smile made its way to her lips.

As she drove, a crisp breeze filtered through her opened window, and a hint of wood smoke clung to the air, a gentle reminder that days would soon turn even cooler, and eventually, the surrounding mountains, too, would bow to the winds of change. Saffron, russet, and scarlet-tinted treetops would, of course, make their triumphant departure before surrendering their majestic cloaks to subtler shades of brown. It was a bittersweet season, but necessary, and for the most part, welcomed.

Mel slowed the car to a crawl and found a parking spot beneath a tall, shady pine. She stepped out, smoothing the hem of her cinnamon-colored skirt as she walked. She paused a moment before entering the century-old church where her family had been members long before she was born.

A magnificent white structure with elongated, green shutters and a towering steeple that reached toward open blue sky, the place smacked of regal reverence and nostalgia. How many times had she entered this beloved building of her youth? Besides regular church services, Mel couldn't even guess how many weddings, fellowship dinners, church socials, and Vacation Bible Schools she'd attended there over the years. Sadly, even some funerals punctuated her memories.

It was a place rife with history, a place of comfort. A place where God dwelled. And one day, the very place where Mel hoped to be married. Naturally, it might help to have a groom first, and her only prospect at this point was one she'd rather not think about. While she'd dated Spencer off and on for a while now, Mel had definitely decided the time had come to cool their "association." Their date last Friday evening clinched that.

As she made her way up the ancient steps, Mel's heels click-clacked against the concrete. In the midst of the crowded vestibule, Gabe, the eldest sibling of the Brewer tribe, greeted her with a grin and a peck on the cheek.

"Missed you in Sunday School earlier."

Brothers. Hers didn't miss a thing. And when a girl had three of them, she had triple the fun. "Had to catch a few extra winks. I'm sure the Lord understands."

"Yeah. I'm sure He does. You certainly had Holms in a lather though."

Mel counted to ten. "For heaven's sake. We're not an item, Gabe."

"He sure thinks you are, Sis. In fact, don't look now,

but Mister Handsome himself is headed our way."

Mel tried her hardest not to look. To glance in the direction her brother indicated would only fuel Spencer's interest. "Great. Keep talking, Gabe. Maybe he'll walk on by."

Gabe laughed. "Uh-huh. Like that old song. Seriously, Sis, Holms is a little different, but he's not such a bad guy. And he's certainly a sharp dresser. Why, he doesn't even resemble the kid we grew up with. Guess he had to ditch his blue jeans and tee shirts when he started teaching down at the school."

"Guess so." Mel's reply was cut short as the topic of their conversation sauntered up beside them.

Spencer's casual black slacks were creased to perfection and the cuffs fell at the exact right spot on his black leather dress shoes. They complemented his light gray dress shirt and a similar shaded jacket. Ironically, this was the man who, as a boy, used to collect lizards and bugs and study what made the earth tick.

Mel hadn't been surprised when Spencer become a science teacher. But other changes over the years took her aback. More citified now, and possibly better suited to a larger, fashion-conscious climate than modest-sized, laid-back Ruby, Spencer seemed to have outgrown his roots. What made him return after college?

Mel chewed her lower lip as Spencer's hand came to rest upon the small of her back.

"Missed you in class this morning."

"I...slept in."

Why did she suddenly feel like a naughty child with her hand caught in the cookie jar? She wasn't one of his sixth-grade students who needed chastising.

"The busyness of yesterday's activities and all," Gabe said rescuing her. "Long hours and not enough sleep, you know."

Spencer studied her, his brows knitting together. "Maybe you should take a vacation, Mel. You put in a lot of long hours at The Meadows, not to mention your home remodeling project. I mean, you rarely take time off. It's something I've been aware of for quite a while."

His observation annoyed her, and the closeness of his physical proximity and the possessive way he spoke, grated on her.

"Yes, that's what everyone admires about Mel," a familiar voice interjected. Matt shortened the distance between them, extending his hand toward Spencer, forcing Spencer to meet his handshake with the very hand that rested upon Mel's back. "She's dedicated and passionate about what she loves."

Spencer's face registered surprise, then his eyes flickered with irritation. Which, Spencer rarely conveyed.

"Enders," he acknowledged as the two briefly shook hands. "I sometimes forget you're a member here now."

"Hmm. They say the memory's the first to go."

Gabe snorted at Matt's witty comeback, giving Mel the opportunity to move past the trio and into the safety of the church sanctuary.

Quietly, she slid into the same pew where she sat every Sunday alongside her family. Mom and Dad beamed happily as her elder brothers, Garrett and Michael, tipped their heads and grinned.

"I take it Spencer found you," Garrett whispered.

Mel loosened the buttons of her sweater and nodded. She couldn't contain the accidental sigh that slipped past her lips.

"Look, Mel..." Michael leaned past his brother. "Let us talk to the guy. We understand that you don't want to hurt Spencer's feelings, and that's very noble and all, but it's obvious you don't share the same mindset. You've tried being polite. Now let us try a more...direct approach."

"Michael, really," Mel groaned. "I'm not sixteen anymore. I'm a grown woman. My personal life is off limits, and I'll handle my own affairs."

Her brother laughed at her use of the word *affairs*.

"That's not what I meant, silly."

Mel perused the church bulletin, dismissing Mike's helpful intent. Why couldn't everyone mind their own business? As much as she loved her brothers, sometimes she wished they'd concentrate on something other than her. Maybe their own love lives, for starters. Thankfully, her parents hadn't felt the need yet to broach the subject.

The sanctuary began filling up, and Gabe plopped down in the remaining space beside his sister. As if reading her mind, he said, "Don't worry. I'm not going to nag you. But if Holms gets it any worse for you, he's gonna need an I.V. 'cause the poor guy's gonna dehydrate himself. He's one sick puppy."

"Gabe, for goodness sake. Not you, too."

Prelude music—a bright, peppy hymn befitting the Sabbath—reverberated off the sanctuary walls and throughout the room, signaling the usual meet and greet time to which everyone stood and meandered in various directions. Mel didn't wander far, because this was her least favorite part of the service, mainly because Spencer usually found her and monopolized her *and* her hand. Today was no exception. He hurried over and thrust out his hand.

Gosh. What now? Mel could hardly refuse his handshake without seeming rude, but when he followed it up with an all too friendly hug, she quickly broke contact and strode toward her pew. *Really?* Why had Spencer done that?

Rattled, Mel nearly bumped into Matt who poked along in mid-aisle and chose that moment to pivot in the opposite direction. The movement all but brought them chest to head. His chest, her head—since he towered over her a good eight inches. Mel stopped short before they collided.

"Whoa, there. No sprinting in the sanctuary."

The low rumble of laughter made his chest vibrate. He thought this was funny?

"Uh, sorry. Wanted to make it back to my seat before worship began. Guess my mind's on other things."

"No doubt." A lopsided grin tugged at the corners of his mouth.

"Yeah, well..."

"Hey, I meant what I said earlier. You *are* dedicated and passionate, Mel, and I really do admire that about you."

She found their exchange awkward, but she appreciated the compliment. "Thanks."

"Certainly." Matt gave a brief nod. As he stepped around her, he murmured something else. "And Holms isn't the man for you."

"Excuse me?"

But Matt moseyed on, his gaze trained on something, *someone* in the pew directly across from them.

Spencer tipped his head in acknowledgement and reached for a hymnal.

The music that morning communicated an upbeat and joyous message. The final song, an invitational hymn, prompted self-reflection. Pastor Bill hadn't hammered home his sermon points with raised vocals, theatrics, or finger pointing, but rather with gentle persuasion backed up by Scripture. No wonder everyone liked the preacher. He didn't beat around the bush, yet he spoke the truth in love. Parishioners gobbled it up.

Now, as Matt exited the sanctuary, a sudden movement caught his eye. What was Holms up to? The guy zipped past some of the older congregants without so much as an "excuse me" and made a beeline straight for Mel. His steps were quick and decisive, his face determined. Mel's smile faded as Holms marched up to her and took her elbow as if he had every right.

Irritation lodged in Matt's chest. Did the guy really not get it? It should be clear by now that Mel didn't share Mister Fashion Plate's level of enthusiasm. In fact, if looks were any indicator, Mel wished the floor would open up and swallow at least one of them.

Matt knew he should just keep walking. That would be the polite thing to do. The *easy* thing to do. But good grief, leaving a damsel in distress didn't seem proper. Not that Mel couldn't handle herself in an awkward situation. Nope, quite the contrary. In fact, it was a wonder that Matt's kneecaps were still intact after a few of their encounters. With Holms, however, Mel seemed more inclined to dance around his feelings, rather than address the obvious. Was it pity? Concern for his ego? Or...did she really care for the man?

Matt refused to play guessing games. Still, he didn't

know why his feet seemed to take on a mind of their own and turn him back around toward the sanctuary. He had no plan. No speech. No idea what he'd even say. Man, he must be nuts.

"Hey!" Laughter met his about-face. "No U-turns allowed. I'd hate to slap the 'cuffs on you today, it being a Sunday and all." The beloved town deputy stepped aside, gently guiding his wife to follow suit.

"My apologies, Deputy Sapp. Miss Hattie. I forgot something."

"Do tell," Horace laughed, his belly trembling. "Does her name start with an *M*, perhaps?"

"Guilty as charged," Matt conceded. "I wanted to ask my co-worker something."

"Hmm..." Hattie nodded, eyes twinkling. "Co-worker. That's a new name for it."

"Yeah, puddin'. It's politically correct, for sure." Horace agreed.

"No, really. Mel's my co-worker. That's it."

"Last I checked, three sides still make a triangle. And I'm not talkin' about a percussion instrument. Have a good afternoon, Matthew."

They chuckled all the way out into the vestibule.

Well, dandy. He gave them a good laugh. It didn't deter him though. He continued his stroll toward Holms and Mel, though he did pick up the pace as Holms's hand traveled from Mel's elbow to her shoulder and then to the small of her back. Matt glanced around. Where were her brothers?

While Mel's parents visited with the Packard family five pews away, Gabe and Garrett headed toward the church office, probably to assist with that morning's tithe count. Mike helped tidy the pews, gathering spare bulletins, pens, and miscellaneous items. Holms, apparently, had appointed himself Mel's designated guardian and it appeared he was reveling in the role. What made him think it was okay to impose himself on Mel this way?

Spencer might think nothing of his physical proximity or busy hands, but Mel's pretty, blue eyes flashed with frustration. Rosy cheeks faded to pasty white and her spine went as straight as a board. Holms spoke in hushed tones, but Matt heard enough to set him on edge.

"Mel, please. Let me take you to lunch today. I know everything here is closed, but we could drive into Sapphire. We could go someplace new."

"No, thank you. Like I said, I'm having lunch with my family."

"For Pete's sake, you do that every Sunday. Surely, they'll understand if you break with tradition this once."

"No, thanks, Spencer. I meant what I said Friday night. I think it's best if we don't—"

"Mel, it's lunch. A lunch between friends. You said we could still be—"

"Ah, there you are," Matt broke in, coming to a standstill in front of the pair. "Are you about ready, Mel?"

Holms's hand dropped to his side about the same time his mouth fell open.

"Yes, I suppose we should be going." Mel flushed, but played along. "Have a good day, Spencer."

Matt could have left it there, but he didn't. "Yes, it looks like Mel's parents are leaving soon, and we don't want to be late for lunch." He met Spencer's glower with a grin. "Mrs. Brewer's Sunday roasts are about the best in the county."

"Thanks. I owe you one," Mel said when they were out of earshot.

They ambled out of the building and walked the length of the church parking lot together, their steps in sync with one another's.

"Don't mention it. Besides, I wasn't kidding about your mom's roasts. The Come and Get It has nothing on her, and I gotta admit, I can't wait to sink my teeth into those fresh baked pies again. Peach is my favorite, but I'll sample them all, of course. To be polite, you know." Matt beamed from ear to ear, as if the smirk he wore was stitched in place.

"Excuse me?"

"Your parents invited me last week—for Sunday dinner today."

They did? Was he serious? Their dinner guest wasn't Pastor Bill after all?

"Oh. I didn't realize..."

"Yeah. I bet you didn't," Matt laughed.

Mel fidgeted with her handbag and Bible. Out of the corner of her eye, she spotted Spencer as he stomped toward his new Lexus. He gazed at her, as if daring her to look his direction. When she didn't, he quickly got in his car and drove off.

"I take it Holms's interest isn't mutual?"

While she was grateful that Matt rescued her, her personal life was none of his business. Even so, Mel shook her head *no*.

"The thing is...maybe I've given him false hope. I mean, not intentionally. Over the past year, I've tried to be honest with Spencer about our relationship falling more in the friendship category than anything else, and I thought he'd accepted that. I shouldn't have continued to go out with him, though, even as friends. It encouraged him, I think."

"Don't be so hard on yourself." Matt grew serious. "They say hindsight's twenty-twenty."

"That's no excuse. I knew he was having difficulty with my decision. I tried to talk to him about it again—on Friday night after he..."

Her voice trailed off, but not before Matt caught her innuendo. She'd already over-shared, and she didn't want or need her male co-worker, of all people, as her confidante.

"Mel, he *forced* his intentions on you?"

"No. Nothing like that," she responded a little too quickly.

She certainly wasn't about to go into the specifics of Spencer's goodnight kiss. In fact, Mel preferred to forget about it. She wouldn't give Spencer the opportunity to extend their good-byes anymore. Going out even as friends was no longer an option. In fact, she should have put a stop to it way before now.

Matt continued to study her. He cleared his throat, prolonging the pause. "No man has the right to take liberties with a woman."

Mel squared her shoulders. "I know that. He didn't exactly take 'liberties.' He attempted a kiss, and I dodged it. And besides, I've decided not to see him anymore. Well, as far as a dating thing goes."

"Wise choice." A muscle ticked in Matt's cheek. "Holms may be one of Ruby's own, but clearly, he needs a lesson in manners. *Attempting* a kiss, or however you want to politely spin it, is not okay. Not when the lady's unwilling."

His tone had an edge to it. Not characteristic for Matt. Mel didn't have time now to dissect whatever it was and didn't really want to. Though...he couldn't be jealous? No. That wasn't it. It had to do with integrity. Despite their rocky road to friendship, Matt was a principled guy. Mel couldn't see him pulling what Spencer had.

When she didn't reply, Matt added another thought. "Want me to talk with him?"

Oh, no. Not him, too. It was bad enough that her brothers wanted to meddle in her business. The last thing she needed was for her co-worker to take up the cause.

"Of course I don't want you to talk with him. Spencer understands my position now. Didn't you see the way he looked at us when he left? I don't think he'll ask me out again." She forced a calmness she didn't necessarily feel. "Guess I better scoot on out to my parents' place before my casserole cools off. Insulated containers only retain the heat for so long you know." To deter further commentary, she quipped, "Oh, and even though you probably remember the way, I suppose you can follow me."

He brought his hand up in a mock salute. "Yes, ma'am. Lead on. But remember, Mel—Holms's actions reflect *his* character. Not yours. Okay?"

Matt just had to have the last word, but she appreciated his reminder.

Later, as her dad and brothers visited with Matt in the family room of their home, Mel helped her mom put the final touches on the Sunday meal.

Billie Gail Brewer tied a red and white gingham-checked apron around her waist and busied herself with various tasks. Every Sunday repeated itself. Same routine, same pleasantries, same apron. With the boys living out on their own, and now Mel, too, they relished their family time. Togetherness symbolized unity. They might not agree on everything, but they agreed each member deserved the right to be heard.

Though they all still lived around the Ruby area and remained close-knit as a family, Mom loved having all her chicks back under one roof as often as possible. To break with "family tradition," as Spencer put it, never even occurred to Mel. She enjoyed their special moments together and never took for granted the blessing of family. Her family wasn't perfect, but it was hers.

Mel peeked through the kitchen doorway at the five men as they directed their attention to the football game on television. Matt, broad shouldered, tall, and striking, appeared completely at ease. Gabe, Garrett, and Michael resembled the Brewer patriarch, built like Mack trucks with sturdy, towering frames, each one with his own distinguishing characteristics and qualities.

At thirty-two, Gabe was the oldest, then Garrett at twenty-nine, and Michael at twenty-eight. All of them attractive and single with challenging, successful careers, though they still carved out time to help Dad down at the feed mill in town or out on their property here. And twenty-seven years ago, with the toddler boys still in training pants and diapers, God had smiled again on Jake and Billie Gail Brewer, presenting them with a wide-eyed, rosy cheeked baby daughter. To hear her parents tell it, the celebration went on for weeks. Growing up as the kid sister to Gabe, Garrett, and Mike, and only daughter to Jake and Billie Gail, hadn't left Mel lacking for attention. Even the town folk doted on her. As if breaking the baby boy winning streak deserved elevated status.

"But we didn't let it go to your head," her dad often joked. "We made sure you kept your feet on the ground and your head out of the clouds...most of the time."

Laughter drew Mel back to the present. "Magpies today, aren't they?"

"I think the Chiefs just scored a touchdown, Mom."

"Well, that's good." Billie Gail reached for the salad tongs. "But touchdown or not, they know the rule. No T.V. during Sunday dinner."

Yes, everyone knew the rule. There'd be a few groans, but Daddy would turn off the television at dinnertime. Ball games and rules didn't matter at the moment, though. "What made you invite him?"

Her mother, petite, pretty, and even youthful at fifty-five, continued tossing the salad. "Who, dear?"

"Matt Enders. It's not like he's new in town anymore."

"Why, lamb, I realize that. Your father and I realize, too, that Matt doesn't have family nearby. His parents live in St. Louis, which is more than three and a half hours away. It was the Christian thing to do—to extend a dinner invitation. It's played on our hearts for him to have nowhere special to go on Sundays."

Really, Mom? She fervently hoped that's all it was. Surely, her mom and dad weren't trying their hand at matchmaking. Even with Spencer, they'd taken a hands-off approach. They couldn't be worried about her marital status—could they? However, they did seem to know an awful lot about Matt and where he was from and what he usually did or didn't do after church on Sundays.

It unsettled her to think that Matt might be here for a reason other than Christian hospitality. And for heaven's sake, although they each had their share of admirers, her brothers were older and still unattached. Her parents had never meddled in any of their children's private lives...well, that she knew of anyway.

Today men and women married later, and some chose not to marry at all. It was a different era than it used to be. Thankfully.

Mel filled seven iced tea glasses and set the tea pitcher down on the counter.

"Mom?"

"Yes, lamb?"

Billie Gail Brewer tossed the lettuce greens, grape tomatoes, cucumbers, and matchstick carrots with gusto.

"You and Daddy know that Matt and I are co-workers, right? I mean, we're just friends. And barely, I might add."

Her mother paused for a moment, and then resumed tossing, not making eye contact. "Mmm-hmm. Friends. That's exactly how it should be."

Mel smiled, relieved.

"That's the way it was for your father and I, too, at first. Oh, could you call the group together, darling? We're ready to sit down at the table. I added an additional chair for Matthew. He'll sit next to you—like last time."

As the Brewers bowed their heads in prayer, they linked hands around the table.

Mel's hand was warm and so much smaller than his own. *A perfect fit.* Her palm trembled as Matt clasped it. He'd noticed her reaction before when he shook her hand at various times.

What did it mean? Same thing he thought it did? His heart banged against his ribs. Good thing no one could hear it because Mel's brothers would have a heyday with that one. Matt knew the Lord worked in mysterious ways, but this was something he hadn't counted on. *Man, oh man.* The woman had rubbed off on him, too.

Mel had made it clear theirs was to be a working relationship only. Of course, what she verbalized and what she didn't were two different issues. Now that the tug-of-war had eased between them a little, Matt wondered if Melinda Brewer would remove her blinders. Obviously, something more than friendship crackled between them.

Spencer Holms certainly wasn't the right man for her. Maybe he was a believer. Maybe he was a decent guy. Maybe he even had Mel's best interest at heart, though, the jury was still out on that one. Infatuation had addled Holms's brain and skewed his rationale. For Mel to make a clean break from the guy was definitely for the best.

Matt attempted to concentrate on the deep, rich timbre of the Brewer patriarch's voice. Assessing the situation during a mealtime prayer hardly seemed proper, but maybe the Lord understood because Matt, too, uttered his own silent prayer. *God, there's a lot at stake here. Sure would appreciate your continued guidance. I don't know what's going on in Mel's head...or heart...but you do. And I'll be honest. I hope it's the same thing that's going on in mine...*

During lunch, the Brewer family laughed and joked. It reminded Matt of his first visit here months ago. Gabe, Garrett, and Mike guffawed and teased while Jake and Billie Gail added their two cents. Mel wasn't exactly Chatty Cathy, but she was less reserved than the time before.

"So, Matt," Jake Brewer said as he buttered a second biscuit, "I understand some exciting events are underway at The Meadows."

Had Mel described it that way? He sort of doubted it.

"Yes, sir, that's true. And if yesterday is any indication, I believe our residents and the fine folks of Ruby will rise to the occasion. Your daughter and I will work closely together to make some great things happen."

Mel glanced up from her plate.

"That's wonderful!" Mrs. Brewer's voice rose a notch. "Everyone at church was all abuzz this morning—about the new programs and...various things. Jake and I were so sorry we couldn't make it to the fall gala this year, but we had more than we could say grace over at the mill yesterday."

"I'll say, Mama. But that's a good thing in this economy." Mr. Brewer leaned over and planted a kiss on his wife's cheek. "And thankfully, I had my right-hand gal here to assist me."

"Well, that's how it's supposed to be. I've been your helpmate for nearly thirty-four years, Jake Brewer, and I'm not about to jump ship now."

The Brewers made Matt think of his own parents. Married a year longer than Jake and Billie Gail, their union, too, emulated selflessness and sacrifice. Besides loving one's partner unconditionally, Matt had never contemplated the many facets of marriage before. He'd never had the inclination. Until now. Until he sat smack dab next to Melinda Brewer with his heart hammering double-time and his mouth suddenly as dry as cotton.

Why hadn't he seen it coming? Why hadn't he realized the tug-of-war he'd played for months with Mel wasn't merely borne out of work-related issues? It should have dawned on him sooner. The ritual, unsettling and thrilling, manifested itself at the most unpredictable times. For some, conflict wasn't a catalyst, but for him and Mel, the dynamic presented new possibilities. The thought danced around in his brain as he grappled with the enormity of it. *The mating game.*

Matt recognized the magnetically charged undercurrents between he and his co-worker. However, until this moment, he'd not realized why. *You have to be kidding me. It's Mel Brewer, God? You've thrown Mel—this pint-sized fireball—in my path to get my matrimonial attention?* Heaven, help him! He was attracted to her, yes. But marriage?

He didn't need a wife. Did he? He'd never really thought about it. Until recently, school and work had preoccupied his thoughts. Now, more mature and settled in a new vocation and town, Matt pondered *what if.*

Who was he kidding? The reason no one had landed on his radar yet was because no one had lit his fuse like the bullheaded beauty who'd all but throttled him six months ago.

Fantastic. Here he was knee-deep in *like* with his freckle-faced co-worker, and she'd made it abundantly clear that's as far as it went—co-workers, or possibly friends. Attraction or not, Mel wasn't likely to change her mind on the issue. At least not anytime soon.

Loud snorts erupted from the far end of the Brewer dinner table, snapping Matt out of his trance. What had he missed?

"...So, as I was saying, it's a good thing your offices are in close proximity to each other." Garrett paused to take a swig of iced tea. "Sounds like you'll have to chew the fat pretty often."

Mel fumbled with a loose tendril of hair. "And as I told *you*, dear brother, GIFTS is in its preliminary stages. I'm sure Matt won't need my input on a daily basis."

Ahh. So, Mel's family had decided to help the good Lord out and play Cupid. How fitting.

Well, no time like the present to dance on hot coals. "Actually, I expect we'll have to chat at least several times a day. With the launch of GIFTS, frequent communication will be key."

"And didn't I understand that with this new program everyone will be invited to pair up with a partner?"

"That's right, Mike." Matt kept his voice even, but inside, his heart banged against his chest. This could get sticky.

Mel sawed away at her salad, eyes glued to her bowl

Gabe helped himself to another round of mashed potatoes. "Well, Sis. Don't keep us in suspense. About this new program—who's your sidekick?"

"Me."

Mel's head snapped up. Every pair of eyes lit on Matt.

"To get the ball rolling, I posted a sign-up sheet on Saturday—in the community room right after our speech."

"But I didn't sign up yet."

Uh-oh. He hadn't intended to tell her this way. "No. But I did—and I listed you as my partner. I hope you don't mind."

Chapter Five

Why does this keep happening? Does the guy really have a death wish? Okay. 'Death wish' might be extreme. What about *very slow, painful torture?* Did the prospect delight him?

Mel pictured him, then, in various predicaments. For starters, tied to his desk and forced to eat his words, beginning with that stupid sign-up sheet he'd slapped her name on. Without her permission!

She yanked off her sweater and stamped through the front door of her home, kicking the door shut behind her. She'd never thrown anything, but now, the thought crossed her mind. *Not my Bible or casserole dish. Purse, maybe? A shoe?* She flung her sweater at the sofa instead. Poor piece of furniture. It always got the raw end of the deal lately.

As she made her way to the kitchen, Mel set her purse and Bible on the coffee table and delivered the already washed dish to the cabinet where others like it were stored. She hoped everyone enjoyed her green bean casserole, because to her, it had tasted like wallpaper paste. Along with the rest of the meal.

She didn't know how she'd made it through lunch at all. It took a lot of self-restraint, which wasn't one of her best attributes when Matt was around.

She opened the refrigerator and grabbed a diet soda. Popping the top, she slugged back a good measure of the drink.

Icckk. It even tasted off.

Placing the can on the counter, Mel paced. Usually, her own surroundings gave her comfort, but today, she was too keyed up to find solace even in her beloved cottage.

She wondered what Doc Burnside used to do when troubled. No, not a strong enough word. *Livid.* That was more like it. What had he done? Most likely, nothing. Angry thoughts probably never crossed Doc's mind. And if they had, true gentleman that he was, he wouldn't have acted on them.

Disgruntled, Mel raked a hand through her windblown tresses.

I'm trying, Lord. I really am, but Matt Enders makes me so...so...bonkers. Just when I think we've come to an understanding, the guy springs something else on me! Who does he think he is? What's his angle?

Come tomorrow morning, she'd set him straight on a few matters. First, they'd discuss his lack of communication—an all too familiar pattern. Then, she'd navigate her way around *respect* and what the word meant in *her* dictionary. And finally, she'd chart a course on simple manners and ask him whether or not he owned any. And if those tactics failed, she'd present him with one of those old life preservers she'd found in Doc's shed out back. Matt would need one when he was drowning in his sea of knowledge.

Matt adjusted the water temperature and allowed the spray to pelt his face and chest. *Yeah, you nailed it, buddy. You made Mel so mad she'll probably never want to be in the same room with you again, much less team up for joint*

projects. Good job, man.

He lathered his washcloth and started scrubbing. Well, it could be worse. He didn't know how, but it could be. Maybe tomorrow things would look brighter.

He showered quickly, changed into lounge pants and a tee shirt, and padded downstairs to the living room. His place seemed quieter tonight—a silly thought since his house was always quiet, but that never bothered him before. When he bought the house from Sam Packard, Matt didn't pay the square footage much mind. He liked the wide-open floor plan and room to spread out. He'd outgrown his rental back in the city, so when he relocated to Ruby, two thousand square feet appealed. New job, new town, new digs. Perfect.

He liked the place when Jerry Marshall first showed it to him, and still did...except, sometimes, the silence seemed a little loud. The extra space, unnecessary.

As the last vestiges of sunlight faded on the horizon, Matt studied the old Ozark hills off in the distance. Homes, brightly lit and well-loved, dotted the landscape. It made him think of Mel and her little cottage, and he wondered if the silence bothered her, too. When single, square footage seemed a mere side note. Alone was still alone no matter the size of one's home.

The more he thought about it, the more he wanted to know about the woman who drove him nuts. What made her happy? What troubled her? What were her dreams? Her fears? Her thoughts for the future?

One thing he knew for sure. He couldn't backtrack now. The past couldn't be undone, but the present had shifted in a heartbeat...and the future beckoned them forward.

Dusk fell, punctuating the thought.

Sleep came in fits and starts. Images of Doc, Matt, and Clinton Farley dominated her dreams.

Clinton Farley. His name made Mel's heart ache. How could she possibly help him? She had to think of something. There had to be a way to reach the wounded man. Matt's words echoed as she dozed. *I think God's got some plans for Clinton Farley, and I believe you and I can help Clinton see that—if we work together, that is.*

How could they work together? How could she possibly work with a man who'd proven multiple times, that regardless what he spouted about teamwork, he still marched to the beat of his own ear-splitting drum? Her head throbbed with the thought of it and another thought, too.

Service above self. Doc Burnside's mantra seared her brain. Why hadn't she taken the wooden placard from Doc's old medical building to her office? That it remained on her dresser, unseen, seemed pointless. Other than the fact she knew it was there, and now the words convicted her in a way they hadn't before. Surely, a coincidence. She rolled over and punched the pillow, counting to fifty, then to one hundred.

At number 379, slumber descended again. And somewhere, a rooster crowed. How was that even possible? It couldn't be much after three a.m. Could it?

When early morning sunlight eked past the blinds and nudged Mel awake, at first, she squeezed her eyes shut. Had she slept at all? She reeled and regrouped as she clawed her way through the fog. No need to lie there, waiting for her cell phone alarm. She didn't need "Tale as

Old as Time" from *Beauty and the Beast* to announce the time. The sandman had shortchanged her and delivered a headache in the process.

Mel stretched her legs and attempted to shake off the sluggishness. What a weekend. Limited downtime and too much Matt. *Ugh.* Normally, Monday mornings excited her. Today, not so much. She dreaded the inevitable summit with her counterpart and wondered how she could barricade her office door. Could she move her desk by herself? She contemplated the possibility.

Knowing Matt, he'd go outside and crawl through the window. Taking no for an answer wouldn't occur to him. He'd made that clear.

Well, okay then. She'd be ready. A mirthless laugh wobbled past her lips.

Mel chose her attire carefully—fire engine red slacks and matching cropped jacket, paired with a crisp, white blouse. Power colors. It was the outfit she usually reserved for the Christmas season, but today, she wasn't going for a festive mood. No, today her choice of dress reflected confidence and strength. Nothing fun about it.

She secured her up-do with a pearl hair clip, slipped on a pair of red heels, and resisted the urge to use more blush. Definitely not the day for a fashion show, and why worry about make-up?

She downed some OJ, grabbed her purse, and scurried out the front door. No way would Matt beat her there this morning. She'd bet this month's paycheck he'd not even made it past his coffee pot yet.

The headache drummed at her temples, but she refused to acknowledge it. Who had time for that? Mel poked her key in the ignition and her VW roared to life.

Atta girl. I can always count on you. She maneuvered around the circle drive, down the sloping incline, and headed toward her home away from home. The familiarity of routine calmed her, but as The Meadows came into view, Mel frowned.

There, in the Employee of the Month parking spot, Matt's big blue truck gleamed beneath a sunlit sky. Forty-five minutes early. She might have known. To underscore the perfect start to her Monday, white-blue globules rained from the sky and landed with spot-on precision across her windshield and hood. *Splat-Splat-Splat.* Just her luck. She glanced upward as the cloud of black starlings flapped their ugly wings and flew off toward their next target.

What else? It was the predictable icing on her Monday morning cake.

Well, no matter. Mel slapped on a smile as she parked, stepped out of her vehicle, and prepared to enter the cheery brick building. She wasn't about to let a little bird poop *or* Matt Enders deflate her spirits or her mission.

Whoa.

Matt did a double take. Was that gorgeous blur of red really Mel Brewer? He could hardly tell. The image evaporated so quickly.

Stepping away from his office window, Matt listened for the clickety-clack of her heels on the hallway tiles. He'd give her a few minutes to get settled and then he'd go pay little Miss Hardhead a visit.

He swigged the last of his coffee, wishing he had another cup of the strong brew. Matt rarely drank more than two cups a day, but this morning he could almost bet his next paycheck he would need more. Much more.

Mel might have been all smiles just then, but the rest of her countenance had conveyed a different story. Her quick stride, the glint in her eye, and the determined set of her jaw told him everything he needed to know. Matt knew that look. He also remembered their parting words as she'd left her parents' yesterday.

"I'm so done with this," she'd whispered. "Your manipulative behavior is offensive, and it has to stop."

"I apologize, Mel. That wasn't my intention. I truly wanted you for my partner. I thought this project would grow us and that we'd make a remarkable team."

"Isn't it customary to get the other person's input first before committing them to something like that? Or are you really so full of yourself that my feelings don't matter one iota? You're supposed to be a professional!"

"I *am* a professional. Please don't turn this into another battle. I really think joining forces is a good thing, and maybe we'll gain some insight about Mr. Farley. You want to help him, don't you?"

Her pretty little mouth had snapped shut as she'd mulled over his words. Then her lightly tinted lips parted ever-so-slowly. With barely restrained anger, she'd ground out her next words. "I'm not into games or popularity contests, Matt. Your motives better be genuine, or you might find yourself out of a job. People here don't like being played for fools."

Matt shook his head, recalling Mel's words.

Did she really think he was toying with her and the rest of The Meadows' staff? What had he done to merit that? Good grief, GIFTS was an innovative new program— not a nutcase reality show!

He set down his empty coffee mug as a shadow fell across his doorway. Mel's blue eyes flashed with fire and her cheeks grew crimson. Her mouth turned to granite.

"May I?" she snapped. She marched into his office, hands at her sides, palms clenched.

In his time at The Meadows, he'd never seen her so mad. Their previous encounters hadn't even come close. He hoped she didn't hyperventilate.

"Would you care to have a seat, Mel?" Matt nodded toward a chair.

"Not on your life." Mel retraced her steps to close the door. When she faced him again, disdain emanated from every pore.

"Why don't we have a seat?" Matt tried again, gesturing to the matching pair of chairs on the opposite side of his desk.

"Communication. Respect. Manners. Are they really too much to ask?"

She stood stock-still. The five feet distance that separated them might as well be five hundred.

"Mel, please... Let's sit down."

"Quit patronizing me, Matt. I'm not a five-year-old who needs fussed over and babied."

"I'm sorry. That wasn't my intention."

What was going through her mind now? Besides the urge to kick him in the shins with those fancy red shoes of hers. Man, oh man, was she ever a knockout. Why hadn't he noticed before? Well, maybe he had. Maybe that was part of the problem. Conflict had become the norm—no, the dynamic—between them.

Just like his train of thought yesterday, Matt's mind began to race full steam ahead. He knew the psychology behind his thoughts, and he understood all too well the interplay between adrenaline and heightened emotion. He needed to diffuse the situation and quick. Before he kissed the daylights out of her.

"We're on the same team here, Mel. Okay?"

"Team?" She laughed, the sound more like a growl than a stab at genuine humor. "You've got to be kidding. What team? Team Enders and Enders? Like you so eloquently espoused recently, Matt, teamwork is dependent upon two. Teamwork involves asking the other person for input. To use your words, teamwork means working together rather than apart. Teamwork—"

"Mel, please. Believe me, I meant no harm. I thought if we joined forces it would be a good thing. For Mr. Farley—and us."

Matt crossed the distance between them, noting the glazed appearance of Mel's otherwise beautiful blue eyes. Her splotchy red cheeks and smattering of freckles seemed almost cartoonish against the sudden paleness of her skin tone.

"I really think you should sit down."

"Stop it, Matt. I won't be treated like a ch—"

And with that, Mel's five-feet-four-inch frame propelled forward into Matt's awaiting arms.

Why was he looking at her like that—like someone who'd lost his last balloon? He probably realized better than to plead his case at this point.

But...wait...What was wrong with this picture? Matt gazed *down* at her, his penetrating, dark eyes mere inches from her own. She was looking *up*. The room buzzed and her thoughts scattered.

No! She fainted?

"Don't move, Mel. I'll page the nurse." He shoved a coat under her feet and reached for the phone.

"Wait!" That was all she needed—staff and management to come running over a minor thing like fainting. It would only upset the residents and cause needless concern. She couldn't let that happen.

Mel willed the fog to lift. She'd never fainted before in her life, and it took a minute to get her bearings. Her cheeks blazed and her eyeballs burned. Surely, not the typical reaction to fainting. She didn't just feel lightheaded. She felt off—hot and cold at the same time. *But... I'm never sick.*

Matt hovered over her, his hands skimming her forehead. "Wait. Mel, you're burning up with fever. Why'd you come in today?"

"I—didn't realize I was sick. I thought it was exhaustion. That and—"

"Me?" He shook his head. "We'll save all that for another time. Right now, we have to get you home."

"I can't leave. I just got here. And besides—there's too much to do. There's the sing-along at ten, art therapy at one, the book club at three. Not to mention paperwork and meetings." She tried to sit up, but Matt wouldn't have it.

"Huh-uh. You stay put for a sec until we figure this out."

"Matt, really. Don't treat me like a child."

"Then don't act like one. You're ill, Mel. There's no way you're working today. And maybe not tomorrow either. Say, you did get your flu shot a few weeks ago when they were vaccinating, right?"

"No. I got busy with fall carnival prep and I

rescheduled it. I'm supposed to get it this Friday."

No one at The Meadows had the flu yet, but a few people at church did. *Fabulous*. That's probably where she'd caught it. She knew better than to risk infecting the residents or her co-workers if it were indeed the flu. And even if it weren't, Matt was right. As much as she hated to, she should really go back home.

"Okay." Matt's voice softened. "You'll probably have to reschedule it again when you've recovered from whatever bug this is, but right now, I'm driving you home."

Mel's head pounded and her legs ached. The urge to argue evaporated. Still, what about her car? And her activities with the residents?

"Don't worry." Matt read her thoughts. "Your car will be fine where it is for today. I'll see that it gets to you. And I'll step in for you while you're out. You know how it is here—we all pitch in for one another. I'm happy to help."

"Yes. I don't doubt it."

"Ah. Glad to see you've still got some bite left in you. It's reassuring." Beneath the concern, his eyes twinkled. "Now—think you can walk?"

"Of course, I can walk," she snapped.

But when she tried, her legs turned to Jell-O and the room spun. And to make matters worse, any additional protests vanished when Matt scooped her up in his strong, capable arms.

"Shh. Just hold onto me. We're getting you to Urgent Care."

Why did women always fuss with their hair when there were more important things to worry about? Matt didn't get it. "Relax. You look fine. Extraordinary even, considering your temperature's one hundred and three."

Mel's palm trembled as she finger-combed the auburn-colored waves. "But a week? I can't take medical leave for an entire week!"

Fever and chills caused her teeth to chatter. Matt centered the cool washcloth over her forehead and covered her with the blanket he'd found in her hall closet. "You heard what the doctor said. Since you tested positive for the particular flu strain that's going around, you won't be released to work for at least that long. Maybe longer. The antiviral medication should help shorten the duration of your symptoms, but you'll still be contagious for a while. Don't worry—I've already spoken to Foster and relayed the situation. His exact words were 'You tell our little gal not to fret. The Meadows will miss her, but her health trumps sentiment *and* work.'"

"Wonderful. Our boss knows me so well." Mel shivered beneath the blanket. "I'm never sick. In five years, I've only taken sick leave twice. Once because of a nasty head cold and once because of a stomach virus."

"See? No one questions your commitment, Mel. Stop worrying." Matt lowered his tall frame to the edge of the couch, careful not to move quickly. Poor girl. He didn't want to exacerbate her aches and pains. "Would you like me to phone your parents? Your brothers?"

"Absolutely not. I don't want them exposed to this. And besides—they'd just hover."

"But they'd want to know."

"I mean it, Matt. No calls. I'm a grown adult. I can take of myself."

Right. Obviously *stubborn* was Melinda Brewer's middle name.

"Then I'm staying. At least for today."

"No. You have a job to do—and besides, I don't want you to catch this either. I've taken the first dose of the prescribed medication, and some aspirin, and I'll follow the doctor's orders and drink plenty of fluids. I'll be fine. Really." Mel yawned and covered her eyes with splayed fingers. "And do you mind drawing the curtains and turning off the lights on your way out?"

Catching influenza was only a minor concern compared to this gal's pigheadedness. At least he'd had his flu shot. Wasn't much one could do to prevent a bad case of mule-itis. But two could play that game. "I'd be happy to."

Mel's lips curved upward, satisfied she'd won. "Thanks. For everything."

As her eyes grew heavy with exhaustion and illness, Matt stood and did as asked. He drew the blinds and pretty lace curtains over the picture window and tugged the lamp chains to the off position. Then, as Mel's breathing grew even, Matt smiled. He sank into the comfy chair opposite the couch and texted Foster Pearce.

Pearce's reply was immediate and not surprising.

Sure. Great idea. You stay with Mel today and we'll see you tomorrow. No worries. Keep us posted.

Score one for the team. His—for now.

Watching Mel sleep eased Matt's mind. Under normal circumstances, observing a sleeping woman would be out of the question. It seemed far too intimate—too voyeuristic. But this was not a normal circumstance, nor was Mel just any woman. Mel was his friend, and at the moment, a very sick one. He wasn't about to leave her.

As the hours ticked by, Matt waited. He sponged off Mel's forehead. He readjusted the blanket. He watched. He prayed. He did all the things he remembered his mom doing when he'd been sick as a kid.

Late afternoon, Mel stirred. "Matt? Wha...What are you doing here?" She pushed at the blanket and tried to sit up.

"*Whoa.* Easy. Here let me help." Matt cradled her neck with his palm and offered his free arm, giving her the leverage she needed. Her hands were like hot coals against his skin. "Your fever's spiked again."

"I know." She stretched her legs and groaned. "Every bone in my body aches and—" Her eyebrows creased with awareness. "You never left, did you?"

Well, not gonna lie. "No."

"Why not? I asked you to."

"Yes. Yes, you did." He reached for her insulated mug of ice water and tipped the straw toward her. "Here. Drink this."

For once, she didn't protest. Mel inclined her head and sipped slowly. "Thanks."

"You're welcome. Now, how about a trip to the bathroom while I warm up some soup. There's chicken noodle in your pantry. Hope you don't mind—I already checked."

"Matt, really. You don't have to do this. I'm perfectly capable of taking care of myself. I've done it for years."

"Okay. I believe you. But today you don't have to. Can't you just go with it? Please?"

The urge to debate ceased. He sensed it immediately.

Mel simply nodded and attempted to swing her legs over the side of the couch. Matt didn't know whether to be relieved or alarmed.

Any other day the Melinda Brewer he knew would've dressed him down and sent him packing, but thankfully, today wasn't that day.

"What happened to my shoes? And my jacket?" she asked as Matt steadied her on her feet.

"Over there."

Her gaze traveled to the wing chair where he directed. On it was her handbag, and her jacket, neatly folded. He'd placed her heels nearby on the floor. "Uh...thanks."

Didn't she realize by now that he was happy to help? She didn't need to feel beholden or embarrassed. He wasn't there just to be polite. He cared about her. "No need for further thanks, all right?"

"But I appreciate it, Matt. I really do." Her voice trembled and sounded out of character. And was that a tear?

"Hey, now." Before she could swipe at the errant tear, Matt captured it with his fingertips. Her cheek was soft...and hot. Mel being ill kicked his instincts into overdrive, but instead of alarm bells sounding, the need to take charge guided him. It wouldn't do for her to see him fret. "Today's rough, I know, but tomorrow will be somewhat better I think."

"Yeah. You're probably right. It's just that—you're being so nice and all."

"But I *am* nice, Mel." He tamped down the laughter that begged for release. "Remember that when you're feeling better, okay?"

Fresh ice water, chicken noodle soup, and another round of medication—Matt tended to her most pressing needs in a by-the-book fashion. As daylight dwindled into evening, he readied a tray of additional things for later—a thermometer, aspirin, and a cold, insulated mug of orange juice. He placed her cell phone on the coffee table within easy reach of the sofa.

"You know your mother would want to stay with you tonight."

Yes. Mel knew that. She also knew that Mom would fuss and hover in the most loving, unintentional way. Neither of them would sleep a wink.

"Promise me you won't call her, Matt."

"Mel, I—"

"Promise. Please?"

His eyes held hers for the briefest of moments. In a not so by-the-book fashion, he took her hand. "On one condition."

Oh, goodness. Did he have to do *that*? Her heart tripped as his palm circled hers, the warmth of his hand surely equal to her own. Sick or not, she couldn't deny the pleasant reaction. "Which is?"

"Call or text me if you need anything—anything at all. I mean it."

"I'm perfectly capable of—"

"I know." He quashed further protests with pleading eyes.

Illness wasn't an excuse for being impolite, and contrition silenced her tongue. Hadn't Matt gone above and beyond today? First, Urgent Care. Then the pharmacy. Back home and respite care all afternoon. Selflessness and compassion. Her heart softened at his attentiveness. "But I will call or text if I need to."

"Good girl. I'll be going then." He squeezed her hand and stood. "I'll see you back at work in a week or so. Follow the doctor's orders and don't overdo. Got it?"

"Got it."

"And Mel?"

"Hmm?"

"If you really have an aversion to being my partner, I understand."

What was he talking about? "Partner?"

"GIFTS, remember? Our dynamite new program."

"Oh. That." Again, Mel's heart did a curious thing. It swelled at the word *partner* and expanded with the joy of it. "Yeah, maybe I'd like to be your partner after all. If we could find a way to help Clinton Farley, that would be awesome."

Matt smiled and stepped out into the cool, October night.

Toward the end of the week, the walls of Mel's little abode seemed to close in on her. She'd never been prone to stir-craziness, but she'd never remained stationary for so long either. She still battled a slight fever, but she felt much better than she had in days. She'd recuperated, watched a little television, and lazed around, willing away the last vestiges of flu.

Her mother had sensed something was amiss and dropped by twice, armed with baskets of food, groceries, and magazines. Dad delivered firewood two weeks ahead of schedule and stayed one afternoon as she napped. And not to be outdone, Gabe, Garrett, and Mike insisted on checking in, too, under the guise of various yard activities—leaf blowing, fence row clearing, and shrub pruning.

Foster sent flowers from The Meadows' crew, and Sarah texted a few times to update her with work odds and ends. One day, she phoned her with a particularly interesting tidbit.

"We all miss you around here, Mel. Even old Clinton Farley's been in a snit—well—much more than usual, that is. He asked Matt if you'd taken off for parts unknown."

"Ha! What'd Matt say?"

Sarah giggled on the other end of the line. "That was the cool thing. He told him, 'Not likely. This place would go belly up in a hurry without Melinda Brewer at the helm. She wears a dozen hats to my one.' And, of course, Clinton agreed. To be precise, he said, 'Best to remember that, Enders. Glad you know your place around here.' Priceless, Mel. You would've had to have been there."

Mel nearly spewed out her orange juice, but managed to swallow it just in time. "Wow. Drawn and quartered in a single breath by an eighty-one-year-old! How did Matt respond?"

"As you might expect—like the gentleman he is—but with a witty retort. 'I agree, Mr. Farley. And I trust you'll keep me in check by being an active participant in GIFTS.'"

"Ohh. Touché. Go, Matt!"

"Huh? Has the wind shifted where Matt's concerned?"

Leave it to her big mouth…and Sarah's keen intuition. How much should she say?

Three quick raps at her front door scattered Mel's thoughts and, thankfully, negated a reply. Thank heaven for timely interruptions. "Sorry, Sarah. Gotta scoot. Someone's at the door."

Chapter Six

A speckled pup couldn't be cuter.

Mel's eyes shone bright and her cheeks glowed. The smattering of freckles smacked of God's provision and glistened against fresh, creamy skin and the warmth of a smile.

"*Wow.* What a difference. You look *great.* Wonderful, in fact."

"Thanks. Flattery will get you everywhere." She stepped aside, permitting him entrance.

"No. I'm serious. Here." He handed her the gift basket he'd made himself. *Good grief*—the woman wasn't just cute. She was stunning. Pink sweats, fuzzy slippers, hair askew and all.

"You shouldn't have." Even as she said it, her fingers floated over the basket's contents, lightly touching each and every item—trail mix packets, protein bars, and a small box of chocolates. Her hand stilled and lingered on the small furry teddy bear dressed in PJs and adorned with a bow.

"You never called." It sounded harsher than he intended. "I...kind of thought you might."

"But I texted. And you texted back. Remember?"

"Yes. But it's not the same. You can't hear inflection in a text."

Mel closed the front door and motioned for him to have a seat. "Well, I'm feeling much better. Tons, actually. Mom made sure of it."

"Ah. So, your family found out, huh?" No wonder. In a family as close-knit as the Brewer clan, it was only a matter of time before they guessed something was wrong. "And did they hover as you feared?"

"Not exactly. They were pretty sweet about it. Sneaky, but sweet." She joined Matt on the sofa and set the basket down on the coffee table beside the vase of flowers. "And speaking of sweet—thank you, Matt, for your compassion, the extra work, and the gift. For everything really."

Had he heard her correctly? Was this the same Mel Brewer who wanted to take him down a peg or ten only four days ago? Well, like his folks always said, the good Lord worked in mysterious ways.

"My pleasure. I hated seeing you so sick. I only wish I could've done more."

"You went above and beyond." She swept a loose tendril of hair away and studied him with the bluest of eyes. "Being sick humbled me. Over the last few days, I've done a lot of thinking, and I'm sorry we got off to such a rocky start in the beginning. I'm sorry if I was petty and unreceptive."

Whoa. Matt swallowed. In fact, he gulped. Had she read his mind? "Mel—I came over to tell you the same thing."

"Excuse me?"

"That *I'm* sorry. It must have been hard, to say the least, to have an outsider step in and bombard you with new ideas and odd approaches. I should have handled things differently." He shook his head. "I must have seemed like a big jerk with an even bigger ego."

"Change is...well... change is difficult sometimes. It

wasn't anything personal, Matt. Not really."

"*Whew.* Good to know." The sound of her laughter lit a fire in his soul. He laughed, too. "Because if it had been, I might have thought you liked me or something."

"Oh?"

"Yeah. Sometimes sparring is a smokescreen. You know. To hide deeper feelings."

Mel gave an exaggerated sigh. "You know that ego thing?"

"The one I don't have?"

"Uh-huh. That one. I think it's time you admit it, own it, and move on."

Wow, the gal must be on the road to recovery. Her wit was showing. "Only if you join me. Which means hurry and get well so you can set me on the straight and narrow."

"I'll be back to work on Monday so get ready. Until then, I trust Clinton Farley will help with any attitude adjustment."

Ha! Sarah had snitched. "Yeah. He sure put me in my place, all right."

"Told you how the cow ate the cabbage, did he?"

"Yes, ma'am. He sure did."

Matt stayed long enough not to wear out his welcome. They talked about work, GIFTS, and town. They discussed family, politics, and principles. They bonded over hot tea and chocolate chip cookies. And when Mel walked him to the front door, he did a dumb thing. He brushed a kiss atop her head because it seemed like the perfectly natural thing to do.

"I'm contagious, remember?"

"Good thing."

The blush that stole across her cheeks again brought him immense satisfaction.

Who would have thought having influenza would add a new dimension to their relationship?

Since she'd returned to work, Mel resolved to put the past behind her and focus on the present. GIFTS kicked off with much fanfare, and resident and community involvement increased two-fold. She and Matt brought new ideas to the table, and together, they helped facilitate small groups within the new program framework. Though Clinton declined or outright ignored their invitations to join them, Mel continued to pray for the man.

Please, Lord. Show us a way. Show us how to get through to Mr. Farley.

As Thanksgiving approached, the holiday brought an increasing awareness of another year spent. The passage of time highlighted not only the season, but it also punctuated the urgency.

"How can we help him, Matt? How can we draw Clinton out of his wall of hate and distrust?"

Matt took the chair opposite her desk and leaned forward, elbows on knees. "By continuing to do what we're doing. We demonstrate love."

"Yes, but there has to be something more. Something we can do to make him realize how much God loves him, too. The man's not getting any younger. What if something happens? What if he dies like this—hardened and bitter?"

The burden weighed heavily on her heart. Surely, Matt grasped the gravity of Clinton's spiritual condition.

"Sometimes, Mel, all we can do—the best thing we can do—is pray."

Mel nodded. He was right, of course, and an idea formed in her mind. An idea that seemed outlandish, but one that might work or at least start the ball rolling in the right direction. "Yes. Prayer. That's it!"

"What? I see the wheels turning in those pretty blue eyes of yours."

"Well, as you know, holidays are huge events here at The Meadows—especially Thanksgiving, Christmas, and Easter. The week before Thanksgiving we have a big community meal in the dining room, complete with turkey and all the trimmings. Usually, Foster's the master of ceremonies and I assist him with organization and the day's activities." Her idea gathered steam. "We always ask a Meadows' resident to pray—to ask the blessing over the food when we gather together for the meal. Last year it was Edwin Ramsey."

"Mel," his tone was kind. "I see where you're going with this, and I like the way you think, but I don't believe it will work."

"Why not? Why won't it work, Matt? It would be another way to include Clinton. You know, make him feel like an asset to our community here."

Matt shook his head. "I applaud your inspiration, but Clinton's not even a believer. He'd only refuse."

"Well, we won't know for sure until we ask him, will we? Besides, we don't really know the condition of Clinton Farley's heart. I mean, we surmise, but maybe this will make him reconsider."

"It's worth a shot, I guess."

"Good. When will you ask him?"

"Me? Mel, Farley has about as much use for me as a snow cone in a blizzard."

She smiled at the analogy. "Just try, okay? And don't underestimate the influence of a good snow cone."

But as Matt predicted, Clinton refused their request. Not only did he refuse, He cursed and shuffled away in a huff, leaving his coffee to chill and his lunch tray untouched. Mel's eyes misted as she watched the whole thing unfold from the serving line in the dining room. She should have known better. Matt was right.

She made her way to the dining table where he stood, her heart a wellspring of emotion. "It was a bad idea. You called it."

"I wish I hadn't. And Mel—your idea wasn't bad exactly. Clinton's attitude is."

They commiserated over meatloaf and mashed potatoes, and then, peach pie and coffee. The guy was a good eater. Attractive. Compassionate. Loved God.

Oh, dear. When had it happened? When had she fallen for the man?

"Well, we'll just keep trying."

"Yeah. That, and pray." He reached for her hand and gave it a gentle squeeze. "Where two or more are gathered..."

Matthew 18:20. She knew the scripture well. She was raised on it. "...there I am in the midst of them."

"Amen."

At home that evening, Mel curled up on the sofa beside the warmth of a roaring fire. It had been a long day. Meetings. Activities. Holiday prep. Fretting over Clinton Farley. And then curiosity—about the new job posting on the employee website. The one for Assistant Director of Sunset Meadows.

With Foster traveling overseas more with mission

work, the newly created position not only made good sense, but it also set the grapevine to chattering and Mel's mind to wandering. What if she were to apply? What would it be like to spread her wings? Have a little more freedom to try new things? She was young, but still, she met most of the requirements, and with Sunset Meadows being a private, good ol' boy facility, her shot at the job was as good as anyone else's and certainly better than an outsider's. Interviews would begin soon, and the opportunity kick-started a cornucopia of ideas. Fitting, considering the season at hand.

While Mel loved her job as Activities Director, lately, she'd wondered what it might be like to venture beyond her comfort zone. She liked people. Staff and residents liked her. They were family. And since she was still single, the world was her oyster. She could pursue whatever path she wanted.

Mel frowned. Of course, it might be nice to share the path with a special someone. But who?

Her thoughts flitted to the previous few weeks and to the one who insinuated himself in her brain on a daily basis now. *Matt.* Somewhere between the throes of influenza and today, the man had hijacked her heart and scattered her emotions. That kiss on the top of her head sealed the deal—and made her realize her feelings for the man had morphed into something more than *like.* Obviously, he knew it, too.

But as much as they might like to pursue a relationship beyond the parameters of work, the idea seemed awkward. What would her co-workers think? There was no official policy on office romance at The Meadows, and as long as they remained professional on the job, it shouldn't be a problem. Still, the situation could easily turn sticky. She and Matt certainly had a knack for sticky. The last several months bore testament to that.

Mel settled back into the comfy throw pillows, thinking. What if she were to get the job? That would make her Matt's superior. Now, that could be uncomfortable. But she had to try. If she didn't pursue this career opportunity, she'd always wonder what might have been. *Guess I'll polish up the ol' résumé.* She tapped the laptop keys with confidence.

Before bed, she pored over the updated document. *A double major. Summa cum laude graduate. Continuing education credits. Geriatrics specialties. Endorsements. Volunteer work. Exemplary work history. Unquestionable character. A self-starter.* An outstanding career snapshot, if she did say so herself. She printed a hard copy.

In the kitchen, Mel pulled out a manila folder from the built-in secretary and perused the copies of her résumé one more time. Goosebumps danced down her arms. For five years, she'd loved her job as Activities Director and excelled at it. Was it silly to consider something new? The thought of career advancement both excited and terrified her.

In addition to responding online, tomorrow, she'd personally deliver a packet to Foster's office. According to the job posting, interviews would begin after Thanksgiving. The board of directors, which consisted of community locals, would make the ultimate hiring decision. Since Sunset Meadows was a privately owned and operated retirement community, things worked differently. The hiring dynamic was unique and so were the politics. Thank goodness. It alleviated some of the stress.

As a smile formed on her lips, Mel flipped off the desk lamp and padded off to bed. She drifted to sleep considering all the new and wonderful possibilities that now seemed within reach. A new relationship. A new job. A new future. If only the Lord would grant her the insight to deal with Clinton Farley.

Maybe she and Matt could put their heads together and continue to work on that one.

The week before Thanksgiving dawned dreary and overcast, and there was a new nip to the air as the fall season turned sharply cooler. Seven-fifteen and there sat Mel's Volkswagen. He had to hand it to her. He didn't know anyone who worked as hard as Mel. Matt flipped up his coat collar to shield himself against the cold and hurried into The Meadows.

"At it early, aren't you?" He paused at her office doorway, taking in the warmth of her smile. The way her lashes fluttered jarred his insides.

"I could say the same thing."

"Yeah. Guess you could. Today's going to be another big one, huh?"

"You bet. The Thanksgiving banquet is almost as big as the ones at Christmas and Easter. It's a community affair and friends and family come and go all day. The camaraderie is so much fun!"

Her enthusiasm hopscotched its way around his heart and landed on all the right squares. Lord have mercy, the woman addled him. *Focus, man. Focus.* He was on the clock. Later? Well, he'd figure that out soon. Right now, responsibilities beckoned. "Yeah, that's the best part of this paying gig. It doesn't seem like work. Is this the usual way of it?"

"From what I've experienced, it is. I interned here during college and I've worked here for five years since. We're a pretty tight group."

"A reflection of the town...a good thing."

"Yes. Ruby is different. Of course, this area—the Ozarks—is a friendly niche. We have our ways, but neighbor is another word for *friend*. Always has been, and I hope, always will be."

"I know I've said it before...but I'm glad we're friends."

"Me, too." She'd ceased tapping the computer keys and folded her palms beneath her chin, as if waiting for him to say more.

Like what? Like *where do we go from here?* Like *how about a date?* Or *would you mind very much if I come over there and kiss you?* The third choice probably not appropriate, though, he'd sure like to say it. And do it, for that matter.

"Say, Mel..."

Enough of this chit-chat in the doorway business. He crossed the length of the room and seated himself in one of the matching blue wingbacks across from her desk. Admittedly, he wasn't very good at this sort of thing. Dating had taken a back seat to education and work-related goals. Worthy pursuits, but neither offered quite the same intimacy as that human connection. Kind of hard to hug a textbook, tap an app, or enjoy success with the same zeal a romantic meal shared with the right woman might garner.

How to say this? He leaned forward, elbows on knees, and heaved out a breath.

"I really mean it, Mel. I'm glad we've gotten to know each other better."

"Mmm-hmm. It took a while."

"Sometimes, good things do. Take a while, I mean."

At that, her cheeks colored the prettiest shade of pink. She lowered her hands to her lap, where her fingers remained laced together. A hint of something played across her face. Shyness, maybe? Surely not. Mel was a lot of things, but shy? Nuh-uh.

"I'm glad you think it's a good thing."

"Not 'it.' *We're.* We're a good thing. Is that an awkward concept for you?"

"No. But...we started out pretty wobbly. Plus, we're co-workers. It's still kind of jumbled in my head, and I don't know where this might go. It's new territory for me."

"Yeah, for me, too. But I think we're both mature enough to not let anything between us interfere with our jobs."

"I agree."

"Well, then." Man, he was botching this. He'd never been one to mince words, and he wasn't about to start now. He plunged forward. "Would you like to have dinner Saturday? I know it's the weekend before Thanksgiving, so if that doesn't work, maybe after the holiday?"

Mel studied him for a moment. "Have dinner as in *a date?*"

"Yes. A d-a-t-e. You're acquainted with the word, right?"

"Matt, really." She tossed him the look. The one that could freeze ice cubes in July.

"Well, like I said before, if I asked you out on a real date, you'd know it. Now, I'm asking. And you well know it."

"Okay. What did you have in mind?"

"*Okay?* Contain your excitement." The laughter rumbled deep in his chest, then slipped past his throat and tongue and lingered on the space between them. He glanced at his watch and stood. "Tell you what. Let's keep it a surprise. Does six on Saturday work for you then?"

Her mouth curved upward. She relaxed her shoulders. "Yes."

"Great. Nothing fancy. We'll keep it simple. You know—like me."

"Perfect. I wouldn't expect anything less...or more."

"Ahh, Mel. Your wit charms me like a chilly brook." He headed toward the door, but turned before leaving. "See you later this morning. Let the festivities begin!"

A rush of adrenaline fueled his steps. He hadn't even had his coffee quota yet, but he didn't need it. That one word wound around his heart and tugged all the right strings for good measure. *Yes.* A date with Mel Brewer. Who would've imagined?

Matt fist-pumped the air as he entered his office. Today was getting better all the time. Might as well get 'er done while he seemed to be on a roll. He sat down at his desk and powered up his laptop. Five-four-three-two-one. *Terrific. Here we go.*

When the job opening initially posted, he wasn't sure. He wanted to let the idea gel for a while. Now that he'd had time to consider the position and opportunities it afforded, Matt knew he had to go for it, and for the time being, place a secret dream on hold. The Assistant Director would assume the new role in addition to his other duties. In other words, he'd be Foster's right-hand man and assist in day-to-day operations. Too, it would be a generous salary increase, and it would also allow him to further expand his gifts and be an even bigger asset to The Meadows' retirement community.

Matt perused his documents and clicked on the one named *M.Enders _Résumé*. He scanned it a final time. *MBA. MSW. Certifications. Honors. Awards. Experience.* Everything seemed in order. He attached the file to his letter of interest and application, pointed the mouse, and clicked "send." Done. No turning back now.

Though interviews wouldn't begin until the first week of December, excitement drummed at the quiet spot in his chest—the spot reserved for possibilities. This place, the people, GIFTS. Somehow, all the pieces fit together. Somehow, Matt knew he belonged here. And the one person who seemed to be at the center of it? The woman three offices down from his. The one who drove him crazy in all the right ways. *Mel Brewer.* Between the two of them, surely, they could hatch a plan to help a disillusioned old coot like Clinton Farley.

Matt closed his document. A stray ray of sunlight danced across his desk shifting his attention to the window. Early morning drizzle paused as golden sunshine eked its way past wispy, gray clouds. Beyond the blacktopped parking lot, the view afforded him a visual treat. The Ozark Mountains, old and majestic, rose in the distance beyond country roads, quiet meadows, and a sleepy, little town ripe with promise. Far removed from city life, Ruby, Missouri captivated and lured with her picket-fenced yards, cozy homes, and steepled churches.

And yet—Clinton reminded him unpalatable aspects of life existed even in delightful, quiet towns. The man snarled and muttered something as he ambled past Matt's open door. What was it this time?

On a different day, it might not bother him. After all, grunts and groans of dissatisfaction were nothing new where Clinton was concerned. Sadly, that pretty much defined the man. Today, though, Clinton's deportment wore on Matt's soul. Could the guy not find even an iota of joy in today's celebration? Didn't he have one thing to give thanks for?

Matt rose from his desk. Did he really want to do this? Face off with Farley so early on an otherwise perfect day? Riding an elephant would be easier. He expelled a breath, resigned.

"Mr. Farley... Wait up for a minute!"

Farley continued to shuffle down the hall poking the floor with his cane. The guy might be old, but he still moved at a pretty good clip. Matt hurried to catch up.

"Join me for a cup of coffee?"

"Don't try to engage me, Enders. I know what you're up to and it won't work. Save your breath."

He refused defeat. Matt fell in step with the grump. "Mind if I ask you something?"

"*Hmpf.* If it's about that crazy blessing nonsense again, my answer's still the same. Won't even be there today."

"That wasn't my question, but now that you brought it up, what do you mean you won't be there today? Surely, you'll attend the Thanksgiving banquet with the rest of us?"

Farley froze in mid-step. Angry gray eyes flashed beneath silver brows. "And why, for the love of pickled pigs' feet, would I want to do that?"

Why, indeed. Still, Matt nudged. "Because today's a celebration. Today's when The Meadows family joins together and thanks God for our blessings. A time where we feast and fellowship and maybe make a memory or two."

"Look, Wonder Boy. I'll speak plainly. Folks here aren't my besties, and we sure as shootin' aren't family. Don't have any blessings. Don't need to make memories." Farley poked out his bottom lip. "Oh—and I'll eat lunch in my room. Me, myself, and I. Does that cover it?"

"Almost."

"What else is there, Mister College Boy?"

"I still didn't get to ask my question—the one I wanted to ask in the first place."

"Well, spit it out. Pull up your big boy trousers and ask already."

He could couch it with pleasantries, make it more palatable, but what was the point? Matt stood his ground and held Clinton's gaze. "What do you think Marabel would say about your behavior?"

Clinton's jaw tightened. His face darkened. For a moment, Matt thought he might actually take a swing at him. Had he overstepped? Had his method backfired?

A muscle ticked in Clinton's cheek and he stepped back, distancing the physical proximity between them. "You don't know one blame thing about my wife," he ground out. "Don't you ever say her name again or I'll have your blue-jeaned butt fired. You hear me, Enders?"

"I hear you, Mr. Farley. Loud and clear. Now, you hear me. Maybe it's time you stop feeling sorry for yourself. Maybe it's time you behave like the man God made you to be. And maybe—just maybe—it's time to do something honorable with your life while you still have the chance."

Clinton's lips parted to speak, but Matt added one last

thing. "And if you want to have my blue-jeaned butt fired, go for it. I'd rather tell you the truth in love than live with regret about things I never said."

Matt squared his shoulders and strode down the hall. Clinton stared. Every nerve ending tingled as Mel watched, too, from the doorway of her office. Silence weighted the air.

Seconds ticked by. Then, without glancing her way, Clinton resumed his objective and headed toward his suite—room forty-two on the Laurel Lane residential wing.

Oh, Matt. Mel's breath whooshed out in a rush. She grasped the doorframe and leaned her head against its cool, hard surface. He'd confronted Clinton with eye-opening truth. He'd said the very words maybe no one else had the guts to say. Not out of retaliation. Though, who would blame him?

Matt was a complex man. A wonderful man. He wasn't vindictive. The things he'd said to Clinton addressed wounds that needed attention. The interaction between the two men—one, callous and bitter, and the other, fearless but frustrated—reinforced the obvious. Matt excelled at his job. He could have said a lot of things when Clinton unleashed his wrath, but he didn't. Matt responded with maturity and wisdom. He counseled in love. And that last part—when he told Clinton to "go for it"? He'd meant it.

Matt Enders championed the truth, and certainly, truth for a higher cause. He'd rather be unemployed than sacrifice conviction.

Mel turned and stepped back into her office. *If I get that Assistant Director position, I'll speak to Foster about making some changes.* This, from the woman who once despised the word. But the idea that bounced around in her brain was a positive change. One that would benefit every resident at Sunset Meadows—especially residents like Clinton Farley. Though, at the moment, she could think of no one else who shared Clinton's life view. In fact, he was the only resident at The Meadows who seemed to be in a constant state of mean.

Mel selected a sparkling water from her mini fridge and twisted off the cap. The day could only go up from here. Clinton Farley, notwithstanding, there was a celebration today, and while he may choose not to participate, others would.

She sipped the vitamin infused drink and scanned the stack of files on her desk. Still so much to do before the banquet, and yet, progress notes and activity planning no longer appealed. What was Matt doing now? Reliving the play-by-play? Surely, he wouldn't let the verbal altercation ruin his day. She doubted he would, but still...

Okay. Why stand there and wonder? Additional work could wait. Retracing her steps, Mel exited her office.

She found him in the dining room, coffee mug in hand, paused beside the bank of windows overlooking the crimson-colored hills.

"Beautiful, isn't it?"

"Exquisite." He acknowledged her with a smile and took a sip of coffee.

"Matt...I heard...I mean, I saw..."

"My encounter with Farley?"

"Yes. And I wanted to say you were right. Someone needed to say those things to Clinton. We've sidestepped or whitewashed the truth for too long where he's concerned. We've hoped his attitude would improve, but it's only gotten worse. Why, I don't know. Maybe it's old age. Senility. Possibly other things."

"God's chasing him, Mel, and Clinton's afraid. Afraid of his past. Afraid of his future. The only way he can reconcile his fear is to manipulate the present."

That was something she hadn't fully considered. It made sense. "Meaning, he uses abrasiveness as a form of control. He pushes everyone away before they get close, right?"

"Something like that." Matt's eyes scanned the hillside again. "Clinton Farley's kind of like those hills off in the distance. Right now, those colors are striking. Magnificent, even. To get that way, though, conditions must be right. A gorgeous fall often requires seasonal rains and the right temperature. Sunlight factors in, too, of course. Without those elements, this old earth stagnates. Things wither and die without proper attention. That's Clinton. He refuses God's goodness and he's grown rough like old tree bark. He's color-blind."

"A colorless, empty world. Sad, isn't it?" Mel followed his gaze. She couldn't imagine life like that. Nights were long, sometimes, and lonesome. But still, she had her cottage, her family's love, a cool job, and friends. And of late, new possibilities. Clinton could boast none of that.

Matt surveyed the horizon where sunshine danced. "See, Mel, the thing is I don't believe Clinton's a lost cause. To paraphrase our friend Paul, to bear fruit, we first have to share it. We endure. We wait. We serve others." He turned to face her. "And in doing that, we serve Christ."

"That's a profound passage from the book of Colossians, Matt. I've pondered that lots of times. You know, the good stuff in chapter three about clothing ourselves with compassion, kindness, humility, gentleness, and yes, patience, and the thing we're supposed to put on above all those—love."

He grinned. "So, we're on the same page. Good to know."

"Yes. I remember most of it from Pastor Bill's sermons and my own studying, but I also think GIFTS has opened my eyes to a deeper understanding of that little book of the Bible. And I want to believe you...about Clinton not being a lost cause and all. Maybe, though, I underestimated how tough it was going to be. Clinton's always been a difficult man, but since Marabel died, he's almost impossible."

"Mel, think about that. If a persecutor of Christians can become Christ's greatest champion, then why should we think a guy like Clinton can't change? Besides..." Matt touched her arm, letting it rest there. "He has a soft spot for you."

Mel's pulse quickened. His touch—almost a caress—rattled her. "He does?"

"Yeah. When you were out that week with the flu, you should have seen the way the old guy moped. He was crankier than usual. Meaner. My guess is he missed you."

Hmm. That was a new one. Although, come to think of it, Mel couldn't remember Clinton ever being as ugly to her as he was to others. "Maybe you're right, but what can I do? I've tried everything. Nothing's worked."

"Maybe we should pray for new insight. All I know is we can't give up on him. Not now."

His hand lingered on her arm. Something soft and unspoken stirred between them. Be it holiday sentiment or renewed commitment for a mutual cause, the unnamed thing danced. It lit on her shoulders and wound its way down her chest and into her heart. So much emotion, and yet so new. Like other instances, lately, the feeling jarred her. Had she answered him? She didn't think so. *Oh, for the love.* Where was her level-headed logic? Her cool, calm, and collected self?

"Don't you agree?"

"Yes, you're right. We can't give up on him, Matt."

"Super. We're a bang-up team." His smile softened. He drew his hand away and let it fall to his side. "Team Enders and Brewer. Or, Brewer and Enders, if you prefer."

She remembered another time when they talked of teamwork. Obviously, so did he. The memory teased the corners of her mouth until she gave in and laughed. "Let's just call it Operation Teamwork, okay?"

"Good call."

Kitchen staff stirred around them, readying tables with pretty lace cloths, dinner napkins, and Thanksgiving-themed centerpieces. Delectable scents of percolating coffee, roast turkey, and baked pies wafted in the air. In a few short hours, the dining room would come alive as residents and guests joined in a glorious celebration of thanks, and they'd do it all over again next week on the actual holiday. There would be fewer guests there on Thanksgiving, certainly, as many gathered in their own homes to celebrate with loved ones, but nevertheless, it wouldn't diminish the excitement.

How would Matt celebrate Thanksgiving? Would he go home—to St. Louis? Shifting gears, Mel inhaled deeply. "Ahh... Smell that?"

He tipped his head and sniffed. "*Mmm.* Sure do.

Smells divine, huh? The Meadows' culinary staff know how it's done. I think I've gained a few pounds since coming here."

Yes, Mel had, too. About ten, to be exact. Two pounds a year. *Ugh.* At least her job as Activities Director kept some of the calories in check. "What are you doing for Thanksgiving, Matt? Will you visit your parents?"

"No, not this time, I'm afraid. I'm on call. I'm required to stay within a twenty-mile radius. You know how it goes." He shrugged his shoulders. "I'll head home for a few days at Christmas, though. No worries."

Poor guy. Being on call wasn't a requirement for Mel's position. Still, he seemed to take it in stride. "Will your parents drive down here, then?"

"No, they host a pretty big crew, but we'll Zoom or video chat. Naturally, it won't be the same, but it's all good. I'll stop by here for a while, maybe do dinner again, and later, there's football."

"You're kidding. You're going to be alone on Thanksgiving?"

"No, not alone. After I visit with our friends here, it'll be me, my recliner, and the big screen. A winning combination, if you ask me."

Matt always saw a silver lining. She liked that about him. Still, the idea of anyone being alone on Thanksgiving saddened her. She'd never had to face that. Dinner at Mom's and Dad's was a given. Besides her and her brothers, her parents usually invited Pastor Bill and his wife Sharon and a few others from church. One day, Mel expected Gabe, Garrett, or Mike to show up with a young lady on his arm. It was common knowledge that Erin Shaye, the new veterinarian in town, seemed to have taken a shine to Mike. Time would tell.

"Listen, Matt…" Mel knew Mom wouldn't mind. In fact, she'd welcome the additional dinner guest, especially, given the fact it was Matt. In the Brewer stable, what was one more? "Consider your holiday booked. Dinner's at noon. And Mom would want me to tell you—don't bring a thing. Just yourself."

His quick smile jiggled a little piece of Mel's heart. Okay, a big piece. But there wasn't time now to analyze it. He also knew that. Too many things vied for their attention at the moment.

He simply said, "I'd love to. Thank you."

"Great." A week should be enough time to figure this out. Whatever *this* was. "I have a few things I have to take care of now before guests arrive today. See you back here in a few?"

"With bells on, as the saying goes. Oh, and Mel…"

"Yes?"

"Saturday at six. Our date, remember?"

Like she'd forget. By Thanksgiving, surely, she'd know if this thing between them was even a thing at all. "D-A-T-E. Got it. See ya in a few, Matt."

With that, she retraced her steps and proceeded back down the hall. Call her crazy, but it was now or never. She continued walking until she reached her destination. Her conversation with Matt emboldened her. Finger poised, she pressed the buzzer at Forty-Two Laurel Lane.

Chapter Seven

Matt watched her go. The fact they'd reached a turning point in their relationship wasn't lost on him, nor did he take it for granted. Besides agreeing on some things, their newfound camaraderie boosted him, body and soul. Maybe, between the two of them, they'd win over Clinton Farley yet.

Matt sipped the last of his coffee. *Cold.* Still, the warmth of Mel's presence enveloped him and propelled his thoughts forward. The woman fascinated him. More than that, she awakened a part of him he hadn't even realized was dozing. *Aw, man. I'm a goner. Not that it's a bad thing.* Except...now that he knew, what would he do about it?

Well, their date this Saturday was a great start. A new beginning. And then there was Thanksgiving at Mel's parents. And he was pretty sure they liked him. For that matter, as far as new beginnings went, even Mel's brothers seemed open to the undercurrents between him and their sister. That pleased him. Nothing like having the entire family onboard where new possibilities were concerned.

Once more, Matt gazed out the window. What would happen if he were to get the Assistant Director position? He'd be Mel's superior. Would that resurrect resentment? Would it hinder their relationship from moving forward? He wanted the job and he'd be terrific at it, but he didn't want the position if it meant sacrificing a future with Mel. He didn't know where, exactly, the future was headed, but he did know he wanted her in it. The timeframe and logistics weren't something he'd fully explored. Maybe, he should.

"A body could get lost in that masterpiece." Edwin Ramsey waggled a wrinkled finger toward the scarlet hillside. He stepped closer, following Matt's gaze.

"Yes, sir. You're right." Matt wondered how long Edwin had been standing there. Had he watched the interchange between him and Mel? Not that it mattered, really. They'd conducted themselves professionally. "I'm still awed by the fact that this is where I get to live and work every day."

"So, you think Ruby's where you'll settle down?"

"I do, Edwin. There's something about this little town and the Ozarks that captivate me. I've seen a lot of pretty places, met a lot of wonderful people, but this area is different. I don't know that I can even put it into words…"

Edwin squeezed his shoulder. "No need, Matthew. I think I understand." He bobbed his head toward the doorway. "And I daresay there's one person, in particular, who's enhanced your outlook."

Was he that transparent or was Edwin just a wise old fellow? Matt watched a pair of squirrels scamper across the parking lot and into the mottled grass. "You have me there, friend. I'm still trying to figure it all out, though."

"It does take some figuring, all right. I think you're on the right track."

"You do?"

"Yep. Known the Brewer family for a mighty long time. Cream-of-the-crop folks." Edwin faced him. "Miss Melinda's never set her heart on anyone. Until now."

"That's quite an astute observation."

"I'm rarely wrong about such matters, Matthew. Just

ask Sam, your former homeowner. And Chuck and Ida Mae Farrow down at the diner. I have a knack for knowing these things. Dunno how or why."

"Good to know, Edwin. Good to know."

The only thing that tickled Matt's brain was a little matter of direction. Specifically, his. Would it matter that his role at The Meadows could be about to change? Again, he wondered. And again, he didn't have the answer.

Mel pressed the buzzer a second time. Was Clinton watching her through the peephole? Did he stand on the other side fuming?

Well, no matter. Hands on hips, she waited. She stared at the tiny round opening centered at eye-level and rehearsed what she wanted to say. *Look, Mr. Farley...I know you may not want to talk now. I realize you're upset. I'd just like you to reconsider something—your presence at today's banquet isn't only about you. It's bigger than that. It's about unity and love. About joining together with your fellow residents and friends who...*

The door whooshed opened, taking Mel by surprise. Clinton regarded her with pinched lips and brooding eyes. "Yes?"

Everything she thought she might say, vanished. She grappled for the right words. Were there any? "Hello, Mr. Farley. May I come in?"

"Suit yourself." He moved aside.

The room, or "apartment" as The Meadows preferred to call them, was small and tidy. Like many of the rooms here, it was actually a suite, except more compact. The tiled entryway led into a well-appointed sitting room, flanked by a diminutive kitchenette. Beyond that were a bedroom and bath not quite visible from Mel's immediate vantage point.

"I thought we might chat for a moment. Would that be okay?" The room held the essence of lavender and lemon. No doubt, housekeeping's handiwork. They usually cleaned and straightened residents' rooms during breakfast hour. "I'd normally check with you beforehand. Before buzzing you, I mean."

Clinton waved his cane toward the far wall. "Well, have a seat now that you're here. Chair or sofa, take your pick."

Mel chose the sofa. Clinton pattered up behind her and eased himself into the chair. Obviously, conversation wasn't his strong suit. He waited for her to speak.

"I'll be honest," Mel began. "I understand you and Matt—uh, Mr. Enders—had words earlier."

"If that's what you want to call it."

"How would you describe it, Mr. Farley?" Mel treaded lightly. Accusations wouldn't solve the problem.

"How would I describe it? Bunch of hogwash. Boy's an idiot."

Okay, maybe she should try a different approach. "You know, when Matt first came here, I thought the same thing."

That got Clinton's attention. He sat up a little straighter.

"But I realized that, actually, for some silly reason, I felt threatened. He had a lot of good ideas, but I resisted them because I liked the old ways. I thought they worked just fine." Clinton's mouth twitched. Mel continued, "Change is hard, sometimes. When we've grown accustomed to having things one way and, suddenly, we're forced to confront new issues, it makes us uncomfortable.

Life is like that, too. Wouldn't you agree, Mr. Farley?"

His eyes narrowed, but still, he didn't speak.

"Matt's a lot of things. Bold, confident, perhaps, a little over-eager at times. One thing he's not is an idiot. He's also not apathetic, lazy, or unkind. He's a man of integrity and he has The Meadows' best interest at heart. He cares about the community here, and that includes you." A frank assessment, but Mel didn't want to leave any stone unturned. This might be her last opportunity to speak candidly with Clinton Farley, and he'd hear her out if she had to glue him to that chair. "Matt Enders doesn't have a malicious bone in his body. What he said to you, he said out of love. He didn't sugarcoat it with sweetness and light. He put it in terms he thought you'd appreciate. Man-to-man. From someone who cares to someone who needs to."

Clinton's Adam's apple bobbed, though, his face remained hard. He rolled the end of his cane back and forth over the short-piled rug, the noise magnifying the sudden silence. What was he thinking? Had he even heard a thing she said?

"Enders doesn't know jack about my wife."

"Excuse me?"

"Marabel. My wife. And if he brings up her name again, I'll lay him out flat. Man-to-man."

Mel's heart nosedived. She'd struck out. What had she expected? A miraculous come-to-Jesus meeting? She blushed at the notion. She'd been as effective as a broken lightbulb. Clinton had seen through her tactic and turned the tables on her. *Failure. And you call yourself a professional?*

Tears, so carefully held in check, formed at the corners of her eyes. She willed them away and stood. "I hope you don't mean that, Mr. Farley. And I really hope you'll reconsider joining us in a few hours. I'd love to see you there." She extended her hand to him, which he ignored. "I'll let myself out."

Like The Meadows' previous celebration, today dashed forward at a breakneck pace. If Matt thought the fall gala bustled with excitement and busyness, today's banquet promised all that and more. Matt fielded calls, made rounds, and attended two brief meetings. Staff readied cozy niches and visiting areas as guests arrived early to visit loved ones. He had barely enough time to straighten his desk and do one or two other tasks before festivities began. *What a morning.* But, other than the encounter with Farley, a great one. He'd rather be busy and productive than idle and unchallenged.

Matt started with the manila file folders at the far end of his desk. The stack was small so those found a home quickly. He closed the file cabinet drawer and turned his attention toward this morning's mail. The local newspaper, a workshop pamphlet, and some geriatrics literature. Those, he placed in his inbox.

"Got a minute?" Foster poked his head inside the doorway. He leaned in a tad, his right hand visible, holding his favorite coffee mug. The one with the logo *Heaven-bound. But today...coffee's the next best thing.*

"Sure. Come on in." Matt motioned toward a chair. "Have a seat."

"Thanks, but this'll only take a minute." Foster tapped his watch. "Ruthy's arriving soon and I need to help her unload some additional baked goods. At last count this morning, I believe she'd baked and iced about four dozen cupcakes. That's not including the monster batch of butter mints and two containers of homemade fudge."

He couldn't help but laugh. Ruthy Pearce's culinary prowess was legendary, and her husband's slight paunch bore testament to the fact. "Okay. What's on your mind?"

"Rumor has it that you and Clinton exchanged sunshine and rainbows."

Boy, that didn't take long. Matt braced for a reprimand. "Well, more like showers and thunder, minus the unicorn."

Foster clapped him on the back. "Good job, Matt. Over the years, we've all tried to get through to Clinton. You're the only one who's ever drawn that kind of response. That tells us something. You've cracked that old bird's shell. Maybe just a mite, but it's a start. Congratulations."

Huh? Foster was complimenting him? For exchanging words with a resident? Matt scratched his head. "Thanks. I think."

"You're welcome. Keep up the dandy work." The men shook hands. "And for the record. Clinton didn't come to me. Tilly did. She saw it unfold as she restocked goodies in the breakroom. She was worried about you."

"Tilly Andrews?"

His boss chuckled. "Yep. Everyone's grandmama. She's rather sweet on you, in case you didn't know. Anyway, well done." He hurried toward the door. "Now...I best scat. Ruthy'll have my hide if I'm not Johnny-on-the-spot when she arrives."

Matt rather doubted that. Foster's wife of twenty years didn't have a cross word in her. From all accounts, in addition to his own observations, Ruthy Pearce adored her husband. And it was a well-known fact that he felt the same about her. Two decades together and three kids later, they were a couple still very much in love.

Matt wanted that. And the woman who made him think about it was the one he wouldn't have guessed. A lot had happened in almost seven months. And despite their differences, he'd rather have someone who rocked his world than pacified it.

The thought trailed him to the dining room where he spotted her in an instant. Mel stood at the coffee bar, chatting with guests and residents. She'd gathered her hair into a ponytail, accentuating high cheekbones, freckles, and full, pink lips. To her sweater and slacks ensemble, she'd added a fall-themed scarf. Their eyes met briefly and she smiled. *Whoa.* This morning's coffee did the backstroke in his gut. Someone could douse him in ice water and he probably wouldn't notice. *Yeah. I'm in that deep.*

Matt summoned a shot of confidence. Voices swirled around him as residents and guests arrived and mingled. He spotted Horace Sapp who, evidently, was on duty and wore his dress browns today. Beside him were his perpetually happy wife Hattie, Pastor Bill from church and his wife Sharon, Sam and Charla Packard whom Matt had grown quite fond of, and Chuck and Ida Mae Farrow, owners of the Come and Get It Diner. Nora and Ned Brewster, proprietors of Nora and Ned's General Market, moseyed in, wearing matching orange sweaters complete with cornucopia motifs. Others followed suit as Matt made his way over to Mel.

"Here's the man of the hour." Edwin Ramsey grinned and stuck out a hand.

Oh, boy. Had word made it around that quickly? Matt

didn't want to discuss Clinton with other residents, even if they were friends. It risked integrity. "Nah, Edwin. Appreciate that, but I believe that designation is for someone far more deserving. Say, like Horace here. I understand he snagged the male lead in the Christmas cantata next month."

"That he did," Pastor Bill chimed. "I can attest to it. Best bass pipes around. And I have it on good authority that this year's cantata is shaping up to be one of our finest."

"Well, Matthew, Pastor—thanks for that vote of confidence. The choir's working really hard, that's a fact." Horace slugged back a swig of coffee. Edwin looked from Horace to Pastor Bill and back to Matt again.

"Yep. Can't wait. We're in for a real treat. But what I meant is look at you, Matthew, all nonchalant and all, when chatter on the vine has it that your new program here is a smashing success. GIFTS is the biggest jolt of excitement around here since they installed this fine coffee bar." Edwin's old eyes darted to Mel. "And this lovely lady can't stop singing your praises, so we know where there's smoke, there's fire."

GIFTS? Edwin hadn't been referring to his exchange with Clinton after all? And then, Matt had another thought. Mel—singing his praises? About the project he'd initiated? It was one thing for her to soften her heart toward him, but to pay such accolades publicly? *Wow.* Forget the backstroke. Anything left in his gut from this morning plunged from the high dive and plopped to his toes. The recognition didn't matter. That Mel affirmed something he'd spearheaded and wholeheartedly believed in, skipped on Matt's heart and squeezed.

"That's very kind of her." He noted the pink that stole across Mel's cheeks. "It's great to have a cheering section. I can't take full credit, though. This woman's a powerhouse."

Mel shrugged. "Thanks. I've coordinated some new activities and scheduled additional speakers, but GIFTS is totally Matt's brainchild." Her gaze traveled around the circle of smiling faces, landing, finally, on him. "This is your baby. Don't be modest. Own it."

The crowd laughed. Pastor Bill raised his coffee mug. "To teamwork, then."

Others raised their mugs, too, as they toasted the sentiment. It seemed only fitting that Jake and Billie Gail Brewer should bustle through the dining room's arched entryway at that moment. And of course, Mel's dad, affable guy that he was, immediately took up the cause. "Hear, hear! I like the sound of that."

Again, laughter bounced around the massive room where their merriment echoed. The crowd eventually dispersed, and several rushed over to unburden the couple of their coats and baked goods, but not before Billie Gail winked at her daughter as if they shared a secret.

Matt tipped his head and whispered, "I'm guessing teamwork is the operative word."

"More like *team*. Mom seems to think you and I would make a good one, I'm afraid." Mel shook her head. "I'm sorry. That was rather embarrassing, and it would have to be in front of everyone."

He tried not to grin. "Well, that's a compliment if I ever heard one."

Mel's brows wrinkled. It took her a minute. "Oh, no! I didn't mean that like it sounded. Sure, we'd make—we are—a great team. Just not like Mom thinks. That's all I meant. And I'm sorry she winked. Hopefully, no one thinks we're an item or something..."

"Yeah. Or something. Because that would be terrible, right?"

"Yes. Well, no." Her hand flew to her face. Through splayed fingers, her mouth twitched. "Sorry. This is awkward."

He couldn't do it. His mouth twitched. One by one, he pried her fingers away from her eyes, forcing her to look at him. "Not awkward at all. We've never crossed the line on professionalism at work. But Saturday? We'll be off the clock."

She blushed and her eyes widened. "Matt! Are you flirting?"

"No, ma'am." He glanced at his watch, and then, back to her. "We still have about five hours to go...before today's work day ends."

Thanksgiving dinner at Sunset Meadows never lost its thrill, and this year, Matt added to the excitement. As friends and residents gathered 'round the tables, Foster asked the blessing on the meal. Clinton Farley didn't join the group, nor had Mel expected him to. Still, disappointment pricked her spirit.

She shook off pangs of sadness, and as Foster prayed, she did the same. She asked for insight, resilience...and patience. After this morning, she didn't know what to do. She wanted to talk with Matt, but clearly, now wasn't the time.

After the blessing, Foster directed everyone to two separate serving lines where mountains of turkey, dressing, mashed potatoes, and all the fixings waited. Staff assisted residents in their choices and helped them carry their plates to tables where drinks had already been poured. Unlike a skilled nursing facility, The Meadows retirement community was home to more ambulatory folks—individuals who still navigated well, albeit a little slower, and comfortably managed on their own. Clinton Farley was the oldest resident, with Edwin Ramsey about five years his junior.

Clinton's attitude wasn't doing his health any favors, though. Meanness had certainly aged him. What would happen if his health declined and he had to move somewhere else one day? The man may have a nasty streak, but Mel hated to think of him somewhere less attentive and without friends...or those who wanted to be his friend.

"This is quite the spread, lamb." Mom caught her as she mingled about the tables. In her hands, she juggled two salad plates and a dinner platter. "Your father missed his greens. He thinks I didn't notice."

"What would he do without you, Mom?" Mel planted a kiss on her mother's cheek. "Here. Let me help."

She followed her mother over to the table where Daddy sat, flanked by Pastor Bill and his wife Sharon, and Horace and Hattie Sapp. Daddy stood when they approached. "Ah. Busted."

Mel set the salad plate down at her father's spot and hugged him. "Eat a few of those cherry tomatoes and a few lettuce leaves and that should satisfy her," she whispered.

"You're a good girl, princess." He lowered his voice, too.

Mom sat down, and Daddy did the same. Pastor Bill

gestured at the remaining two chairs. "There's room for two more, Miss Melinda. Will you and Matthew join us, perhaps?"

There it was. The grouping of the two of them together. The town of Ruby had matchmaking down to a science. Several couples in the community could, in fact, testify to that.

"I can't speak for Matt, Pastor Bill. I think he's carving more turkey, but I'll be back after I take care of something."

"Wonderful, my dear. Sharon and I are eager to hear about everything you've been up to."

She excused herself and made her way toward the kitchen. "Tilly, I need your help. Where would I find a couple of those insulated food containers? The ones we deliver to residents' rooms when they want to dine there instead of here?"

Tilly Andrews finished slicing a pumpkin pie and moved on to another. "Now, Miss Melinda... Please tell me you're not taking dinner back to your office? Work can wait. Today's a celebration, child."

"Oh, no, ma'am. It's not for me. It's for someone else. I don't think he's joining us today and I want to take him a meal."

"Well, in that case..." Tilly ceased cutting. "Wait a minute. Let me guess. Clinton Farley?"

"Yes, ma'am."

Tilly made a *tsk-tsk* noise. "That old fellow is one sad stinker. He sure raked Matthew over the coals today."

"Yes, I know. But I'm not ready to give up. Are these the ones?" Mel reached toward the containers that looked like what she needed.

"Yes, dear. Those are the ones. Help yourself." Tilly wiped her hands on her apron. "And you'll need a tray. Here."

"Thanks, Tilly. You're a gem."

"No. You are, child. But let me slice this other pie and I'll help you fill those."

The two women gathered salad, dinner, and dessert plates and filled each with tantalizing goodies. They wrapped rolls in foil and extra cookies in napkins. Tilly filled an insulated mug with iced tea and tossed a straw on the tray, too.

"It's a bit crowded, huh, Tilly?" Mel grabbed a small serving cart. "This will help. I'll return it soon."

"No worries." Tilly waved her on.

Mel negotiated the cart around the serving tables. She'd almost made it to the dining room entrance when Matt ambled up beside her. "Do tell."

"Nothing to tell. I'll be back in a minute."

Matt nodded. Obviously, he knew what she had in mind. "Want me to tag along?"

"No, thanks. I'll be fine."

"Okay, but if you don't return in a while, I'll venture down."

"Don't worry. I've got this."

Crazy or plain stubborn, Mel didn't know which fit her best. For the second time that day, she rehearsed what she might say. *I thought you'd like turkey with all the trimmings, Mr. Farley. Since you didn't come to the dining room, we came to you.* No. Make that *I. I came to you...* Personalizing it sounded better. More sincere. Because she was sincere. She wanted Clinton to enjoy a nice Thanksgiving meal even though he'd rebuffed her previous invitation. The man needed tending to in the very worst way. Or...make that *best way*. He had no one. Except for Edwin Ramsey, Clinton continued to alienate other residents. Staff tried to engage him, but it wasn't the same as having one's own peer group.

Mel rolled the cart down the shiny waxed floors. Scrumptious scents of turkey and dressing lingered in the halls and made her stomach growl. She hoped the luscious aromas found their way to Clinton's nose, too, when he opened his door.

She maneuvered around the bookcase, chairs, and sofa in the little wing adjacent to Laurel Lane and continued her trek toward room forty-two. Sarah met her in the hall, halfway there.

"I'm not even going to ask, but I applaud your efforts, girl."

"Thanks. I know it seems pointless, given Clinton's rotten attitude, but I have to keep trying. I can't give up."

"Nor would anyone expect you to. Don't be long, though. Deliver the goods and then come eat." Sarah patted her shoulder. "Maybe he needs some space today."

"Well, that's the problem. I think we've given Clinton too much space. Granted, he's scared off a lot of people with his nastiness, but seclusion isn't good for anyone— especially an elderly guy like him. Just makes him cranky."

Her friend hiked an eyebrow.

"I mean more than usual."

"Yeah, you may be right. And I have to admit, if anyone can draw Clinton out of his self-imposed exile, you can." Sarah pointed toward the cart. "That's a great idea. I'm guessing there are lots of goodies tucked away in those containers. What red-blooded male can turn down a spread like that?"

"Tilly helped me, and I hope you're right."

"Carry on then, my little turkey fairy. I better run— Andy's joining me today."

"That's nice. Tell him I said hi."

"I will. Though, you can probably tell him yourself. He blocked out an hour and a half for the banquet today."

The upside of owning one's own business. Knowing Sarah's husband, Mel bet he gave his employees an extended lunch hour, too. We've Got Nails wasn't known only for their hardware supplies. Integrity and compassion topped Andy Dawson's good qualities' list. That, and a "servant's heart" as Sarah often said.

Good thing, or they might never have married. Andy's penchant for pranks preceded the Dawson's premarital bliss. Thankfully, life had a way of maturing even the worst offenders, and Sarah had long since forgiven him for infractions during their teen years. Specifically, those things—however stupid—teenage boys do to get the girl of their dreams to notice them.

"And that's why I work here instead of with my husband. I want him to fully appreciate what a catch he got. Absence makes the heart grow fonder and all that." Sarah told her once. "Not saying that doesn't work for your parents, Mel. It's a personal choice."

A personal choice. Sarah had a point. In today's twenty-first century world, men and women could certainly work and perform on equal footing when given equal advantages. Case in point—Mom had always worked part-time as Daddy's bookkeeper and right-hand "man" at the feed mill, and their marriage thrived. Still...life was different now. Today, sometimes, too much togetherness didn't allow for partners to function individually or, perhaps, to reach their full potential.

The thought brought Mel up short. Would a relationship with Matt hinder her goals? Would it blur lines? She'd considered it plenty of late, but as she thought about Sarah's words, the idea of dating Matt seemed peppered with conflict. If she got the nod for the Assistant Director position, that would certainly put a new spin on things. Sunset Meadows was fairly laid back and operated differently than most places, but being Matt's superior could definitely complicate the matter.

She arrived at Clinton's door and put those thoughts on hold. At this moment, Clinton needed her attention. She'd dissect the other stuff later. Sucking in a breath, she counted to ten and pushed the buzzer.

Nothing. She released her breath and tried again. Was Clinton napping? Maybe she'd caught him in the bathroom. Behind the closed door, a cane tapped. Movement from inside the suite penetrated the silence. Mel envisioned him shuffling toward the door and peering out the peephole. Should she say something? Break the ice?

"Mr. Farley, it's Melinda... Mel Brewer. I brought lunch. May I come in?"

Again, nothing. Well, she wasn't giving up that easy. "Come on, Mr. Farley. I know you're in there." A grunt came from inside, along with a few choice words. Marabel would thump him on the head if she heard him talk like that. Mel gazed toward the ceiling. She glanced back down and trained her eyes on the peephole where she knew, by now, the old fellow peeked.

"Look, Mr. Farley—Clinton—please, at least see what

I brought. There's turkey and dressing, mashed potatoes and gravy, green bean casserole. Salads, rolls, pie, and cookies. And sweet tea...your favorite." Another minute passed. Defeat hovered on her shoulders and pressed. Though his rejection stung, she reminded herself that Clinton's attitude wasn't personal.

Once more, she tried. "Please, Clinton, let me bring in this cart and then I'll go. I promise."

She could leave the cart sitting there, but it would probably remain untouched. Besides, she doubted Clinton could wheel it inside and handle his cane, too. At eighty-one, the guy still moved pretty well for his age, but a fall couldn't be ruled out, given the right circumstance.

Mel's spirits sagged. She drummed her fingers on one of the stainless-steel container covers. Why would anyone choose this? Why, when surrounded with so much love and holiday revelry, would anyone willingly choose loneliness? Sure, Clinton had alienated lots of folks in recent years, but people here were a forgiving lot. The little town of Ruby, including the Sunset Meadows' retirement community, doted on their own and loved without question. What would it take for Clinton to recognize that or believe it?

"I know you're listening. Please open the door." The cart taunted Mel with its bounty. Sadness dulled any attempt at charity, bringing home the reality of how deep one could wound another. "Please..."

Nothing.

She pressed her cheek close to the door. "Just so you know, I'm not giving up. I'll be back. You matter to me, Clinton. And you matter to God."

Mel turned to go. Despite her better judgment, she left the food cart right where it was.

Chapter Eight

Mel's eyes were rimmed in red when she returned from Farley's. Her cheery façade didn't fool him for a minute. Matt knew Clinton had rebuffed her efforts. *Mean old coot.* While the man in him wanted to give Farley a piece of his mind, Matt, the believer, harnessed his emotions.

They met at the serving table farthest from her parents. Mel's hands trembled as she reached for the salad tongs.

"Here. Allow me." Gently, he took the tongs from her hands and captured a generous helping of mixed greens. "Dressing?"

"Pear-honey, please." Her voice was soft. Detached.

Matt spooned a dollop of in-house dressing over her salad. "Okay? Need a little more?"

"No, this is perfect. Thanks."

They moved on to the relish trays where he speared a pickle, some olives, and a few artichoke hearts and added them to the side of Mel's salad plate. "You know, sometimes, God uses us to plant seeds. We don't see the entire garden right away."

"I know. I told Clinton I'm not giving up. I'm sure he heard me even though he never opened his door."

"Good for you. Clinton's old, not deaf." Matt added some cherry peppers to his own salad plate. They moved on toward the dinner rolls. "And closed doors aren't always forever."

Mel smiled. "You're right."

On Saturday, Matt replayed that moment in his mind as he approached Mel's front door. He'd never been as inclined to kiss a woman as he'd been then. For propriety's sake, naturally, he hadn't. It wouldn't do for two department heads to lock lips in front of a few hundred people, but man, he'd wanted to.

That face. Those freckles. Her smile. Her *heart*. Melinda Brewer cornered his and set up camp. Their date couldn't come soon enough. He hoped he didn't mess it up. Why even think that? Dating a co-worker didn't have to be complicated. As professionals, obviously, they'd use discretion. They could do this.

He hid the box of American Beauties behind his back and knocked. Then, he waited.

The sight of him made Mel's breath catch. He wore the jeans well, and the brown flannel shirt beneath a black jacket highlighted his dark eyes. Waning sunlight glinted off sable waves, combed and neatly trimmed. His mouth inched upward in an all-too-familiar grin.

"These are for you." He held out a long white box, secured with gold ribbon and matching bow. The grin morphed into a full-fledged smile.

"Oh, Matt."

"If you'll invite me in, you can open the box and see if you like them. Or we can do it here and give your neighbors a good peek, too."

Funny, yet, so true.

"The fact that your truck is parked out front will set a

few tongues wagging, but yes, do come in." She accepted the box and stepped aside, closing the door behind him. "You shouldn't have done this."

"Hey, never *ever* say 'You shouldn't have done this' when accepting a gift. That diminishes the blessing." He helped her remove the ribbon. "And makes the giver want to pinch you."

Now, it was her turn to grin. "You're right. Sorry."

Gingerly, Mel lifted the lid. The dozen long-stemmed red roses and accompanying Baby's Breath lay cradled in white and gold tissue, their aroma, intoxicating. She brought the box closer and sniffed. *Oh, my goodness.* They smelled divine. Better than Mom's homemade apple pies. Better than her mother's Sunday rump roasts. Certainly, better than anything she'd ever smelled in her life, including the gift basket Matt brought her when she was sick. And, most certainly, better than the discounted roses Spencer gave her once. No comparison there.

"There's something else."

Overwhelmed and giddy, Mel fingered the miniature envelope. Matt helped her juggle the box as she tugged out the card and read. *To the woman who upends me, yet strengthens my resolve. You make me a better man. Thanks for being you. P.S. Next time you want me to hold you in my arms, just ask. You don't have to faint to get my attention. Fondly, Matt*

Her face warmed, and she laughed, remembering. "Thank you. I'll keep that in mind." She leaned forward and hugged him from the side with her free arm. Her five-feet-four-inches to his almost six-feet-tall frame didn't allow for cheek-to-cheek intimacy so the hug seemed more neighborly than affectionate. "You spent a fortune, but the roses are gorgeous. Really, they are."

"Tut-tut. A simple thank you will do." Matt returned the hug with one arm as she'd done. "If you have some pruning shears, I'll help you trim the stems and we can set those in water. I think I spotted a nice vase last time I was over. If I remember, it looked about the right size."

The vase he referred to—a hand cut, lead crystal beauty that graced one of her second-hand shelves—was left behind in some of Doc Burnside's things. A wedding present, probably, and sentimental girl that she was, Mel wouldn't think of parting with it.

They worked together and had the roses arranged and displayed within a few minutes.

"Perfect." Mel stepped back to observe from a different angle.

"I agree." Even as Matt said it, he looked past the roses and at her. "Exceptionally perfect."

Nothing about his words were suggestive. Yet, his tone—quiet and almost reverent—raised goosebumps beneath her sweater. She'd known Matt Enders almost eight months now, and in that time, she hadn't considered him anything more than a royal pain. Until, recently.

For heaven's sake, the guy had grown on her. Like it or not, co-workers or not, there was no going back. She would never think of Matt in the same way she had before. Their relationship had...evolved. Like her affinity for broccoli-rice casserole. Broccoli once appealed about as much as chopped liver, but when paired with rice and all that cheesy goodness? *Oh, my.* She'd jumped on board quick as her tastes expanded beyond the ordinary, same old thing.

Granted, Matt was more appetizing than broccoli, but

the principle still applied. For seven months, they'd been at odds. Then, this past month? BAM. His finer qualities ambushed her, revealing deeper layers and details she'd missed.

"Penny for your thoughts?"

If he only knew. But not yet. The timing wasn't right. For now, their connection was enough. More could come later. "Nope. It'll take at least a dollar. Maybe five."

"Ma'am, you drive a hard deal. Next time then. Shall we head out?"

"Sure. Let me grab a jacket."

The cool air nipped their noses as they ventured out into the early night. Overhead, the moon inched high in the sky, illuminating the quiet street and distant hills. Smoke from a burning fireplace licked the dusky horizon and wound its way above barren treetops. Matt offered a hand as he helped her into the passenger side of his pickup.

"Thank you." The strength of his grip belied the gentleness of his touch. "You never said where we're going."

"No. I didn't, did I?" He winked but added nothing more.

Matt turned at the edge of town and headed north toward Sapphire, a "city" to the locals, but really, just a large, sprawling town when compared to bigger metropolises. During the twenty-minute ride, they chatted about various things—the holidays, family, what he liked about the Ozarks. For the time being, they didn't discuss work, Clinton, or his refusal to attend the banquet, much less sample anything from Mel's hand-delivered food trays.

They approached the freeway and drove another ten minutes to the historic part of town, home to family-owned delis, restaurants, and businesses. Matt slowed to a crawl and guided the vehicle to a small, tightly packed lot adjacent to an older brick building. Mel recognized it immediately and a tiny thrill coursed through her.

"Oh! I haven't been here in years. I used to love this place when I was a little girl."

"I know." Even in the darkness with nothing but the reflection of the neon sign nearby, she sensed Matt's pleasure. "I got that straight from the horses' mouths."

"Excuse me?"

"That would be your brothers."

"My brothers? You told them about our date?" *Fantastic.*

"You might say I asked for their input. I weighed all options and made the final decision myself."

Those rats. Gabe, Garrett, and Mike hadn't said a thing to her. She'd never known the guys to be so tight-lipped. And it wasn't like them to not quiz her about her dates or lack thereof.

"I wonder if it's still the same."

"Well, why don't we go find out? Our reservation is for seven."

The vintage charm of Fryin' Pan and Into the Fire washed over Mel and transported her to another era, to the days of her childhood when she'd come here with her family for birthdays or special occasions. Nana and Papa had known the owners, the Teagues, personally. Deceased now, she'd heard the Teagueses' grandchildren had taken ownership and operated the little restaurant in the same vein and with the same careful attention to detail that

Chester and Zelma had.

It reminded Mel of Chuck and Ida Mae's place back in Ruby except the Come and Get It, while unique and sigh-worthy in its own right, was more of a diner, while Fryin' Pan and Into the Fire exuded a restaurant-like quality. Brimming with nostalgia and bursting with personality, both eateries swept patrons away to a different time, yet in a different way. Scents of fried chicken and spiced apples and cinnamon wafted across the room and made Mel's stomach growl.

The hostess, whom Mel recognized as the Teagueses' oldest granddaughter, greeted them warmly. "Matt and Mel, welcome. Very nice to meet you in person, Matt, and goodness, Mel, it's wonderful to see you again. What's it been—ten years?"

"At least. How's everything with you, Lisa Ann?"

"Couldn't be better. Hal and I are due at the end of April. Well, strike that. I'm having the baby. He just thinks he is by the way he struts around, proud as a peacock."

Now that she mentioned it, Mel did notice the vague swelling of Lisa Ann's abdomen. A definite baby bump protruded from her middle to fill out her slender frame.

"Congratulations! That's wonderful. May I share with Mom and Daddy? They'd love to know."

"Well, I can't imagine anyone in our neighboring towns not knowing yet, but sure, share away." Lisa Ann giggled, her blonde curls bouncing like springs on her shoulders. "Now, if you'll follow me, your table's ready. It's the best in the house, as per your request, Matt."

The young woman, a few years older than Mel, led them to a cozy alcove toward the back of the restaurant. The small round table was appointed in red and white gingham and flanked by two Windsor chairs. An oil lamp, lit and glowing, graced the center of the table. Lisa Ann drew the chairs back and presented them with twin menus.

"Our special this evening is the fried chicken meal for two. That includes two chicken breasts and two wings, smashed garlic taters and cream gravy, bacon-wrapped green beans with a brown sugar glaze, angel biscuits with honey butter, and apple turnovers with homemade ice cream for dessert. That also comes with your house salad for starters and iced tea or the soda of your choice. I can bring the wine list, too, if you like."

"Wow." Matt gave a low whistle. "Can you give us a moment to decide, ma'am?"

Lisa Ann nodded. "You bet. Take all the time you need. May I get you something to drink?"

Matt gestured with his hand. "Mel?"

"I'll have the iced tea, please. Unsweetened."

"Iced tea for me, as well, but with sugar, please." He helped Mel out of her jacket, and then slipped off his own. Lisa Ann reached for their things as they were seated.

"Teas coming right up."

When they were alone, Matt leaned forward. "So, what do you think?"

"It's everything I remembered." From the distressed hardwood floors to the antique-white wainscoting, and overhead, to the vintage metal ceiling tiles, the place smacked of nostalgia. Some features, like the fans and lighting, were newer, but the woodwork was still original and remained intact. "It probably seems strange that I like old things."

"Not at all. I've always held a certain esteem for eras

gone by. Maybe we're just a pair of sentimental souls who appreciate the past and what we perceive as a gentler way of life. Come to think of it, a lot of people around here are like that." His voice softened. "We respect those who've gone before us, and yet, we understand the mission we're charged with—to think with open minds and receptive hearts when considering the future. Can't advance and improve without a little give and take."

Mel knew he referenced more than his life philosophy. Like, for instance, their personal history.

"Yes, I agree."

He cocked an eyebrow.

"Okay. Maybe it took me a while to warm up to change, but I do think good things happen when people move forward together."

"Speaking of good things..." Matt paused as Lisa Ann sat down two, large mason jars brimming with iced tea. "Now, these are what I call some fine glasses. Thank you."

She flashed a smile. "You're very welcome. Starla will be over in a moment to take your order. Enjoy, my friends."

And not even thirty seconds later, Starla, a younger, trendier version of Lisa Ann appeared. Judging by their similar features, they had to be sisters. "Hi. I'm Starla. Would you like more time?"

Matt grinned. They'd barely skimmed the menus. "I think so, Starla. Could you give us a little while?"

"Absolutely. Take all the time you need."

They scanned the menus, finding so many choices, it made it difficult to decide. The fried chicken special. Red beans and rice. Beef stew and cornbread. Ham steak with red-eye gravy. Shepherd's Pie and more. Not to even mention the dessert selection. Pies. Brownies. Custards. Cake. Everything pictured and described sounded heavenly. And with the holidays right around the corner, too. Mel might as well kiss her waistline good-bye.

She perused the options and shook her head. "This is hard. Surprise me, Matt."

"Really? This could be fun."

When Starla returned, he positioned the menu so Mel couldn't see as he pointed. "Starla, the lady suggests I surprise her. We'll start with this. And end with this. And this. Oh, and we may need boxes for leftovers, please, ma'am."

"You got it, sir. Now, sit back and relax and let Fryin' Pan and Into the Fire work our magic." Starla bounced away, humming.

"Goodness. Am I going to regret this?"

"No worries. Trust me." He took a swig of tea, exaggerating an *ahh* after he'd swallowed. "Now, getting back to my question."

"What question?"

"The one I didn't finish asking earlier. I was going to ask if you'd always wanted to work with the elderly—to be an activities director for a retirement community. Was that something on your radar for a while or did you ever envision doing something else?"

Mel considered the question. "The older generation intrigues me. I suppose it goes back to my affinity for nostalgia and the old days. More than that, though, rather than seeing *old* discarded and replaced with new and improved, I wanted to help others realize age didn't have to define them. Through activity and by living life to its fullest, there's still a place for them in today's world." She drummed her fingers on the table, wondering if that sounded silly. "See. It's that word. Change. For the aging population, change causes anxiety. When encouraged to stay active, they feel better—emotionally and physically. They reminisce about the past, but they're less apt to get stuck there. I like playing a part in that. Does that sound weird?"

"Not at all. I entered the field of social work for some of the same reasons. My granddad kind of influenced my decision, too. He lived in a retirement home for about three years before he died. Great place, but I knew I wanted to do things a little differently. I wanted to do more than push forms and agendas. The position at Sunset Meadows was the perfect opportunity to expand my gifts." Matt swirled his tea with his straw. For a moment, he seemed carried by something else.

"So, social work was—is—your dream career?"

"It's a career I love, yes."

"Is there something else?"

"I don't know. It might lead to something else someday. Granddad always encouraged me to think beyond my comfort zone and reach for the stars...whatever they may be."

His answer intrigued her. Was Matt being evasive or reflective? Did he have a secret or was he merely recalling affirmation from a loving grandparent? Nevertheless, they'd been close.

"It sounds like your grandfather loved you very much."

"Yeah. We were alike in many ways."

They talked easily, without pretense. When Matt spoke of family, they connected on a deeper level. She appreciated family roots and loved her family in the same way he loved his. He hailed from a blue collar, Bible-believing background. He championed love, truth, and underdogs. He liked the color blue. He despised apathy. He favored homemade over store-bought. He never met a cookie he didn't like. Telling tidbits, and yet, so much left to discover.

When their meal arrived, Mel realized another thing about Matt. Timid, he wasn't. Not really a surprise. She'd already guessed that.

"How does everything look?" Starla whisked the now-empty tray to her side and stepped back.

For a moment, Mel simply stared. Had he passed the test or not?

T-bones. Fried potatoes and massive sides of gravy. Corn on the cob slathered in butter. Creamy cole slaw. Cinnamon-apple sauce. Texas toast. Their dinner platters could barely contain it all.

Mel gasped. "Oh, my gosh!"

"That's everyone's initial reaction." Starla laughed and lingered a moment. "I'll check back soon, but if there's anything you need before then, please give me a shout. And remember, save room for dessert."

"Will do." Matt unfurled his silverware from the gold dinner napkin. "Thank you, Starla."

Starla nodded and bounded away. Mel remained motionless and continued to stare. Had he made a bad call? She liked steak, didn't she? He trailed a fingertip across her hand in an effort to coax a response.

"*Wow.* This looks incredible."

"Good. For a minute, you had me worried. I did all right, then?"

"More than all right. Thank you." Mel glanced down where his fingertips remained nestled next to hers. Then, surprisingly, she linked her fingers with his. "You're tough on a girl's willpower."

"Yes, ma'am." He tried to keep a straight face, but couldn't. "That's what they tell me."

Laughter bubbled past Mel's lips. "Riiight."

"Oh, you meant the entrée I chose?"

Her cheeks flamed and she continued to smile. "Tame your ego, Matt. Certainly, I meant the entrée. I can now kiss my Christmas diet good-bye, thanks to you."

"Diet? What diet? You're beautiful." Their eyes met and held. "I mean it. You enter a room and hearts flutter. And it's not just your physical beauty, though, I admit— you're pretty easy on the eyes. It's also your aura. The way you carry yourself. Your countenance."

She shifted in her chair. Clearly, his appreciation made her uncomfortable, which was not what he'd intended. But good grief, didn't she know? Maybe not. Television and movies had their own version of beauty and declared it gospel. Another reason Mel endeared herself to him. Authentic appeal, she didn't lack.

Maybe he should lighten the moment and lessen some of the awkwardness. "Need I continue, or should we dig in before our food grows icicles?"

That garnered another laugh.

"I say we dig in."

As they dined and chatted, Matt sensed their bond deepening. The tip of her head. Eyes fixed on his. Body language, open and receptive. Subtle, unintentional cues that his honest praise resonated.

They exchanged stories, memories, and ideas. They

shared. They listened. When dessert came, it hardly seemed like an hour had passed.

Starla made a grand production of the chocolate chess pie, spooning generous dollops of homemade whipped topping over each slice. Then she shaved dark chocolate over the slices, and with a gloved hand, plunged the remaining blocks of chocolate into the clouds of whipped cream. She returned only a moment later with matching red coffee mugs, full and piping hot. Beside the mugs on the matching saucers were gingerbread stirrers drizzled in—what else? More chocolate.

But that wasn't all. When Starla delivered their take-home boxes, she discreetly slid the check toward Matt and then also presented Mel with one of the restaurant's specialty items—a soy-based, brownie-scented candle inside a miniature fry pan and wrapped in red cellophane. On the sticker was the restaurant's name and their trademark frying pan and fire logo.

Mel's mouth curved upward. "You thought of everything, didn't you?"

"You said 'surprise me.' I obliged."

"And the soy candle is scrumptious. At least I can burn it without feeling guilty. Thank you, Matt. For tonight. For everything."

"The evening isn't over yet. I'd still like to show you something."

"Let me guess. It's a surprise, right?"

Well, she had him there. He hadn't planned it. In fact, this surprise or *secret*, he hadn't planned to share at all. Mel did that to him. She made him want to dive in head first and judgment be hanged.

"It's back at the house."

"Your house?"

"Unless nine's too late for surprises. Make that nine-thirty, considering the twenty-minute drive."

She hesitated for the briefest time. Was Mel second-guessing his intentions?

"Okay. I'll bite." She blotted her mouth with the dinner napkin and slid the remaining food from her plate into one of the carryout boxes. "Should I ask or are you going to make me wait?"

"Waiting's half the fun, don't you think?"

"It depends on the surprise."

"Don't worry. It's not what you're thinking."

"Which is?"

Did he have to spell it out? Matt chuckled and gathered his leftovers, too. He closed the insulated box, snapping the tab into the coordinating slot. "That I may have an ulterior motive. And let me assure you, I don't. If I wanted to kiss you, I'd ask. I wouldn't spirit you back to my place under false pretenses to do it."

Mel gazed heavenward and shook her head. "Matt. Matt. Matt. Am I supposed to be shocked by that?"

"Not at all." Laughter rose in his chest. "A statement of fact. I don't play games. You should know that by now."

She flashed him a smile. "Okay, then. Let's go. I'm all about surprises."

The way she said it made him believe it. Whatever reservations he had disappeared as he slipped three twenties and a generous tip inside the leather binder that Starla had left on their table.

Matt reached for the candle and carryout boxes. "Allow me."

"Oh, you don't have to do—"

"Hey, none of that. Gentlemen always remember their manners." He offered Mel his free hand and they stood to leave.

"Are you sure you can juggle everything?"

He quirked an eyebrow, amused. "If I can rescue a damsel in midflight, I'm sure I can carry two takeout boxes and a parting gift."

"You're never going to let me live that down, are you?"

"Nope."

Laughing, they made their way toward the front of the restaurant, and Lisa Ann met them at the entrance with their jackets. Matt thought it must be true what they said about pregnancy. Lisa Ann glowed.

"Was everything to your liking?"

"The meal and service were outstanding. We'll definitely return."

"Wonderful! That's what we like to hear."

They strode out into the moonlit night, away from quiet chatter and fond memories. They were almost to his vehicle when Mel looked skyward and pointed.

"Look! A shooting star."

It streaked overhead toward the horizon, and in a flash, was gone. *Perfect.* For a moment, neither of them spoke. Matt wondered if Mel sensed it—that it meant something. Something that went beyond words and time. Perhaps, a wish. Perhaps, more.

On the drive home, the moon inched farther up into the sky, bathing the cold earth below in its brilliant white light. Mel craned forward, as if to catch another glimpse of a shooting star.

"Afraid that's the only one we'll see tonight."

"Maybe not." Mel relaxed against the seat. "When I

was ten, Dad and I saw three in one night."

"Wow. Can't say I've witnessed anything like that. Must be a rare phenomenon."

"That's what Dad said. And then I wished upon all three of them. I figured three stars, three wishes. I thought it increased my odds."

"Of what?"

"Of coming true, silly." The sound of her soft laughter bounced around the truck cab, landing squarely on his heart.

"And have they?"

"One did. Still waiting for the other two."

"Which one came true?"

"Doc Burnside's cottage. I wished that one day I'd have a place like his to call my own. I couldn't have dreamed all these years later it would finally happen. Like I've always said, I think God had more to do with that than me wishing on a star, but it's still fun to think about."

Yeah. And he wanted to know what her other wishes were, too. "I'm sure you're right. It's fun to wish and dream though." He leaned forward then and stared into the sky as he drove. "See? You're rubbing off."

"What do you wish, Matt?"

"Huh-uh. I want to know what your other two were."

She stretched, and gently nudged his elbow. "You know I can't tell you that. Then they won't come true."

"Oh. Got it. Well, then. I better not share mine either."

Chapter Nine

Matt turned down his graveled drive. Moonlight fell across the leaf-strewn lawn, lighting the property in soft, glowing shadows. Mel last ventured out this way when Sam Packard still owned the place, and she and Mom delivered some baked goods. Even in the semi-darkness, the home and surrounding area mirrored an ethereal beauty. Almost as pretty as her cottage, the house, matching shed, and larger outbuilding boasted breathtaking appeal with their character and charm. The outbuilding had housed Sam's carpentry business before he remarried, and he and his daughters moved a few miles across the rise. A beautiful residence—this dwelling and location—but what on earth had drawn Matt here? All this space for one person. What did he use the outbuilding for anyway?

Mel's eyes drifted to the front porch swing, a new addition she didn't remember. She noticed other things, too. The quaint cobblestone walkway between the carport and house, recently restored and lengthened. Twin lamplights, lit and welcoming, flanking each end of the home. Elongated shutters, repainted the previous red, a color she adored. The entire setting, surreal, and definitely, magazine-cover worthy.

"I'd forgotten how extraordinary this place is." Mel peered through the passenger side window as Matt brought the vehicle to a stop and cut off the ignition. Motion sensor lights immediately illuminated the carport.

"Ooh, nice. Did you install those?"

"Surprised?" Matt laughed. "Besides being book smart, I'm a fairly handy fella. I'm good with paint, tools, and some basic electrical stuff."

"Naturally. Is there anything you can't do?"

"Yeah. Brush my teeth with my eyes closed. That drives me nuts."

"Ha! Good to know."

"Another interesting fact, right?" Matt exited the truck and stepped around to her side. He opened the door, grinning. "But I still have a few things I hold close to the vest."

"Really? Like what? Do you turn into a pumpkin at midnight?"

"Something like that." He slipped his hand around hers, guiding her toward the cobblestone path that led to the house. Then, he paused and tipped his head toward the outbuilding adjacent to the home. "I'd like to show you. That is, if you're interested."

A delightful thrill charged down Mel's spine. The warmth of Matt's hand, combined with the thought of another surprise, made her slightly giddy and not herself. Since when did she respond to a man this way? And not just any man. Matt Enders—her co-worker, once a royal pain—now a friend, and something more. "Well, don't keep me in suspense. You bet I'm interested. Lead on."

"Okay. Watch your step. I haven't extended the walkway down this far yet, and the ground is somewhat uneven through here."

She gripped his hand a little tighter, the nearness of him setting her mind to wandering. Had he purchased this property in hopes of raising a family here? It certainly offered all the amenities. A striking home. Gorgeous grounds. Tons of room. Exquisite views. Everything a couple could possibly want in a place to build a future.

They approached the outbuilding from the side entrance instead of entering through the larger garage door out front. "Sam probably used the bigger entryway because of his carpentry business, but this side door suits me fine." Matt paused. "I've never brought anyone here. You're the first."

Okay. He had her full attention. Goosebumps raised on her arms, and they had nothing to do with the night air. "And the anticipation mounts..."

"I hope you won't be disappointed. I'm certain it's not what you think."

"Well, let me be the judge, all right? Open the door and we'll see."

"Sure." Matt punched in the code at the keypad and twisted the silver knob, allowing the door to swing open. "Here. Let me catch the lights."

Instantly, light bathed the building interior in varying degrees of brightness. Mel blinked, but not from the light. It took a moment to register the sight. Easels, art supplies, equipment, and paintings. Ahh...the paintings! She sucked in a breath. An artist's studio?

Slowly, she inched forward to get a closer look. Several canvases appeared as works in progress. Others, obviously finished and ready for framing. The paintings ranged from small town life and the folks who lived there to the outlying Ozarks' hills and hollows—each painting, magnificent, and accurate in its portrayal of the rural culture and heritage here.

Mel slipped her hand from Matt's and began to

navigate about the room. She noticed the initials "M" and "E" in the bottom right-hand corner of all the pieces, with a definitive swirl emphasizing the "E." Her jaw dropped as the revelation hit her. "*You* painted these?"

He nodded an affirmative, following beside her. "Not to brag, but I told you I was good with paint. I'd like to know what you think though. Your honest opinion."

"I thought you meant you were good with paint in the general sense—like painting a room or rehabbing your carport. Oh my gosh, Matt! You're an artist!"

"Nah. I just tinker around a bit."

How could he not recognize his own talent? His ability to capture every nuance and subtlety of lives well lived? The way he translated his vision from paints to canvas communicated skill far beyond novice ability. How long had he been at this? Months? *Years?*

"I don't paint lavish pieces. I like to capture life through a realistic lens. Neighbors gathered 'round a picnic table on a fall afternoon. Friends chatting over pie and coffee beside a cozy fire. Kids playing softball on a summer day. Stuff like that."

Mel wanted to run her fingers over the seamless blending of colors, but she refrained. "If these aren't lavish, I don't what is. How long have you been painting?"

"Since I was a kid. Granddad gave me my first set of paints when I was ten and what started out as a hobby kind of grew on me."

A hobby? Really? Didn't he realize his gift? "Matt, these are phenomenal. Which leads to my next question." She turned to fully face him. "Why are these here and not in a gallery...or in your own business somewhere? We appreciate you at The Meadows, but *wow*. Are you certain that you shouldn't be doing this instead?"

"Trying to get rid of me, huh?" His eyes danced with mischief.

"Never. Don't be silly. But I've never seen anything like this." Mel touched his arm and held his gaze. "I see your heart in these. Not that I don't at work. But there's a difference here. Something on a deeper level that connects the dots and communicates your love for humanity. Something beyond your job at The Meadows. It's like this is the overflow."

"Overflow?"

"Of everything you've stored up. Until, at the end of the day, you release it. Here. On canvas."

"Now it's my turn. *Wow.*" He reached up to cradle her cheek with his palm, the intimate gesture causing Mel's breath to catch. "I never thought about it like that."

"Probably because, like the saying goes, you can't see the forest for the trees. You're too close." She placed her hand over his—the one that rested on her cheek. "Conflicting passions are like that. We may be gifted at more than one, but usually, there's one that holds the upper hand. It's the one that tugs our heartstrings above all others."

Matt remained silent for a moment.

Well, he'd wanted to know her thoughts. Had she said too much?

"You're a smart woman, Mel." He trailed his fingertips along her jawline and let his hand fall to his side. "I appreciate your perspective. That's one reason I wanted to show you this."

"The other reason?"

"Promise not to laugh?"

His response squeezed her heart. "I would never do that. We may have had our differences in the past, but we've grown beyond them. At least, for the most part. Don't you think?"

"Yeah, I do." Matt studied her, as if debating whether he should say more. "See, painting's always been a private thing of mine. It's an intrinsic part of myself I've reserved for only me. No one knows this is what I do on the side. Or...they didn't. Until you."

A bubble of happiness burst in Mel's chest and expanded, but she didn't want to over-read his confession. "Surely, your parents know you paint?"

"They know I dabble."

"What? They don't know... They haven't seen these?"

"When we lived closer, I'd show them some works-in-progress or even a few completed pieces. Mom would ooh and aah, and Dad would slap me on the back and say how talented I was, but you know. They're my parents. Naturally, they're going to react that way."

"Matt, listen. You're right. Parents often think the sun rises and sets in their children. But believe me, and believe *them*, you have a gift. Your work is extraordinary." Mel allowed her gaze to travel once more around his makeshift studio. Some likenesses in his paintings she recognized. One, in particular wrung her emotions. It was a man, advanced in years, facing an opened window, gazing upward toward a sunlit sky. His face devoid of emotion, except for his eyes. Eyes that held a thousand questions and belonged to Clinton Farley.

"That one I'm not quite finished with yet." Matt wondered if he ever would be. He'd encountered a mental block and couldn't seem to move past it to complete the portrait.

"Oh, Matt."

Tears shimmered on Mel's lashes. Her reaction communicated what she couldn't vocalize, but what he'd felt too with every brushstroke.

"I'm not sure what I'm waiting for. Maybe a surge of inspiration. Maybe a personality shift. Clinton's, specifically. Without a thawing of the old coot's heart, I can't do his eyes justice."

Mel moved closer to the painting, inspecting it further. "I don't know. I think you've painted his eyes with amazing accuracy."

"That's just it. In this case, I don't want to be accurate. I want to be wrong." Could he even explain? He gave it a shot. "I want those questions in the old guy's eyes to convey answers. I want them to mirror a confidence in tomorrow, whatever tomorrow holds. More than that, I want to give those eyes peace."

"The peace that passes all understanding."

"Yes."

"I'd like to see that, too. It'll happen, I think. We have to remain focused and confident."

Matt gave a short laugh. Funny how God worked through folks. In the past few weeks, he and Mel encouraged one another during their low points at precisely the right time. No doubt the woman could still administer a proper tongue lashing if needed. Only lately, he hadn't needed it. Or maybe he had, and she'd resisted.

"Do you find what I said amusing?"

"Not at all. I believe you're right." He reached toward her and gathered her in his arms, something he'd wanted to do all night. Man, she was tiny. The close proximity magnified their significant height difference. "I laughed, not because what you said is funny, but because I realized the irony of our...uh...friendship. We're completely different people, yet the same in so many ways. We share similar core values and beliefs, and despite our rough patch, we want what's best for others, as well as you and me, individually. The way we key into each other's off moments and then try to perk one another up is pretty intuitive."

"I've noticed that. We've even talked about it before." Mel stared up at him, her lips curling in a smile. "I guess it means we kind of care about each other."

"Kind of? Is a qualifier necessary?"

"Given how we started? You betcha."

Now they both laughed. What would it be like to kiss her? He didn't want to pull a Spencer. What if he misjudged the moment? Mel's wishes? And then there was the comment he'd made earlier. That if he wanted to kiss her, he'd ask. That he wouldn't spirit her back to his place under false pretenses to do it. *Aw, man.* Would she think him a liar now? He hadn't planned on kissing her tonight. But this seemed...right.

"Hey, may I ask you something?" He touched her chin with his fingertips. He hoped he didn't blow this. "You know I'm not a game player. I don't talk in riddles. I say what I mean."

Mel tilted her head, those freckles of hers mocking him with their cuteness. "Is there another question there?"

"I'm working up to it. Hang on." *Yeah, bud. You say what you mean all right.* His heart raced and his resolve slipped a notch. Good grief. A grown man should have no problem with this. There shouldn't be anything nerve-wracking about kissing a woman. In fact, he'd kissed a few in his life. But they weren't Mel. And they hadn't cornered his heart like she had. He took a deep breath. Exhaled. *There.* Better. "Earlier tonight, I meant what I said about not bringing you here with other motivations. I wanted to show you my work. To share that part of me with you."

"I'm so glad you did, Matt. I'm honored."

"Well, the thing I hadn't planned on, and that I mentioned, was kissing you. That I wouldn't disguise my intentions with tricks. That I'd ask. Up front. Like a gentleman. I truly didn't plan it this way, and I don't want to give you the wrong impression about me."

Mel's mouth twitched. "I like that about you. I would never doubt you were a gentleman. Except maybe during those times you really got on my last nerve and I considered dousing you in ice water."

"Ah. Keeping me grounded, as always."

"You wouldn't expect anything less, would you?"

"No, ma'am. Not at all. Which is why I should ask before you bolt." He didn't actually think she would, but he sure didn't want to mess up now. Nor did he intend to beat around the bush. "May I kiss you?"

"Hmm..."

Wait. She had to think about it? Mel smiled again and Matt's stomach catapulted to his shins. She didn't say no, but she didn't say yes. What was he supposed to do with that? "Sorry. I misread—"

"I think I'd like that."

She would? "You 'think' or is that a yes?"

"Yes. It's most definitely a yes."

So...a yes, was it? My, oh my. Her answer bolstered his confidence. With that, he bent down—way down because of their height difference—and feathered the lightest of kisses upon her lips. A safe, sweet, but more than friends, kiss.

He'd intended to leave it at that, but Mel reached up and wound her arms around his neck, and the landscape changed. He didn't want to let her go. Until now, they'd kept a respectable distance, but at this moment, he wished he could hold her forever. They'd come a long way from bruised egos and snappy barbs. Tonight, something beyond friendship unified them. It ignited new possibilities and caused Matt to reflect on his little spread here. How great it would be to have someone to share it with. Someone like Mel.

He drew her close, her rose scented shampoo tickling his nostrils. *Wow.* She smelled incredible. Like a rose garden.

Mel brushed her fingertips along his hairline at the nape of his neck. Should he, or shouldn't he? He definitely should. Matt kissed her again. This time, he didn't hold back and neither did she. He deepened the kiss and she responded. Holding her in his arms seemed perfectly natural—like they'd known each other a lifetime. "After all these months, the *us* we're becoming should seem strange, but it doesn't. I believe we've almost nailed this friendship thing."

"Yeah. *Strange* isn't the word I'd use to describe what just happened between us." Mel gazed up at him, her eyes teeming with recognition. "I'm glad we've reached...an understanding."

"Is that what you call it? An understanding?"

She shifted her weight. Her breath came out in a whoosh, as if she'd run a marathon. "Yes. We're on the same page now."

"Which is?" If he had to drag it out of her, maybe they weren't.

"We care about each other. I think I've already said that."

Okay. Still, he didn't want to make assumptions about their relationship. Could she maybe elaborate? "Look, in my mind, we crossed the friendship bridge a long time ago. And I gotta be honest here. For me, where we stand now? Well, it looks a whole lot like something more."

A rosy glow colored Mel's cheeks. "I agree. It certainly *feels* like something more."

"*Whew.* That's a relief. Now, see? That didn't hurt at all, did it?" He tried not to laugh. Or fist-pump the air. Why was the woman so cagey when it came to matters of the heart? She didn't strike him as the type who played hard to get. Maybe Holms had caused her to proceed with caution. But he and the humdrum science teacher were about as different as corn and peas. He'd never foist himself off on Mel like Holms tried to do. Smothering a woman into a relationship wasn't his idea of mutual respect.

"Nope. Didn't hurt one bit." She lowered her arms and scooted back a few inches. "Except we work together, and I'd really like to keep my private life and professional life separate."

"Totally understand. Though, our friends and co-workers probably already detect some undercurrents, don't you think?"

Mel's brows crinkled. "Has someone said something?"

"No. Why would they? We've had one date. We haven't given the grapevine any cause to thrive. But folks aren't stupid, Mel. In time, they'll figure it out. In fact, I bet your friend Sarah already has. Oh, and your family, too, of course. Kinda hard to keep our date a secret since I did ask your brothers for suggestions where to take you."

"Yeah, I know. I just want to make sure we don't become story fodder around town. People mean well, but in Ruby, even innocent chatter can circulate quickly. Today, we're dating. Tomorrow, we're engaged. Life in a small town—nothing like it."

A hint of affection underscored Mel's words, yet Matt knew she spoke the truth. He'd heard enough matchmaking tales to make a believer out of him. Still, dating a co-worker didn't seem problematic as long as it didn't affect work. It wasn't like one was the other's subordinate, which would certainly demonstrate bad form. As separate department heads, they weren't breaching personal ethics *or* company policy. Needless to say, they'd use discretion.

Matt gently placed his palms on her shoulders. "If the time ever comes where our private life infringes on my ability to do my job, you can bet I'll rethink my employment. Deal?"

"You don't have to say that. I know you well enough to confidently state that'll never happen. You'd never cross that line, and neither would I."

"Exactly. Now, why don't we head back to the house and grab a cup of coffee? Unless it's too late and you'd like to go home." Though, he hoped she didn't want to leave yet. He wasn't ready to let her go. *Oh, boy.* He'd dived into the deep end. Not that he minded.

Mel wouldn't have guessed the interior of Matt's home to

be so traditional and cozy and somewhat on the vintage side. His tastes almost mirrored hers. For a late twenty-something-year-old guy to like the same homestyle vibe as her? Maybe she wasn't as weird as she thought.

While a few bare areas still needed a woman's touch, as well as some furniture rearranging, without a doubt, the home embodied warmth and cheerfulness. Guests could easily lose themselves in the comfy, cushiony sectionals, Sherpa throw blankets, and retro wall art.

"I like it." Mel allowed her gaze to roam. "It isn't what I expected."

"What did you think it would be—a messy man cave littered with beer cans and stinky socks?" Matt chuckled.

"Well, maybe not beer cans. I was thinking moldy coffee mugs."

"Ha!"

"Glad to see I'm wrong on both counts."

"But you haven't seen the kitchen yet. Or the rest of the house." A mischievous glint sparked in his eyes. "How do you know I haven't stashed the evidence in other strategic locations?"

"See. That's something I've learned about you. Artistic, free spirit that you are, you *aren't* disorganized. Everything has a place. And everyplace has things comfortably and casually ordered. Not to the point you're obsessive about it. It's just unexpected...and sweet."

"That's me. Casual. Unexpected. Sweet. And way too charming for my own good."

She all but snorted. "And don't forget humble."

Matt tipped his head toward the kitchen. "How about joining my humble self for that coffee? I think it's cool enough that your leftovers will keep okay in the truck for a few more minutes until I take you home."

"Yes, I'm not worried about the food spoiling, but on second thought, may I take a raincheck on the coffee? Unless you have decaf, it's kind of late for a caffeine jolt. Got any vitamin water?" She'd seen him carry those into work. Maybe he stocked them in his fridge.

"Ask and you shall receive. Come with me." He flipped on extra lights as they went, coaxing dark corners awake.

They entered the kitchen, a large, welcoming space that reminded Mel of her childhood home where her parents still lived. Like the main living space, this room held a pleasant appeal, and a colorful but relaxed, vibe.

"Matt, what were you like in school?"

He studied her and grinned. "Why?"

Because I want to know everything about you. "I'm curious. Were you always an extrovert?"

"You mean the loud and obnoxious kind or the go-getter, outgoing kind?"

"What do you think?" She nudged him with her elbow. "Not the excessive, rowdy type, but yes, were you always so sociable and goal-oriented?"

"Hmm." He headed toward the fridge. "Sociable. A good word. An adjective I'm glad you now associate with me." He grabbed two vitamin waters and motioned toward the kitchen table. "In answer to your question, yeah. I knew from an early age I wanted to help people. Obviously, I'd always had an interest in the arts, but I realized I had to temporarily shelve other interests. Painting wouldn't sustain me financially. Like I've said before, though, my granddad encouraged me to consider new dreams, and now, so have you. Who knows what the future holds? As far as the sociable part, I enjoy interacting with all sorts of people. Always have. Even the cranky ones like Clinton Farley."

Mel opened her drink and sipped. Matt definitely had great people skills. She recalled how they'd clashed so many months ago, grateful they'd grown beyond those early days. "I'm glad you're in Clinton's corner. Someone needs to be. I hope we can figure out how to help him."

"Me, too. Then I'll finish the painting."

"I know you will."

Matt reached for her hand and clasped it. "We're good together. I really enjoy being with you."

Happiness burst within her, unearthing all kinds of emotions, but for the moment, Mel only wanted to savor one. It wasn't every day that a girl fell in love.

Chapter Ten

If he hadn't lingered at Mel's place when he took her home last night, maybe he wouldn't be as apt to nod off during Pastor Bill's sermon this morning. As convicting as the preacher's sermon was, Matt fought a persistent case of the yawns. The busyness of the past week and a late date night made the twenty-five-minute sermon seem more like a slow backstroke against an incoming tide. He wanted to be attentive, but his brain wouldn't cooperate.

Matt sat up straighter. Tightened and relaxed his toes within the confines of his dress shoes. A pew over, Mel intently studied the church bulletin. Was she having trouble concentrating too? She glanced up and her eyes locked with his. He'd give a dollar for her thoughts. No. Make that five bucks. She blushed and returned his smile. Could she be remembering their date? The kisses they'd shared?

Not exactly sermon related thoughts, Matt attempted to refocus. Surely, God understood his preoccupation. The woman unraveled him. Had from the time he'd come on board at The Meadows. The good Lord knew this, of course.

They'd be sitting together now if not for the whole Brewer clan taking up the entire church pew. Matt had a feeling, though, if he'd planted himself next to Mel at the start of service, none of her family would have voiced an objection over someone moving. In fact, if their reception toward him were any indication, they'd be delighted to accommodate the budding courtship. Mel's parents, and certainly her brothers, too, seemed pleased by the recent turn of events.

Another five minutes and Pastor Bill began to wind down. "And so..." He retrieved a starched white handkerchief from his suit pocket and patted his forehead. "The truth is, folks, our Heavenly Father loves the sinner as much as the saint. Because, really, friends, even those who are sanctified by the blood still err. Sometimes intentionally. Sometimes inadvertently. We acknowledge our transgressions, repent, and turn from our wrongdoing. We try again, and we tell others about this free gift." Here, Pastor Bill closed his Bible and gazed intently at his congregants. "No individual is too wounded, scarred, or sinful to redeem. Every soul matters to God."

Every soul matters to God. Every soul. Even hard cases like Clinton Farley. Especially him. The thought darted across Matt's mind and he shifted in the pew. But how to reach him? How to reach a man who emanated disgust from every pore of his being?

As the service drew to a close, Matt ruminated on this and considered various scenarios. Several ideas formed, but as quickly as they fired, he dismissed them. He wouldn't reach Clinton with compliments or praise, not that he could think of a worthy accolade at the moment. A polite nicety wouldn't do either. He'd tried that. Well, he'd have to ponder it some more. Surely, Clinton had a soft spot for something. Or someone. *Mel.*

Matt had noticed that Clinton's rough edges and harsh demeanor softened around Mel. A subtle change, and unpredictable, but noteworthy.

They exited their pews at the same time and Matt refrained from kissing the lingering smile that played at the corners of Mel's mouth. No need to give their fellow parishioners a preliminary peek into their personal lives. The cat would be out of the bag soon enough, but until then, he'd let Mel decide when that would be. Matt, did, however, fall into step with Mel, their arms almost touching as they moseyed down the aisle and into the church vestibule.

"Sleep well?" Or had she replayed their date far into dreamland as he had? Specifically, the kisses they'd shared in his studio? And what about that goodnight kiss—that *amazing* goodnight kiss—before he'd left her place? That one, especially, kept him awake a while. Definitely not in a bad way though.

"Hey, if my date hadn't kept me up so late, I wouldn't have nodded off during the sermon." Mel giggled and continued her pace.

"Not exactly what I meant. I was asking if you slept well last night?"

"Oh. Sure did. Just not long enough. You?"

He laughed too. "Same."

Mel's brothers sauntered up beside them. Gabe cleared his throat and poked Garrett in the ribcage with his elbow. "Hey, what do you say, bro? Think their date went okay?"

"Hmm. I'd wager Pastor Bill's sermon notes it did." Garrett turned to Mike and repeated the playful jab. "What do you think, Mike?"

The youngest of the brothers stroked his chin, as if deep in thought. "From the grins on these two faces, I'd say you'd win that wager. Fryin' Pan and Into the Fire still do it up right, kids?"

Mel's siblings high-fived each other. The brothers' easy camaraderie with each other tweaked Matt's heart. Their connection made him homesick in a way, but the fact that Gabe, Garrett, and Mike had accepted him enough to tease, warmed him.

"Yeah, I'd say you fellas made a great call. But as a gentleman, I'll defer to the lady. Mel?"

Mel's cheeks bloomed with color. "I'll second that. Anything else you boys might like to know is really not church conversation."

"Oh?" Gabe cupped his hand to his ear in an exaggerated motion.

"Wait! I said that wrong. That's not what I meant."

Matt also struggled not to laugh. The woman could certainly keep him on his toes with her range of emotions, but obviously, her love life was a subject she preferred her brothers not gab about. At least in a public place.

"Hey, guys, I think what Mel means is that date talk best wait since we're on our way to shake the preacher's hand. Suffice it to say, men, you did good." Matt gave them a thumbs-up and guided Mel forward, away from the good-natured ribbing of her brothers.

"They aggravate me to no end, but I love 'em. My personal life is none of their business though."

They made their way toward Pastor Bill and his wife, Sharon, who stood in their usual spot shaking folks' hands as they departed church. The preacher and his better half had to be in their seventies, but their exuberance made them seem much younger.

"So, how's life treating you kids? Matt? Mel?" Pastor Bill shook each of their hands, a glint of cheerfulness making his senior eyes sparkle. If Matt were to guess, the local grapevine had sprouted some new tendrils.

"Good. Good." He paused as Mel confirmed his assessment with a nod. "GIFTS is rolling along, and we've received a lot of excellent feedback. So far, folks have enjoyed the various speakers and presentations, and the program seems to have struck a positive chord."

Pastor Bill smiled. "That's what I hear, along with a few other things."

"Yes, tell us, dear," Miss Sharon piped up, patting Mel's arm. "What do you recommend at Fryin' Pan and Into the Fire? We hear they still make a mean steak and taters."

"Well, that didn't take long." Mel shook her head, laughing, and stuffed her church bulletin into her Bible as she stood on the paved parking lot. Out of earshot now, she turned to Matt. "Aren't small towns fabulous?"

"They are. Less than twenty-four hours and word's already out. Can't say I mind. You?"

"No, not really. Like we've already talked about, our seeing each other isn't a problem as long as we remain focused and professional."

"Agreed." Matt linked his arm through hers. "When we're off the clock, I don't think a kiss is unprofessional, do you?"

Oh, goodness. The way he gazed at her caused goosebumps to rise on her arms. "Of course not. I think we already established that last night, didn't we?"

"Yes, ma'am. I believe we did. I suppose, though, the church parking lot isn't the most private place to discuss kisses, huh?"

"No, it isn't." She held her breath. Surely Matt wouldn't test the notion. Not with half the town still pouring out of church. "Let's table this discussion, okay?"

"Sure. Maybe after dinner then?"

"Dinner?"

"Rump roast. Potatoes. Pie. You know the drill. Your mom and dad invited me over today."

Sure, they did. Boy, had things changed. She couldn't even be aggravated. All she could do was giggle like a schoolgirl with a bad crush. "And you're still coming for Thanksgiving dinner on Thursday?"

"You bet. But hold the cartwheels. Save those for later." Matt winked and unlooped his arm from hers. "See you in a few over at your parents' house."

"Okay. But you know that razzing we got from my brothers? Prepare yourself. I have a feeling they're just warming up."

"Not a problem. Doesn't bother me if it doesn't bother you."

"It did once. Not now."

Where they were headed, she didn't know, but what had once been a contentious relationship with Matt had blossomed into something carefree and sweet. They'd entered a new phase. A future filled with possibilities...and each other.

The shooting stars she'd seen with Dad so long ago popped into her mind. Could it be?

First, the cottage. Someone to share it with. Career advancement. Yeah, still considering those two. Loneliness had never inserted itself into Mel's life until she met Matt. Since then, the silence and contentment her home once afforded now stirred questions and unease.

Building a life with someone other than pretty walls and nostalgia appealed more these days. Too, career advancement that used to be a mere blip on her goal radar rocketed front and center. Interviews for The Meadows Assistant Director position would begin after Thanksgiving and she'd be ready. In fact, Mel had ordered a new outfit for the occasion. Red, naturally.

Later, as she sat next to Matt at Mom's and Dad's, Mel mulled over something else. If Foster and the hiring committee offered her the job, one of the first things she'd suggest would be a scheduled break time. Not specifically for staff but including them while pairing them with residents throughout the day.

She'd given this some thought. Formed the concept in her mind. While residents were always encouraged to come and go at their leisure in the community and dining rooms, an organized break between staff and residents would facilitate even more interaction.

Staff could stagger their breaks throughout the day and visit with residents on a more intimate level than solely at mealtimes or special events. Maybe this new routine would draw Clinton Farley out of his shell. Maybe the change of pace would encourage him to join others his age for coffee and companionship. Mel would ask Foster to schedule her break for late morning, pairing her with Edwin Ramsey and Clinton. A long shot, initially, that Clinton would participate, but she'd sweeten the pot with something. She didn't know what yet, but something.

"*Yoo-hoo.* Earth to Sis." Garrett leaned forward and waved his dinner napkin. "So...as I was saying, it seems like you're pretty busy these days. What's on tap for the holidays? Will you finally take some vacation time?"

"That's a great question." Her father took a swig of iced tea and set down his glass. "Will you grace us with your presence? Work some jigsaw puzzles and watch Christmas movies with Mom and me?"

Bless his heart. Mel resisted the urge to laugh. But Dad's sincerity and the longing in his eyes made her all gooey inside. For the Brewer family, the Christmas season meant a time to reflect and recharge and celebrate God's goodness. Faith, family, hearth, and home. Every Christmas, it was the same. Gabe, Garrett, and Mike would take time off, and up until last year, Mel joined them and her parents. Last Christmas, she'd deviated from the norm, opting to spend Christmas Eve and Christmas Day, but beyond that, no additional break.

Work had been particularly busy around that time, with some of the residents needing extra TLC. Clinton being one of them, though, he'd never admitted it, nor appreciated her efforts. During that period, he'd refused to participate in anything she'd organized.

"Hey, that sounds like a blast." Matt stabbed another slice of roast beef from the platter Mom offered. "My family does something similar. All the relatives descend on Mom's and Pop's for the week and we do 'er up right. Mountains of food. Games. Church. Sledding, if there's snow. All the stuff that a lot of folks don't seem to have the time for anymore."

"Well, hats off to your parents, Matt. They sound like our kind of people." Mel's father beamed approvingly. He reached for another potato roll and started the basket around the table again. "Nothing like family. Quirks and all. Not that we have any, you know."

To emphasize the point, her father dunked his potato

roll in a side dish of gravy and tackled the thing in two bites. To which Mom shook her head and sighed.

The day before Thanksgiving, Matt captured Mel by the elbow and propelled her into his office. "In our commitment to remain professional while on the clock, I wanted to say this privately. You look especially beautiful today."

"Thanks. But I think that borders. On professionalism, you know."

Her laughter bounced off the walls and into his heart. He didn't elaborate. He wanted to, but it was enough, for now, that she knew. Matt gestured toward a chair. "Then in an effort to steer our conversation into more work-related territory, let's chat about a mutual concern."

"Love to. Clinton?"

"Yes." Evidently, the old fellow occupied Mel's thoughts as much as his. "I had this crazy idea."

Mel hitched an eyebrow.

"Okay. Crazier than some others."

"Go on. You have my full attention."

She asked for it. "What if you invited Clinton to your family's home for Thanksgiving tomorrow? If he agrees, I can bring him, or you can, since he seems to hold you in higher esteem—though it might be somewhat difficult to fold him like an accordion and get him in that VW of yours. What do you think?"

Mel's smile faded. "Is that a joke?"

"No, ma'am. I'm as serious as a heart attack. Thoughts?"

Mel relaxed in the chair, letting her head go slack against the tufted back. "He refused to attend last week's

Thanksgiving celebration here at The Meadows. Wouldn't even eat the food I took down to him. My parents would be thrilled to have Clinton, but what makes you think he'll say yes to an invitation to their Thanksgiving dinner?"

"I dunno. Lots of hope and prayer." Matt rose from his desk opposite Mel and began to pace. He knew this was a long shot. An utter improbability, really. But still, he believed in miracles. "Look, I know Clinton rebuffed your efforts last week, but we have to keep trying. When you were sick with the flu, you should have seen the guy. He moped for you, Mel. Maybe he wouldn't admit it, however, the old codger worried about you. He missed you. Gave me a tongue lashing like you wouldn't believe. Rumor had it he even asked Foster if I'd been the one to make you ill. I guess he had the notion that I'd actually driven you away with mean talk and germs."

Mel burst out laughing. "Now, that's funny. Wish he'd share some of that heartfelt sentiment with me. Getting back to the dinner invitation, though, I'll give it a whirl. All Clinton can say is no."

Which he promptly did a few hours later when Mel asked. She caught Matt by the coffee bar in the dining room as he was filling his mug with Tilly's holiday chocolate mint brew.

"I think *you* should go ask him." Mel's shoulders sagged. Her mouth inched downward in a frown. "The more he rejects us, the more it makes me wonder what God's plan is."

It pained him to see the defeat in Mel's eyes. He wanted to reassure her. Wanted to say Clinton wasn't a lost cause. Because nothing was impossible with God. But the harder they tried, the more they nudged, the more

Clinton drew into his shell. Yet, they couldn't give up either.

"I will. I'll ask him."

"Okay. Tell him we're having all the traditional favorites that he missed the other day. Tell him I've baked up a storm and if he doesn't want to hurt my feelings any further, he better come. I'll drop by here a little before noon tomorrow and we'll head over to my parents' house then."

"Didn't you mention all that earlier when you spoke to Clinton?"

"Yes. But rephrasing it may help."

"I'll do what I can." Matt sipped his coffee, the hot liquid washing over his tongue and down his throat, the brew infusing warmth in his bones. Just the shot of confidence he needed. "I'll meet you back in your office soon. Hang tight." *Let's do this, God.*

A few gents sitting at the far corner of the dining room raised their coffee mugs to Matt on his way out.

"Here's to you, Matthew!" Edwin Ramsey called. "We understand Tilly added this specialty blend because you suggested it. Hearty and robust, with subtle hints of chocolate and mint. Enough to turn a sour lemon into a peach at Christmastime, or Thanksgiving, as the case may be. *Scrooge's Favor*, Miss Tilly calls it."

Does she now? Matt paused at the doorway, mug in hand. *Scrooge's Favor.* Christmas charity in a coffee mug. Who could resist this heavenly concoction? Surely, not Scrooge himself. Matt lifted his mug and saluted the men. "Glad you fellas approve."

With that, he did an about-face and headed back toward the coffee bar.

"What are you doing?" Mel's brows wrinkled as Matt placed his partially drunk mug in the pick-up tub and reached for an insulated to-go cup and coordinating lid.

"I have an idea. I'm going to deliver *Scrooge's Favor* to one of his very own. Cross your fingers. No. Scratch that. Pray."

Matt didn't have the faintest idea what he'd say to Clinton. Like he often did, he'd fly by the seat of his pants. He filled the mondo sized cup and turned back toward the door. *Go with me, Father.*

The Meadows was quiet today. Several staff had taken leave early, and some of the residents had already left to spend the Thanksgiving holiday with family. Matt's footsteps echoed down the freshly waxed hall. When he got to the Laurel Lane wing, he slowed his pace. Midway down was Clinton's small apartment. What would he do when Matt rang his doorbell? Snub him as he'd done Mel?

No. Matt wouldn't believe that. For whatever reason, God had called him to this task. Though he didn't consider himself a holy roller, he did believe in divine appointments.

Matt licked his lips. He raised his finger to the buzzer, which sufficed as a doorbell, and looked directly at the peephole. He might not be able to see Clinton, but he for sure wanted Clinton to see him. He didn't know why, but he suspected Clinton might open the door. If not for any other reason than to voice his disapproval.

Matt waited. Seconds ticked by into minutes. Well, fine. Two could play this game. Shoot, he might even pull up a chair.

The insulated cup all but burned his fingers. Matt pressed the buzzer again. Had the old guy given him the once-over yet? Clinton's gruff utterances bounded off the walls inside. Yep. Farley had seen him. Mere minutes morphed into five more.

Finally, muffled words made their way through the door. "Go away, Enders. Don't have time for shenanigans and small talk."

"No worries, Mr. Farley. Neither do I." Matt counted to ten. "Look, I brought you something. A holiday brew from Tilly. Give it a try and I promise I won't bug you anymore."

The door flung open and Clinton glared at him. "Why in blazes should I try a dang cup of coffee? Did you load it with arsenic?"

No, but great idea. Kidding. I'm kidding, Lord.

Matt bit his tongue. "No, sir. But we're wanting to get residents' feedback on which blend is best. Next week is *Christmas Chaos.* It has toasted marshmallow subtleties with whispers of cherry. Everyone knows you and Edwin are the coffee experts around here. Would you please give it a try?"

"Nuts. You're nuts, boy." Clinton moved to close the door, but Matt inserted his foot in the doorway.

"Well, can't help that. Here." He held out the cup. "Careful. It's hot. This one's called *Scrooge's Favor.* What do you think?"

If Clinton's eyes could launch darts, Matt would be aching from head to toe. The grouch's eyebrows knitted together in anger. He stuck out a long, bony finger and shook it at Matt.

"When are you and the rest of the busy bees around here going to get a clue? The Meadows may be where I live, but inside these walls is my space. I pay good money—lots of money—to live here. Don't need nothin' from no one except three squares a day, which, again, I pay for. Don't care about festivals, socials, or holiday dinners, and I sure as shootin' don't care about some dumb coffee contest. Leave me alone, boy, or I'll file a complaint."

"A complaint? About what?"

"Needling old folks is elder abuse, bright one. You're the social worker. Didn't you learn that somewhere along the way? Guess they allow anybody to matriculate these days, as long as they shell out big bucks."

"A couple things, Mr. Farley. Offering someone a cup of coffee is not elder abuse. Yes, I earned a 4.0 GPA throughout school. No, my parents didn't shell out big bucks. I didn't hail from a wealthy family. I worked my way through college, as well as my master's program. In fact, I worked hard as the dickens to graduate debt free. I don't have some deep desire to get under your skin or make you hate me. I want to be your friend. So do a lot of other people."

Clinton blinked. His lips formed a thin, taut line. He retracted his finger and let his arm fall to his side. Matt shifted his foot and stepped away from the door. Was Clinton about to curse and slam the door in his face? The fellow simply stood there, his face a mask of bitterness and pain.

Matt tried again, softening his voice. "Please, Clinton. Please be my friend."

Clinton swallowed. Pursed his lips. "You're pathetic. Know that?"

Yeah. Maybe he was. But in that moment, Matt realized something. He really did want Clinton as a friend. He'd come to care deeply for the malcontent. He'd never known loss in the way Clinton had. Never been in his shoes. But rejection by another human being gripped the heart in a way that singed its perimeters like nothing else could.

"Mr. Farley—Clinton—you're right. I used the coffee as a ruse, but I really hoped you'd like it. I was hoping it might break the ice between you and me." He didn't know what else to say. But this had been his idea, and he'd promised Mel he'd extend the Thanksgiving dinner invitation again. He couldn't face her knowing he'd failed to at least follow through on that. Matt cleared his throat. "Mel wants to be your friend, too. And call me crazy, but I think in your heart of Scrooge's hearts, you want that."

"Ha! You're crazier than I thought."

"Nah. Not crazy. Persistent." Matt extended the insulated coffee cup again. "The Brewer family is hosting a humdinger of a Thanksgiving celebration tomorrow. Come. Mel would like that. If not for anyone else, do it for her."

"Why?"

"Because I believe you think a lot of her, as she does you. The residents here are more than a name to her. You're family." Matt didn't know what to add or how to get through to Clinton. If the Lord wanted him to continue down this path, he needed something. *This is all I have. It's up to You.*

"Scrooge's Favor, huh?" Clinton reached for the cup and curled his withered fingers around it. "Cup's hot as blazes." He took a sip. Then, another. "Tilly done good."

What? Matt's heart pounded against his ribcage. A compliment? Had he heard right?

"Tell Miss Melinda I'm not much for celebrations like I tried to explain earlier, but I do appreciate the offer." With that, Clinton smacked his lips, nodded, and closed the door.

"No kidding, Mel. It's a miracle."

"A miracle? But he still refused to come." How did that rate as a miracle? Mel sunk back in her chair, discouraged.

"Yes, but it's progress. He complimented Tilly's holiday concoction, and then he said, 'tell Miss Melinda I appreciate the offer.' For a guy who has been as mean as a snake, that positivity, however brief, was a full blown, four alarm, heaven sent miracle." Matt leaned forward and clasped her hand. "I think we've made a breakthrough."

Mel wanted to believe that. Anything kind from Clinton's mouth seemed completely out of character. It had to be supernaturally orchestrated. "Do you really think so?"

"I do. No other explanation."

"Then...do you think it'd be pushing it if I showed up here tomorrow and told him I was here to pick him up?"

A slow smile spread across Matt's face. "I think that would be terrific. Catch him while he's still basking in holiday cheer. Hey, I forgot to ask, what time should I come to your parents' home?"

"Around noonish. You can help set up card tables for all the side dishes. Fair warning, though. Mom may snag you for KP duty. She's prepped this big shindig for days, and Dad and the guys always give her a hand with clean-up afterward. Then we set up again with all-day snack tables and watch old Christmas classics on TV. Wear something comfy...and expandable. We always do."

"Sounds fantastic. I'm on call so I'll pop over and

check on things here first. When the new Assistant Director is hired, he'll have holiday and weekend rotation and that'll add another to the crew."

"Or she."

"Pardon?"

"The committee could hire a woman as the new A-D. You never know."

"Hmm. Yeah, they could. Say, you rotate weekend and holiday shifts, sometimes, right?"

"Uh-huh."

"That'll free up your time, as well. Adding another department head to the weekend/holiday schedule is a step in the right direction. Prevents burnout."

"I guess I agree. I probably spend too much time here, but I love my job."

"Except, even good things eventually make Jack and Jill exhausted."

Mel cocked her head. "They're make-believe, you know."

"Hey, it's been a long day. Best analogy I could come up with at the moment." He released her hand and stood. "I guess holding hands on the job is probably a no-no. Sorry. Seemed natural, but from now on, we'll refrain."

She hadn't even thought twice about it, which should tell her something. They'd grown comfortable with each other. A man and a woman so much in sync that holding hands seemed as normal as slathering butter on a biscuit. Except holding hands with Matt was calorie-free, and certainly, more appealing.

Why Mel's mind circled back to his innocent observation about the new hire she didn't know. Was it the fact that Matt naturally assumed the A-D would be a man, or did his comment about workplace burnout raise questions about how much time she already spent at The Meadows? If she got the A-D job, likely, those additional duties, along with her current ones, would substantially increase her workload.

But wasn't career advancement one of the very things she'd wished for? Achieving her work goals meant success and respect. As kid sister to three brothers, the youngest child in the Brewer family, Mel would finally be taken seriously. Climbing up the ranks in her career would earn their esteem and, at last, make them see her for the professional she was.

Naturally, Mel wanted the job, too. She longed to leave her mark in this world. Advance The Meadows into the twenty-first century. Implement positive and productive changes. Wait. Now she sounded like Matt. But change, she'd learned, wasn't so bad. Sometimes, it could be a good thing. An outstanding thing. The thing that separated a well-run retirement community with a fantastic rep from the best of the best in the Ozarks. No matter the reputation, there was always room for improvement.

"Mel? Where'd you go just now?" Matt studied her with serious, dark eyes.

"Sorry." He probably thought he'd overstepped. Which, technically, he had. *They* had. But holding Matt's hand was the farthest thing from her mind, at least right now. How she could possibly convey the conflicting emotions that zigzagged through her heart? "Hey, we're almost off the clock. Enough shop talk for now."

But not all of it had been shop talk. The fact Matt referenced their hand holding indicated his mind drifted to other things, too. "You're deflecting, but I get it. We'll revisit this. I'll wrap up a few things in my office and then I'll be back to follow you out."

"Sounds good. I'm not helpless though. I can certainly find my way to my car. I've done it lots of times in the last five years."

Matt cleared his throat. Grinned. "I know. Helpless isn't the word that comes to mind when I think of you."

"Oh, yeah? I guess that's a discussion for another day." Mel straightened a stack of file folders on her desk and averted her eyes. They didn't have time to continue this conversation now. She had to get home and start various dishes to take to Mom's and Dad's tomorrow.

"Understood." A note of humor punctuated the word. Matt remained rooted to the floor, as if contemplating adding something else. The brief silence underscored what he didn't say. Or maybe she assumed too much?

Mel reminded herself that falling in love didn't need to be announced with fanfare and flowery talk. *I love you*, when spoken aloud, was simply enough. Neither uttered those words, yet they lingered in the comfortable stillness between them.

For now, simply knowing mattered. As her goals aligned, her life picture grew sharper. Clearer. She couldn't wait to share her upcoming interview for the Assistant Director position. As soon as Foster and the hiring committee scheduled her interview, Matt would be the first one she'd tell. What would he think? Obviously, he'd support her goals and dreams. That's the kind of guy he was.

Mel temporarily shoved additional work hours from her mind. Why worry about juggling a few more balls?

Chapter Eleven

The cold November wind sliced through Matt's coat like a meat cleaver. He hurried into The Meadows, mulling over his previous night's sleep, surprised he'd snoozed eight hours. For the first time since coming on board here, he'd fallen asleep without Clinton inserting himself into his dreams. Amazing how a little hope could ease his worry and make him more determined than ever to help the old fellow.

Matt noted Mel's VW stationed near The Meadows' main entrance and he picked up his pace. Had she slept well too? Crazy he should think about that, but lately, besides Clinton, she'd been the one to occupy his thoughts...and dreams. If he were to get the A-D position, he'd be spending less time with her, not more. How did he feel about that? *You know, how, buddy. You already can't get enough of the woman.*

A burst of blessed warmth hit him as he entered the building. Hints of baked turkey and pumpkin pie scented the halls and drew him toward home. He'd miss his family's gathering today, but the Brewers' table had become a second favorite. The way Jake and Billie Gail had welcomed him into their fold, accepting him as one of their own, made Matt realize, again, what special people they were.

"Well, hey, young fella." Edwin Ramsey waved from the doorway of his apartment. "Happy Thanksgiving to you! What brings you back so soon?"

"I'm on call this holiday. Thought I'd stop by early and see what's shaking. What are you up to, Edwin?"

"Oh, you know. The usual. Keeping everyone here in line."

Matt didn't doubt it. "We can always count on you, sir. Say, are Charla and Sam coming today?"

"Yep. The crew's heading over in a while to haul me to their place. Sam seems to think I shouldn't drive the ol' jalopy any longer."

The "ol' jalopy" not being that old, but likely, Sam's sentiments had more to do with Edwin's balance issues and him driving, than the vehicle itself.

"I say let 'em, Edwin. You don't want to rob them of a blessing, do you?"

The corners of Edwin's mouth lifted in a smile. "Of course not. Why don't you join us later, too? The way Miss Charla cooks, they'll have enough for the whole county."

"Appreciate the offer, but I'm invited to the Brewers' Thanksgiving dinner."

"Ahh." Edwin bobbed his head, his smile expanding into a huge grin. "It does a body good to see you and Miss Melinda take a shine to each other after all the months you tried to avoid it. You kids are perfect together. I've said it for a long time."

Yeah, he probably had. And so had a lot of other folks. Apparently, he and Mel had developed quite a cheering section. The Ruby matchmakers had most likely worked overtime contriving ways they could throw them together, which was unnecessary since they seemed to have nailed that themselves.

"Thank you, Edwin. I think so, too. Now, if you'll

excuse me, I need to find our queen bee and see what she's up to. Say hi to Sam and his family for me."

"Will do."

Matt resumed his pace. As he rounded the corner of the Laurel Lane wing, he spotted Mel at Clinton's door. Her knuckles paused in midair when she saw him.

"Have you knocked yet?" Matt lowered his voice to a whisper.

"No. Perfect timing though."

"Let's think positive. Go on. Give it a try."

Mel took a deep breath, squared her shoulders, and gave Clinton's door a couple of sound raps. Matt hung back, watching.

Nothing.

Mel knocked again. "Mr. Farley. It's me—Melinda. Mel Brewer. Happy Thanksgiving! May I have a word?"

Again, nothing.

Matt wanted to thump the fellow. Clinton knew very well that Mel stood on the other side of that door. Waiting. Hoping. Wanting him to answer.

"Mr. Farley?"

Mel shook her head at Matt and mouthed *He isn't going to open the door.*

Patience. Matt mouthed back.

Two seconds later, the door whooshed open and there stood Clinton, stoic, but not scowling. "No need to mime back and forth. I'm right here."

"Certainly. Good morning, Mr. Farley. Happy Thanksgiving."

"Same."

Okay, not a particularly kind greeting in return, but better than an ugly retort he might have once given. Matt continued to wait by the water cooler. He wouldn't insert himself into the conversation unless things went south.

Mel stepped closer. "I'd like to invite you again to my parents' home today. I know there's going to be a wonderful meal here, but I'd really love for you to come, and my mother cooks tons of food. We eat and visit and watch movies, and my brothers sometimes get a little crazy, but it's pretty harmless. I'll bring you back whenever you like. Please say yes."

"I appreciate the offer. I do." Clinton's gaze shifted to Matt for a minute, then back to Mel. "I'm not much of a joiner, as you know."

"That's okay. We don't put on airs. My family would love to have you."

"I remember Jake and Billie Gail and the boys. How are they?"

Clinton was actually engaging with Mel? A good sign. Small talk, no doubt, a novelty for Farley, but a pleasant switch from his usual sour self.

Matt busied himself at the water cooler, this morning's refresher infused with lemon and orange slices. He didn't want to appear nosy, but Clinton surely suspected why he hung around.

While Matt sipped his water, Mel updated Clinton and he seemed to listen with rapt interest. Who knew what went through the man's mind? The exchange both baffled and delighted Matt.

"So, you'll come?"

Clinton shook his head. "Nah. Can't, Miss Melinda. But it's been real nice visiting with you. I mean that."

"Why not? Why won't you come?"

The disappointment ricocheted off her words onto

Matt's heart, squeezing his chest. *Come on, Clinton. Don't do this. Tell her you'd love to.*

"Can't is all." Clinton frowned, then his wrinkled features relaxed. "It's nothing personal."

Mel's shoulders slumped. It was all Matt could do to remain rooted where he stood. What would it take to melt the grump's frozen heart? Maybe this was as good as it got. At least he'd thawed a bit, and that in itself counted as an absolute miracle.

"All right. If you change your mind, will you let me know?"

Clinton squinted. Pinned his gaze on Matt. Focused on Mel again and resumed a guarded expression. "Yes. I'll do that."

Mel stretched out her palm to him. Clinton raised his arm and paused. His hand hung suspended, close to his side. Slowly, the old man's palm met hers, and the pair's eyes communicated a message that, perhaps, neither completely understood. Matt wished he could recreate that moment on canvas.

"Time to gather 'round, everyone!" Mel's mother raised her voice over the holiday chatter and clapped her hands. She flashed an all-knowing smile, satisfied that her announcement would stop the crew in their tracks. The "crew," this time, meaning the entire Brewer household, plus Pastor Bill and Sharon, and a handful of others from church.

"Hey, sugar." Dad came up from behind and encircled Mom with his arms and nuzzled her neck. "Don't have to call us twice."

"Ooh! Jake, you startled me!"

"You'd think by now, you'd be accustomed to my charms. Good to know I've still got it."

Mel observed the easy way her parents interacted, realizing theirs was the kind of marriage she wanted someday. Romantic and relaxed, balanced with a healthy mix of teasing and surprise.

"They remind me a lot of my own parents," Matt whispered, sliding an arm around her shoulders. "I can't wait for you to meet them."

"I'm looking forward to it."

"I was hoping you'd say that. We're FaceTiming later. You can join us."

His wink undid her. A wink, for heaven's sake. How on earth the two of them had grown so close when only a few months ago, they'd barely been on speaking terms still awed her. When she thought of their past encounters before getting to know Matt on a personal level, she cringed. How horrible some of those first meetings were. Thankfully, they'd overcome their differences. An understatement, considering the last several weeks.

"Oh, have you mentioned me?"

The warmth of Matt's breath on her skin amplified his physical proximity as he leaned in closer. "You bet. I've never introduced anyone to Mom and Pop before—well, other than friends—so they're particularly interested."

The knowledge brought a strange giddiness. Parental introductions, formal ones, usually indicated one thing. Mel hadn't introduced Matt to Mom and Dad. He'd simply eased his way into their lives via her parents' Sunday dinner invitation months ago. There wasn't the usual awkwardness because formalities had already been dispensed with. Besides, pretentiousness didn't exist in the Brewer household. Her family was about as laid back and welcoming as they came.

Mel had never introduced Spencer to her parents either. As a homegrown local, they'd already known him. Anyway, there'd been no need to officially present Spencer to her family. She'd never seriously dated him, no matter what the community grapevine spread.

She reminded herself that if Matt's parents were anything like him, she didn't need to be nervous. They'd raised a fine son. They probably shared the same sense of humor and penchant for optimism. Mel did wonder, though, how they'd react to meeting her. Had Matt told them about their rocky start? That, initially, she could barely tolerate him? All right. Now the jitters started.

Not that the past, or any of the rest of it, mattered at the moment. Because, at the moment, the Brewer group and guests assembled around the family dinner table and linked hands. Banter ceased as Dad cleared his throat and bowed his head, a cue for everyone to do the same. As her father offered the Thanksgiving blessing, Mel tried to remain focused and grateful. Nevertheless, her thoughts drifted to Clinton Farley, alone again, on yet another holiday. Beside her, Matt squeezed her hand as if to say *He's on my mind too.*

Matt had never seen three grown men put away as much food as the Brewer brothers. Glory be, could those boys eat! Mounds of turkey and dressing, mashed potatoes and gravy, broccoli and rice casserole, creamed corn, salads, deviled eggs, yeast rolls, and additional sides of every color and stripe—Gabe, Garrett, and Mike socked it away. Not to be outdone, the Brewer patriarch outpaced them by a mile. One would never guess Jake Brewer to be such a big eater, judging by his firm, sturdy frame, where not an ounce of flab rested.

"What else can we pass you, Matt? You're not finished?" Jake carved another heap of turkey slices and fanned them out with the fork and carving knife across the gold-trimmed Haviland platter. "You barely ate enough to keep up your strength, son. Come on. Don't be shy."

"Thanks, sir, that's really kind of you. I'm pausing a minute to get my second wind."

Pastor Bill practically snorted. Laughter rumbled around the table as if he'd said something hilarious. Or maybe an inside joke he didn't know about yet?

Billie Gail glanced his way. "Don't pay any attention to them. They're laughing because second winds in this family are more like a mid-summer tornado. Surely you remember first helpings here are a mere precursor to the main event. And we haven't even gotten to the dessert tables yet. Or the snack tables, which come later."

Mercy, they'd have to hoist him up from the table with a block and tackle if he didn't pace himself. No wonder Mel could cook up a mean streak. Evidently, culinary skills in this family weren't lacking.

"Would you like a refill?" Gabe paused next to Matt's tea glass with a crystal pitcher in hand.

"Yes. Thanks."

"You bet, buddy. This is about as strong as we get here."

"Good thing, because I need to stay focused." Matt held up his glass. "I visited The Meadows earlier, but I thought I'd swing by again on my way home. See what's going on with some of the folks." He didn't mention Clinton by name, but he was one of the few who didn't leave the center today to visit family or have family visit him. Jake and Billie Gail most likely assumed Clinton was among those, though they didn't pry.

"More water?" Billie Gail started to rise. "And certainly, we have coffee to go with dessert."

"I can help myself, Mrs. Brewer, thank you. You sit tight and enjoy."

"Sitting tight isn't in Mom's genetic make-up." Mel leaned over and kissed her mother's cheek. "She's a nurturer."

"That she is." Jake Brewer lifted his wife's hand to his lips and kissed it. "The best half of this marriage, for sure. Runs this home as smooth as butter."

"Oh, go on," Billie Gail laughed. "You'll have Matt thinking I walk on water."

"You almost do."

"Pish posh. Don't let him fool you, Matt. We have our differences like everyone else. We work through our challenges, though. Have for almost thirty-four years."

Her honest assessment warmed him. Again, Jake and Billie Gail reminded him of his own parents. Parents who weren't perfect, but committed to God, and their marriage, flaws and all. It was the kind of relationship he wanted with a partner. *With Mel.* He couldn't see himself without her. Didn't want to. He didn't know when it happened, but something deep and abiding transcended their friendship. They were friends, yes. A friend he loved in more of an intimate way than mere friendship.

"My parents share your and Mr. Brewer's philosophy on marriage." Matt exchanged an appreciative gaze with Jake and Billie Gail. "Mom and Pop always said that difficulties and how we respond to them predict a marriage's longevity. Thankfully, like both of you, they always worked through the rough patches."

"Glad to hear it," Mel's dad said. "A lot of couples want to bail during those rough spots. I'm not talking about adultery, abuse, and the like—those more serious offenses that bear intense examination. I'm speaking of smaller issues which mushroom into bigger problems if not immediately addressed."

"I agree, sir. A healthy marriage is one that resolves the tiny fissures before they become bigger cracks. Pop always said that accidentally leaving the cap off the toothpaste didn't matter a whit. That it's the knowledgeable intention to do ill will that matters."

"Your father's a wise man. Simple oversights aren't even in the same league as intentional harshness. But whatever the issue, it's best to address it early rather than risk emotional distance and heartbreak."

"Hear, hear, darling." Billie Gail caressed her husband's cheek with her palm.

Were they remembering a specific time in their own marriage? It seemed to Matt that Jake and Billie Gail Brewer were an open book. Not without their flaws, but a partnership that valued mutual respect and honesty.

"Careful, you two." Garrett grinned as he spooned more mashed potatoes onto his plate. "Your children are present. And what will the good pastor here think?"

"Your good pastor heartily endorses marital affection. Lots of it." As if to affirm it, he kissed his wife's cheek. Quite loudly.

Then Gabe jabbed his brother with his elbow. "Aww... Leave Mom and Dad alone. What's a little PDA between these young pups?"

"Yeah, we still got it, eh, hon?" To emphasize the fact, Jake snatched his wife's palm and kissed it again, this time exaggerating the smooch. All this kissing business primed Matt's pump. Would Mel mind if he kissed her now? He didn't, but he surely wanted to.

Lively banter resumed, as if this interplay was a common occurrence in the Brewer household. Some parents might be reticent to express their affection in front of their children, much less company, but it certainly didn't seem to bother this family. Matt liked that. Made him seem like part of the group.

Mel eyed her parents with loving appreciation, obviously unfazed by their open affection for one another. Her regard for her mother and father made Matt realize how some families take each other for granted. Not in this household though. Love flowed and spilled over onto each member like water flooding a creekbank. Again, in Matt's mind, it set the bar high how he envisioned marriage and life afterward. Mel must share the same expectation. Was that why he had the sudden urge to spring from his chair and drop to one knee?

Mel couldn't be sure, but if she were a betting girl, she'd bet money that this Thanksgiving ranked as one of Matt's best. Despite being on call and missing his own family's celebration, the guy seemed to lap up all the chaos and craziness of the day. She'd never seen him so animated and talkative, completely comfortable with the zany crew that was her family—both of blood and friendship. From dinnertime to games to movies and snacks, Matt's buoyant demeanor kicked into high gear. She could get used to holidays with him. Another thing to consider if she were to get the Assistant Director position at work.

Goal or not, with it came the increased work load, longer hours, and holidays on call. The time she and Matt now enjoyed together would likely be spread much thinner if she assumed a new role at The Meadows. Did she really want that? As usual, the thought ping-ponged back and forth in her head. Why couldn't she have it all? The perfect job, a great guy, her dream home? *Because ideal is a myth.* But it didn't have to be, did it?

"Hey, a dollar for your thoughts." Matt paused just shy of The Meadows' entryway. Dusk had fallen and they'd stopped to check in with staff and residents and assess the day, and then they planned to return to Matt's place to video chat with his parents.

"What happened to a penny?"

"Inflation." The corners of his mouth tilted upward.

"Ahh. Good point." They fell into step with each other, their hands almost touching, but not quite. Mel wanted to share her thoughts. She wanted to tell him about applying for the A-D position, and how he felt mattered. But now wasn't the right time. Maybe later. "I'm thinking a lot of things. One, I'm happy we spent the day together. Another, how did Clinton manage another holiday alone?"

Matt stopped in his tracks and gave her his full attention. "Spending the day with you and your family and friends knocked this Thanksgiving out of the park. I'm happy we spent the day together, too." He started to add something else but hesitated and seemed to shift gears. "About Clinton. Let's go find out."

What had he been about to say? What she secretly longed to hear?

Mel set her curiosity aside for now and nodded. They entered the bright brick building, already aglow in colorful Christmas lights and holiday wreaths, and Matt gave a low whistle as they approached the gaily decorated hallways.

"Wow. I have a new appreciation for the building maintenance crew. This must have taken hours."

"Yes, it's an undertaking, for sure. The guys actually strung the outdoor lights last week, and then on Thanksgiving Day, the exterior lights are timed to come on at four p.m. and go off every morning at eight all the way through New Year's. The outdoor Nativity matches the smaller one in the activity room. It's a blast the way we do Christmas here."

"I'll say. Not sure how I missed all the decorating last week, other than I guess my mind was on other things. This is absolutely amazing."

Several residents meandered through the halls, cups of hot chocolate, tea, and coffee in hand. Not surprisingly, Clinton wasn't among them. Had he even left his apartment at all today? Or had he ordered room service? Maybe he'd fixed something for himself.

As they approached the Laurel Lane wing, Mel noted the residents' doors where Christmas wreaths, garland, and miniature light strands already decorated many. On some doors, remnants of Thanksgiving—cross stitched turkeys, cornucopias and the like—remained. In the coming days, staff would help residents who needed an extra hand with a festive touch, a fun project that Mel usually volunteered for.

"Think he'll give us permission to decorate his door?" Matt tipped his head toward room forty-two. Clinton's door, stark white, was bare.

"He hasn't before, but maybe this year will be different. Just because he didn't join us today for Thanksgiving doesn't mean I'm giving up." Mel tried to channel some hope. After all, Clinton's countenance seemed brighter—well, bright for him—in the last day or two.

They tarried at Clinton's door, neither necessarily eager to knock, yet reluctant to move on before checking on the old fellow's wellbeing.

"Guess I'll do the honors," Matt whispered. Instead of knocking though, he simply pressed the buzzer, the noise inside bouncing off interior walls and reverberating out into the hall.

They listened for any sound of movement, any indication at all that Clinton would acknowledge their presence, but silence greeted their efforts.

Mel shrugged, disappointed. "Maybe he turned in early?"

"At six? Nope. Don't buy it. He's in there. Probably watching us and hoping we'll beat it."

"Yeah. I imagine you're right." Mel tried the buzzer again. She wasn't ready to give up yet. "Mr. Farley, it's Matt and me. We dropped by again to check on things here. Would you like to have a cup of coffee with us?"

Silence.

"Clinton, you wouldn't want to disappoint Mel would you? Me, it's one thing. But Mel...she's another. Don't keep breaking her heart. Please."

Matt's words soaked into her bones, settling in all the right places. The way he looked at her when he spoke caused her cheeks to warm. For some reason she didn't completely understand, tears sprang to her eyes. *Don't keep breaking her heart.* Something Matt would never do. Without a doubt, Matt Enders would never knowingly do anything to break her heart. The knowledge confirmed her feelings for him. He must feel the same way. Did he? His eyes confirmed what she suspected. *Oh, Matt.*

As she contemplated that, Clinton's door slowly opened. Mel's breath caught. Clinton glared at them, his wrinkles accentuating his frown.

"First time in a long while anyone's actually invited me to coffee here."

"Bu...but just last week, I begged you to come down to our annual Thanksgiving dinner here." How could Clinton not recall that? Maybe senility had colored his thinking more than Mel thought. "And remember," she said gently, "We invited you to my parents' home to share the holiday with us today."

"And yesterday, I brought you a cup of Tilly's special blend," Matt added.

Clinton dismissed their reminders with a wave of his palm. "No matter. Let me throw on a sweater and I'll grace you with my presence. That dining room is colder'n the North Pole. Just give me a minute."

He turned and left them standing there, mouths opened, waiting.

She studied Matt. He studied her.

"What in the world?" Mel whispered. "How do you even explain this?"

"I can't."

The giddiness in Matt's voice buoyed her spirit. He practically bounced on his feet as they deliberated Clinton's change of heart. Could Clinton really be softening? This latest shift both baffled and delighted Mel.

What the man said or did next was anyone's guess, though she hoped for the best.

"Well, are you ready or not?" Clinton's words jolted them back to the present. He stepped from his doorway, poking his arms inside a chocolate brown sweater, and closed the door behind him. "That coffee better be fresh 'cause if it's not, I'm gonna raise all kinds of h—." He stopped short of saying it. "It best be fresh, is all."

Indeed. Mel clamped her mouth shut and Matt did the same. Hoping for the best sometimes called for restraint. Lots of it.

"So, what's the verdict?" Matt drummed his fingers against the shiny tabletop. They'd seated themselves at a table not far from the coffee bar, and Clinton set down his cup after a careful, but prolonged sip.

"Hot as blazes. Decent, I s'pose."

Decent? That's all he had? Though, inwardly, Matt had to admit he was tickled that Clinton even joined them for coffee.

"Personally, I think it's delish." Mel flashed Clinton a smile. "The Meadows' brew is the best. Better than most name brands, in my opinion."

Clinton angled his head and regarded her with narrowed eyes. Then, wonder of wonders, the cantankerous crab also smiled. "Didn't know you to be such a coffee connoisseur, Miss Melinda. You and Wonder Boy here are too wet behind the ears to know what really good coffee is—black as smut with enough bite to curl your toes...like my Marabel used to make."

Matt almost spewed coffee across the table. Instead, he clamped his mouth shut, surprised that Farley would mention his wife's name, but pleased that it signaled progress. That a mere coffee break would draw Clinton out of his self-imposed exile set Matt thinking. What if he proposed a scheduled coffee hour in addition to the leisure come-and-go approach The Meadows already offered? A small thing, but one that could make a big impact on the less sociable residents here. Namely, Clinton. Maybe something as simple as coffee would be a way to bond with other individuals.

If staff expanded the coffee bar and created a warm, inviting space, say, with coffee and various hot drink options, and some new comfy, cozy seating, camaraderie and fellowship were sure to follow. Clinton might be a tough bird, but possibly, he just needed steered in the right direction. The grump wouldn't change his ways overnight, but maybe with a new approach, he might actually make a friend or two.

When Matt interviewed for the A-D position, he'd bring up this idea to Foster and the hiring committee. He couldn't wait to discuss this and some other ideas he had tumbling around in his head. Innovation revitalized an already superb program. Together, he and Mel were already proving that.

"Cat got your tongue, boy?" Clinton eyed him from across the table. "Not like you to clam up without offering some wisecrack."

Was Clinton trying to intentionally goad him? Well, it wouldn't work. Matt inwardly composed himself before responding. "I like my coffee strong, too. Guess we have that in common."

"*Hmpf.* Probably the only thing."

Mel cleared her throat. "Clinton, we missed you at my

parents' gathering today. We really hoped you'd reconsider joining us."

Leave it to her to play peacemaker. But Matt didn't mind. It made him lo—*like* her all the more. *Like? No, buddy. You were right the first time.*

"Now, think about it, Miss Melinda. How would I have gotten there? On my fairy wings?"

Matt bit back a retort and waited for Mel to remind Clinton that they'd both offered to pick him up this morning. The guy's memory must be slipping more than Matt thought.

"Pardon me?" Mel's eyebrows scrunched together above freckled cheeks and a downturned mouth. "You know we—"

"I would have had to roll myself up like a sleeping bag to fit in that tiny contraption you call a vehicle." Clinton interrupted. "And the truck Wonder Boy here drives is so big, a body would need a step ladder and a pulley to climb aboard."

That was why Clinton hadn't come? Because of mobility issues with their transportation? *Blast it.* He remembered wondering about that. Still, The Meadows owned a passenger van and offered shuttle service. Hours were limited on the holidays, but Matt suspected something could have been arranged.

"Clinton, we're sorry for the miscommunication." Matt meant it. He hated to think of Clinton sitting alone in his apartment today because the mode of travel overwhelmed him. Proud fella that he was, he'd refused to admit it. What could he offer to make Clinton believe him?

Matt leaned forward and said honestly, "Mel and I would have moved heaven and earth to have you join us today if we'd only known what the difficulty was. Really. But we're not mind readers. Sometimes, you gotta speak up and say what the matter is."

"Why do you even care?"

Would this battle never end? "Sheesh, Clinton. I care because God cares. I want to serve Him by loving others. That's what brought me to The Meadows to begin with. I want to use my gifts and training to the best of my ability." Matt met the older gentleman's gaze head on. "I knew God had something for me here. Someone I could help, and maybe, too, someone who could teach me a thing or two and grow me in ways I might not have otherwise."

Clinton sipped at his coffee again and set down his mug. His eyes bore into Matt's as if he'd like to slice him and dice him like a basket of garden vegetables. "That spiel sounds real fine. Gifts and training. GIFTS—like your newest project. Guess I'm your next one, huh?" Irritation, though restrained, punctuated his words, his voice almost cracking on *I'm your next one.*

"No, sir. It's not like that."

"Look, you can't possibly care about me. Not to belabor the obvious, Wonder Boy, but you don't even know me. You know nothin' about my life—what makes me tick—other than what's been written about me in those dang files of yours. But believe me, all those jots and tittles rarely tell the whole story."

True. True, also, from where he sat and from what he'd gleaned, he doubted anything in Clinton's file had been embellished. He knew, as well, there was truth in what Clinton said.

"You're right," Matt conceded. "I don't know all there is to know about you. Would you share your story with me? Please?"

Clinton gulped. Clearly, he hadn't expected Matt's reply. The old man frowned. He shifted his gaze from Matt to Mel. "Whatcha think, Miss Melinda? Should I?"

Mel circled her fingers around her coffee mug. She studied Clinton a minute, as if weighing how to respond. "I think," she hesitated. Then she reached across the table and clasped Clinton's hand. "Stories—the best ones—are meant to be shared."

"Even though it might hurt?"

She nodded. "Yes. Even then. Because, often, with the hurt comes healing. And healing revives hope."

"No ill will intended, but you're young. You've never lost a baby son. A spouse of sixty years. A family. Hopes. Dreams." His eyes glistened where moisture started to gather. "It isn't like snagging a fingernail. There's a bit more to it than that."

"I understand that. I'm so sorry for your losses." Now, Mel's voice wobbled. "But here's the thing. I wouldn't begin to minimize what you've experienced, Clinton, but I have known heartache. Maybe not like yours, but I've lost grandparents I loved. I've mourned life events and missed opportunities. I've weighed past relationships in favor of new ones. Each of us owns our stories. One doesn't necessarily trump the other's."

Matt had to hand it to her. She sounded far wiser than her twenty-seven years. Instead of snapping back a quick retort, Mel had responded with sensitivity and kindness—traits that drew out the best in people. Certainly, in him, and Clinton, too, it would seem.

So, what was his story? What else had hardened his heart over the years? Clinton had gone silent, but his hand remained linked with Mel's. Really more her effort than his, yet he hadn't pulled away. A good sign.

Another thing Matt would mention at his upcoming job interview. As The Meadows' new Assistant Director, he'd be sure and toot Mel's horn, also. He'd immediately recommend she be given a salary increase, in addition to an expansion of duties and decision-making prerogatives. She'd earned every kudo and rite of passage that went with job advancement, and as the current Activities Director and multi-tasker extraordinaire, the facility and residents alike relied on her for way more than her organizational and creative gifts. She was the heartbeat of this place. Knew every nuance of The Meadows and its people.

A twinge of unease squeezed Matt's chest. For the dozenth time, he thought about the extra hours involved with the new position. Was he ready to commit to that? His current job already entailed a great deal of responsibility. Did he really want more? Then again, it seemed like a pointless worry at this stage of the game. There were probably other candidates vying for the A-D position—maybe some who were better qualified than him. He might not even get the job. But still...he might.

Matt tamped down variables and misgivings. A lot of couples juggled busy careers and relationships and hobbies. *Hobbies.* Like his painting. A hobby that, in another lifetime, might have been his chosen career path. But hobbies didn't translate to a viable income, no matter how skilled the person.

"And your story, Wonder Boy?" Clinton disengaged from Mel's fingers and rapped the table with calloused knuckles. "You have one with Miss Melinda, right?"

Chapter Twelve

"A-hem." Mel fake coughed. Were they really that transparent? She glanced at Matt who didn't look the least bit uncomfortable.

"We do share a story, Clinton. It's a story that I hope evolves." He met her eyes and smiled.

"Good, good. Don't mess it up." Clinton lifted the coffee cup to his lips and sipped. He swallowed with an exaggerated gulp and sighed. "Ahh. Like I said. Decent. Some room for improvement, but not bad."

"What about your story?" Matt leaned forward. "We'd love to know more."

"In time maybe. Not today."

Disappointment washed over Mel, though she held her tongue. Sitting here with Clinton, talking, was so much farther than she'd hoped to go today. Baby steps, she reminded herself. In the last week, especially, she'd seen a new side of this crotchety, wounded man. Six months ago, she wouldn't have believed it possible, but today on this Thanksgiving evening, their time together— their chat—could only be described as a miracle in the making. Matt had called it right. She wanted to throw her arms around Clinton and hug him. How long had it been since he'd had one? *Go easy, Mel. Don't scare him off.*

"We understand, Clinton. When you're ready to share more, we're here."

"Are you now? That's right dandy of you, Miss Melinda."

Would she ever get used to his passive-aggressive humor? Hmm... She considered that for a moment. Understandably, he covered his pain with bitter barbs. Maybe one day, the barriers would completely crumble away, but tonight they remained firmly in place. For now, she took it in stride and tempered an automatic retort with a pause and kindness. "I mean it, Clinton. My door's always open to you. Matt's is, too. And for the record, if you'd ever like to go anywhere, somehow, we'll make sure you get there. You just have to say the word. Okay?"

"Appreciate it. Thanks. Now, I'm sure you two have other places to be on this fine holiday evening, correct?"

"Actually, Mel and I are heading over to my house for a bit. Other than a quick text exchange this morning, I haven't wished my parents a happy Thanksgiving yet. Thought it might be nice to video chat and introduce Mel while I'm at."

Clinton nodded. "I'm sure your folks would like that."

"May we walk you back to your apartment?" Mel hoped with all her heart he said yes. Something inexplicable had transpired between the three of them tonight. She detected new undercurrents in this, their fragile, blossoming friendship, and she wanted to prolong their time together.

"No, miss. I believe I'll hang out here for a bit longer. You both run along though." He scooted back from the table and stood with some difficulty. "Think I'll grab another cup of coffee."

"Here—let me get it for you." Mel rose quickly and reached for Clinton's cup.

"No. But thank you just the same." His pointed gaze made his intentions clear. Forfeit a man's independence and eventually, pride and self-reliance flew out the window. "You two go on now. I'm rather wiped from all this jibber-jabber."

Jibber-jabber? In Mel's mind, their conversation had been sensible and almost pleasant. Well, civil anyway. Still, Matt stood and extended his hand to Clinton.

"Good chatting with you, Clinton. I'd like to make this a habit."

"Yeah. I bet you would."

And in a heartbeat, the old Clinton reappeared. Except this time, his tone didn't sound nearly as sharp, nor his reply as biting. When he stretched out his withered palm to meet Matt's handshake, hope lit anew in Mel's heart and remained.

Matt's parents completely warmed to Mel, as he knew they would. The four of them chatted a good forty-five minutes before the conversation drew to a close.

"We're so tickled to have finally met you, Melinda," his mother gushed, her full, rosy cheeks growing pinker by the second. "My gracious, Matty, you've hit the jackpot, sweetheart."

"Yes, son, we understand now why you've seemed a tad preoccupied when we've talked lately. We're happy for you," Pop added.

The fact that Melinda joined him in their conversation this evening wasn't lost on them. Other than occasional dates, Matt had never introduced a woman with as much intention as he had Mel. He knew it. They knew it. Now, Mel knew it. Which Matt didn't mind at all. Though he and Mel hadn't fully discussed where they were headed, assumptions leaned toward the obvious.

Judging by Mel's expression, she didn't seem to mind. Her blue eyes misted but sparkled. Her countenance brightened. When Matt curled his hand around hers, she laced her fingers through his and squeezed.

December settled over the Ozarks with surprising ease—except colder. Other than a few errant snowflakes, the only thing that differentiated the subtle transition from last month to now was the underlying excitement of Christmas.

Around town, decorations and lights began to festoon streets, businesses, churches, and homes. Colorful window displays adorned storefronts in various degrees of holiday cheer. Red, green, silver, and gold transitioned Ruby's homespun veneer into a festive feast for the eyes.

At night, the small town twinkled with an ethereal glow. At daybreak, sunlight glazed treetops, steeples, and roofs in shimmering beauty. Different points of day, but equally captivating.

When Mel's phone and laptop simultaneously chimed with an e-mail notification, she strode from her office window and sat down at her desk. Nothing unusual about receiving e-mail. Every day brought tons. Except this week, she anticipated one in particular.

Eagerly, Mel clicked the e-mail tab on her laptop. *Ahh.* There it was! That one, specific e-mail—the official one from Foster. She opened it and immediately her heart started to pound. The hiring committee had scheduled her interview for the Assistant Director position for December 15th. One week from today. There were other formalities and then, Foster added his well-wishes. *Mel, cheering you on as you move toward your goals. You're one of our finest.*

Looking forward to the 15ᵗʰ.

She released the breath she'd been holding and twirled around in her chair. At that moment, reservations about additional work hours and possible infringements on her personal life fled. Scoring an interview at a mere twenty-seven for such an important position ticked off another life goal. Career advancement and industry respect, as well as her family's acknowledgement and pride, mattered as much to her as her own desires. Always had. As the youngest Brewer sibling, and only girl in their brood, moving up the career ladder would ensure her place in the Brewer boy hall of fame. Fire Captain, home builder, and business owner. Next, maybe Sunset Meadows Assistant Director.

Mel had to tell someone. Mom and Daddy? Her brothers? No, she'd share with them later. At the moment, the one she really wanted to confide in was Matt. She knew he'd shoot straight. He'd assess the pros and cons of this new development, but ultimately, he'd be there for her as she prepped for next week. He'd be her sounding board. An encouraging voice and listening ear. Not that her family wouldn't exactly. It was just that Matt had the advantage of being familiar with their workplace and daily demands that her family didn't. She could bounce some things off him that she couldn't her parents or the guys. Matt's professional capacity enabled him to see the situation in a realistic, impartial light.

Mel tucked her cell phone in her jacket pocket and grabbed her near empty coffee cup. She'd pay Matt a visit on her way to get a refill.

As she exited her office, Sarah caught her in the hall. "Hey, girlfriend. How's it going? You seem to have a new pep to your step these days."

"Yeah, this is a peppy place." Mel lingered for a moment to chat. "It's going great, by the way. Your day?"

"Uh-uh. You're not getting off that easy." Sarah pulled her into the nearby ladies' room. "Details, Mel. I want details."

"Details?"

"Don't think we don't know. The whole place is abuzz about it."

Abuzz? About what? She hadn't told anyone that she'd applied for the A-D position, except Foster, of course. Sarah was her best friend, but Mel preferred to keep things on the down-low for now. Scoring an interview didn't necessarily mean she'd get the job. Though chances were definitely in her favor. She'd heard of no other candidates.

"Mind enlightening me then because I have no idea what you're referring to."

"You and Matt, sweetie."

Not the job interview. Her relationship with Matt. Which presented a different complication. They'd been especially careful about keeping their private and professional lives separate. People might assume, but in Mel's mind they hadn't said or done anything inappropriate to call their work into question.

"You mean people are talking? They think we've crossed the line, Sarah?"

"No, not at all." Sarah patted her shoulder. "Don't look so serious. When I said the 'whole place,' what I actually meant is Ruby. You know, town as a whole. Not necessarily here. But I have to tell you, everyone's tickled pink. It's full steam ahead for the local matchmaking train."

"Wonderful." Mel caught a glimpse of herself in the mirror. Her cheeks had turned a soft shade of pink, naturally heightening her freckles. "Not that we're publicizing it or anything, Sarah, but I think we're in love. We're still figuring out some things along the way, adjusting to *us*. Being together. Working together. What the future may hold...together."

"Aww, sweetie. This is so awesome!" Sarah hugged her. "Now, no worries. It's going to be fine. More than fine."

"W...wow. Thanks." Something seemed odd here. Not in a bad way. More like a distinct, unique undercurrent. "Sarah?"

"Yes?" Sarah stepped back, grinning.

"I think another question *is* how are you?" Suddenly, her friend's eyes brimmed with tears. Mel rubbed her arm. "What is it? Are those tears for me or for you?"

"I can't hold it any longer. Andy and me. I'm pregnant!"

"Sarah..." This time, it was Mel who leaned in for the hug. "Honey, this is the best news. Congratulations!"

"Thanks." Sarah reached around her to grab a wad of tissues from the tissue box. "Here."

"How far along are you?"

"About eight weeks. We're waiting until the end of the month to tell everyone because it's still so early, but I wanted you to know. Can you believe it? After four—almost five—years of marriage and three years of trying, just when we put our stork plans on hold, it finally happened. We're going to have a baby!"

"I'm so happy for you guys. Truly. What does Andy think?"

"You know him. He's about to burst. All smiles, every morning. Already planning the nursery and anticipating

Little League events."

"Ha!" Sounded like Andy. Andy Dawson hailed from a large family. Three brothers and two sisters with a passel of nieces and nephews who Andy and Sarah doted on. Now, it was their turn to be on the receiving end. "No morning sickness?"

Sarah shook her head. "No, ma'am. But I'm hungrier than a bear, let me tell you. My pants are already tight."

"What does your OB think?"

"That every woman is different, and that I'm in great health. We have an ultrasound scheduled after Christmas. I'll keep you posted."

"You better." Mel hugged her again and they blotted their cheeks with the tissues. Sarah's news definitely trumped hers. Two years older than Mel, Sarah wore pregnancy well. Mel had been so absorbed in Matt and work stuff, she'd hardly noticed her friend's slight weight gain and additional sparkle. A part of her shrank inside. She resolved to be more cognizant. There was more to life than work. Like friendship. Family.

Family. Again, Mel weighed the pros and cons of possible job advancement. Why anguish over this now? Marriage and motherhood didn't mean one had to forfeit a career. Many women managed both. In today's world, one didn't have to define the other.

Matt re-read the hiring committee's e-mail. His interview for The Meadows A-D position was scheduled for next Tuesday, the 15th, at one-thirty p.m. Foster had added a note. *Thanks for your interest, Matt. Good to see your name in the mix! Excited to hear your ideas.*

Matt gave the air a fist-pump. Wait. *Good to see your*

name in the mix. How many candidates were there? Hmm. Well, what had he expected? Naturally, there'd be other job applicants. The A-D position had been posted internally, as well as various online job sites. Knowing small town unity such as it was in Ruby, he knew they'd try to hire internally, or at least from local candidates, first. He'd been the exception when he was hired. He imagined geriatric social workers were few and far between in the immediate area, so Matt had a leg up there. His qualifications had garnered an immediate interview. His interview snagged the job. God opened the door at a time in his life when he'd known this was what he wanted. Where he wanted to be.

He'd packed away his paints, along with his artistic dreams, and headed to the Ozarks community where he and his training could make a difference. Along the way, he'd held onto his "someday" dream, but now it rested on the periphery of his subconscious rather than the forefront. Serving The Meadows' residents to the best of his ability was his calling. His passion. GIFTS was only the beginning. What he envisioned, long-term, could turn this retirement community on its head.

He loved art. Loved painting. Trouble was his hobby wouldn't support a family. That is, if a guy had one. Again, maybe someday.

"Hi. Got a sec?" Her voice penetrated the morning silence.

Man, just seeing her ratcheted up his emotions. Matt closed the e-mail tab and stood. "Sure."

Today Mel wore a red sweater, black slacks, and ballet flats that accentuated her compact stature, but were perfect considering the steps work generated. Sometimes, she wore heels, but like many of the staff, most chose comfort and common sense over vanity.

Her lips parted in a smile and it all but undid him. "I have some news."

"Must be the good kind, judging by that smile. Come on in." To avoid wagging tongues, he didn't close the door, but instead, gestured for Mel to have a seat, and he did the same. "Does it have to do with Clinton?"

"No. But it does have to do with work." Her smile spread into a humongous, dazzling grin. She flexed her fingers and placed her palms on her knees. "As you know, and as we kind of recently touched on, a new position has opened here. The Assistant Director position. Someone to be Foster's right-hand man. Or woman."

Oh. Boy. Was this leading where he thought it was? Had Mel applied for the job? Surely not. Not when she'd admitted to already spending way too many hours here. But then again, so did he. Muscles knotted in Matt's neck.

Yeah, he remembered their brief mention of the A-D opening and how adding an extra department head, who also had weekend rotation, would free up more of their personal time.

Matt hadn't intentionally tried to dissuade her then, but is that how it would seem since he'd applied for the job, also? That he'd knowingly deceived or misled? He could rationalize it all he wanted, but looking back, maybe subconsciously, he had. But he hadn't meant to. He'd honestly thought the added workload would be a stretch for Mel. In his current role, adding Assistant Director to his title would seem an easier transition than it would be for her. *Keep going, buddy. You'll perfect that double standard yet.*

"I remember we touched on the new position, yes."
Matt leaned forward, resting his chin on steepled fingers.

"Well, guess what?"

"Okay. What?"

"I scored an interview!" Mel practically bounced in her chair. "I'm meeting with the hiring committee next week!"

"I didn't even know you'd applied for the position."

She nodded. "Yes. Several weeks ago, actually. I didn't want to say anything until I had an interview scheduled because I thought maybe there was a slim chance that I would even get one. I know there are likely other applicants who are better qualified than me. Plus, my age. I wondered if that would be a factor."

"Employers can't discriminate based on age, sex, orientation, etcetera."

"Yeah, I know. But I also know that with age comes maturity and the likelihood of more job experience. Experience is a grand persuader." Mel's eyebrows furrowed. "What's wrong? You're not reacting like I thought you would."

"And how's that?"

"Uh...excited. Happy for me."

"I'm sorry. I am happy for you, Mel. If the Assistant Director post is what you truly want, then I'm thrilled for you." Matt rose and ambled over to the window. Fluffy white snowflakes swirled in the air, drifting over the mountains and treetops. He tried to compose how to say it. "So, your interview's scheduled next week?"

"Next Tuesday, yes." Mel stood and met him at the window. "I'm getting odd vibes here."

"Sorry. Not intentional. It's just that...I thought longer work hours were something you were trying to trim, not add."

"I know. But job advancement is a goal I've had. I'll know more after the interview. If we're talking a lot of extra hours or added stress, the A-D position may not be for me. Also, I may not even be offered the job. It's more that I have to do this for me. Find out if I'd be a good fit. You know?"

"I do know. I completely understand."

"You do? Really?"

"Yes. Those are the exact same reasons I applied for the A-D position."

Mel's mouth fell open. "Pardon me?"

Her surprise, and something else, wrenched him. *Hurt*. "I was just reading the e-mail when you knocked. The one confirming my interview. Also, for next week. Tuesday, in fact."

"Wow. The same day as mine." Mel turned her attention to the falling snow. For a second, she didn't say anything. She trailed a finger along the windowpane as a snowflake feathered its way down the exterior glass. "You never even mentioned you were considering applying. In fact, when we recently spoke about it, it sounded like you weren't. Why didn't you say something then?"

"I guess I could ask you the same question." He touched her arm. "Look, I wasn't trying to be sneaky about it. I had no idea you'd applied either. Like you, I wanted to wait to say anything. I'm the new kid on the block. I thought I had a pretty good chance of snagging an interview, but I wasn't ninety-nine percent sure.

"And if you want to know the truth, I've really weighed the additional hours and responsibilities that are sure to come with the A-D position. Yeah, job advancement is nice. Looks good on the ol' resumé. Means more money.

But beyond that—I can continue the work I've started here. Launch new programs. Assist Foster and The Meadows' community in a capacity that's different, yet still hands-on." Matt gently placed a finger under her chin, coaxing her to look at him. "Here's the thing. I understand you and I are both goal-oriented people, but I don't want a job or work or anything else to come between us. That's something we also talked about once, remember?"

She trained her gaze on his, her eyes a mixture of upset and sadness. "I'm still trying to wrap my head around this. The fact that neither of us felt the inclination to talk about it before we applied for the job. I'm wondering what the reason is for that, and I don't think I like the answers I'm coming up with."

"Aw, Mel. Don't. Don't dissect this like there's some hidden motive here. I think we can agree that we each have goals, but those goals are second to *us*. Right?"

"Guess that depends on who's offered the job...and who accepts it. If it's one of us, I suppose we'll revisit this." She heaved a sigh and strode from his office.

Regret punched him in the gut. Why did her reaction startle him? Maybe because he should have mentioned his plans to her. Maybe because he well knew it. Then again, transparency was a two-way street.

So, he'd applied, too. Why did that shock her? Of course, Matt would see the new job post and apply for it. Why wouldn't he? He certainly had the qualifications. An impeccable reputation. Work ethic. Driven. Accomplished. Everything The Meadows' hiring committee would want in an Assistant Director. Especially their innovative, close-knit community.

Recently, the retirement complex had appeared as the feature story in an area newspaper. Foster had fielded calls and inquiries for days after the story ran. More notoriety meant increased visibility and expectations. Good things, indeed. Naturally, Foster would want the best person for the job. The person best equipped to handle the media attention and professional obligations. A right-hand man, or woman, who would not only work alongside Foster in a creative capacity, but who would pick up the slack and take the reins when necessary.

For Mel to suddenly feel a competitive edge where Matt was concerned didn't sit well with her. It seemed childish and out of character. Granted, they'd gotten off to a shaky start, but they'd evolved. Grown beyond that. Fallen...in love. At least, she had.

In a funk, though determined to shake off the doldrums, Mel steeled herself and went about her day. She cued up today's movie in the activity room. Later, she met one-on-one with residents to assess new interests. Organized the afternoon craft. Sat in on a GIFTS presentation by Chuck Farrow, one-half owner of the Come and Get It Diner who rallied attendees to claim their true passion. In Chuck's case, he'd recently penned a cookbook that had garnered praise in the publishing world. He tied in his forty-minute presentation nicely with God's calling on his life, and in closing, he challenged folks not to let age or preconceived notions deter one's earthly mission.

When the presentation ended, the crowd cheered as Ida Mae sauntered up to the makeshift stage and planted a gush-worthy kiss on her husband's cheek. "See why I love this guy, y'all? He's such an encourager."

To which Chuck replied, "Ditto, honey. I have a great example." And then, to everyone's delight, the couple locked lips in a heart-melting public display of affection. Oh, the absolute joy of being in love!

Mel clapped along with the others, certain her face was redder than the Christmas lights that dressed the room in holiday cheer. Being in love was the best feeling ever. And sometimes, the hardest feeling, as well. Loving someone scattered one's emotions all over the map and disoriented a person. New love could be even trickier.

As she made her way toward the exit, Edwin Ramsey tapped her shoulder. "Good afternoon, Miss Melinda, a rousing talk today, don't you think?"

She paused in mid-step. "I sure do, Edwin. Imagine— Chuck Farrow, an author. We have our very own celebrity right here in Ruby."

"Yes'm. A top-notch chef, a smart fellow, and an upstanding guy. Oh, and someone who's figured out that going after one's goals, regardless of age, is something to celebrate."

"I couldn't agree more."

A smile tugged at the corners of Edwin's mouth. "Because when our dreams and goals align with the good Lord's, that's when miraculous things happen."

"Good thoughts there, my friend."

"Thank you, my dear. I believe 'em. Same nuggets I shared earlier with Matthew. Now, you have a real lovely rest of the day." He tipped his head and tottered on his way, leaving Mel to wonder why'd he'd shared the same thing with Matt.

Had Edwin caught wind of the new job opening? Possibly. Had Matt shared his interest in the position?

Doubtful. He hadn't even shared his intent with her until after he'd gotten his interview, and then only because she'd told him first that she had.

Without warning, the exhaustion of the day pressed upon her. Five-fifteen. Well past quitting time. Normally, she stayed behind a few minutes, wrapping up loose ends and readying things for the next day, but today, she was ready to head home. The warmth of a cozy fire and a crock pot full of chili drew her. She'd intended to ask Matt over, but mixed feelings about their prior conversation made solitude more appealing than forcing a lightheartedness she didn't feel.

Mel hurried to her office, closed her laptop, and poked her arms into the sleeves of her winter coat. She contemplated taking some paperwork home, but ultimately, shoved it to the corner of her desk, giving it prominence beside her mail basket. It'd still be there in the morning, along with the usual tasks that awaited her. No sense in carting stuff home if it wasn't necessary. She'd done that far too long, and it had taken precedence over her personal life. If she got the A-D position, she'd have to readjust priorities. Figure out what was best left at the office and what to take home. "Best left at the office" included additional undertakings that were purely "want to" in nature.

Before Matt, Mel's personal life was nonexistent. Spencer didn't count. They'd never been serious. Well, she hadn't been anyway. That's why working extra hours hadn't bothered her as much then. But now... Now it did. What was she thinking applying for a more demanding job when she already had a job that excited and fulfilled her?

You've gone over all this. Don't second guess yourself

because you're afraid of competing with Matt. But did she want the job for all the right reasons? Did she want it if it drove a wedge between them? So much to consider and way too much to mull over at the moment.

On her way out, Mel flipped off the lights and temporarily tabled her thoughts. The halls smelled of this evening's spaghetti and garlic bread and the pleasant aroma made her stomach growl.

"Heading home already?" His voice stopped her in her tracks.

Mel whipped her head around to find Matt following behind her. He quickened his steps and caught her as she was about to exit the building. She waited for him. "It's after five. Why wouldn't I head home?"

"Because you rarely leave work on time. Good for you for being more diligent about that."

"You, too." She longed to reach toward him. Slip her hand in his. But she didn't. For one thing, they stood inside the building, still technically on the clock. For another, their earlier conversation troubled her. She didn't like the conflicting feelings today's revelation dredged up.

"Mel, can we talk?" He stepped forward to open the door for her. "Maybe grab supper at the Come and Get It?"

"The diner's not open. Chuck and Ida Mae closed early to come here for their presentation."

"What about Pennies from Heaven? We can pick up a couple sandwiches. Or we could go into Sapphire and grab a nice meal there."

She shook her head. "No, thanks. I have chili in the crock pot at home."

"Mmm. Sounds delicious. Well, maybe tomorrow?"

Disappointment dimmed the twinkle in his eyes. Guilt

gripped Mel's heart and nipped at her conscience. She definitely couldn't eat an entire pot of chili by herself, nor was she intentionally trying to punish Matt by forcing distance between them. He had as much right to toss his name in the job candidate hat as she did. She simply hadn't expected it *or* the initial secrecy. But she'd been secretive, too. They could spin it however they wanted, but their motivations were the same. They both wanted to pursue advancement for similar reasons. Was that wrong? Nope. But communication in a committed relationship mattered.

Were they committed? It had seemed they were headed that way. Mel drew her coat closed as a blast of cold air hit them. Matt moved in front of her and shielded her with his body as she grappled with the top buttons of her coat. She had trouble with one and he helped her with it.

"Thanks." His fingers remained poised near her coat collar, then he dropped his hands and motioned her to go first while he held the door, but she hesitated. "I made plenty of chili. Why don't you join me?"

"Are you sure?" His face brightened. "I love...chili."

"Great. I make it spicy. That okay?"

"Does a duck love water? You bet that's okay. I love spicy. I do spicy exceptionally well."

Goosebumps scampered along Mel's spine beneath her layers of clothing. *Yes, Matt. I know you do.* Probably a harmless assertion, but his comment drew warmth to her cheeks and made her stomach flutter.

Chapter Thirteen

The tantalizing aroma drifting through Mel's quaint, tiny home caused Matt's mouth to water. Scents of seasoned beef and various spices wafted through the cozy house and briefly carried him back to those glorious days of childhood when Mom would be stirring a pot of homemade chili on the kitchen stove. One of his family's favorite comfort foods, his mother always made enough to last for days. Chili was one of those things that only got better when reheated.

Mel shrugged out of her coat and hung it on the vintage-era coat tree beside the front door. "May I take yours?"

"Sure. Thank you." He slipped his arms free from the thick sleeves of his jacket and handed it to Mel. "I know I've said it before, but I sure like your home. What you've done with it. You've maintained the charm and essence of an era gone by while also incorporating contemporary elements."

"Thanks. Old Doc Burnside's cottage needed updating, but I really wanted to preserve the integrity and character of this house. I scoured estate sales and second-hand stores to locate the right pieces and decorated and revamped on a shoestring budget. I enjoyed it."

"Wow...and that view." Matt peered around the brightly decorated Christmas tree and observed Ruby from the picture window's vantage point. The soft glow of street lamps, twinkling lights, and church steeples rising in the background gave new meaning to "heaven on earth." While he'd been here before, he hadn't fully appreciated the sights that stretched out below.

Situated on a gentle rise above the tree-lined street, the cottage afforded generous views of Ruby and all her splendor. Well-lit homes, churches, and businesses blended seamlessly against the panoramic hills and hollows, save for their Christmas lights, which painted snow-covered lanes in iridescent hues. Man, his fingers itched to paint. No wonder Mel loved it here.

"Sometimes, I still can't believe the cottage is mine." Mel came up beside him and followed his gaze. "When Doc Burnside named me as a beneficiary in his will—deeded me his home—I couldn't believe it. I still can't."

"He must have been an extraordinary fellow. Obviously, you held a special place in his heart."

"He'd been a town fixture for years. Everyone loved him. He practiced medicine in Ruby over fifty years and doctored folks whether or not they had the resources to pay." Mel's voice softened. "He delivered all three of my brothers, and then me, at Sapphire County General where he served on staff for many years. Most of the time, though, he saw patients at his clinic in town here."

"That old brick building at the edge of Ruby? The one with the white shutters and stethoscope cut-outs?"

"That's the one. Dr. Shaye's establishment now. She hasn't gotten around to putting up a shingle yet."

Ahh, yes. That would be Erin Shaye, the new veterinarian who had a thing for Mike, according to his brothers. "Maybe Mike will offer to help."

Mel laughed. "Yeah. She'd like nothing better. Not

sure how he feels about that though."

"The feeling's not mutual?"

"Gabe and Garrett tease him mercilessly about her, but if that's the case, Mike's not talking, He's a hard one to figure out sometimes. He'd rather stick his nose in his sister's business." She inclined her head toward the short hallway. "Would you like to wash up while I set the table?"

"I would. Thanks." He well remembered the direction of the bathroom. He'd located the thermometer there when Mel was sick a few months back. Plus, the entire cottage couldn't be more than a thousand square feet. He wasn't likely to get lost.

A few minutes later, he joined Mel in the kitchen where she'd set the table with festive placemats and Christmas tableware. She stood on her tiptoes next to a kitchen cabinet trying to reach a couple bowls that he assumed were for the chili.

"Here. Let me help." Matt placed his hand on the small of her back as he reached toward the bowls she seemed to be after. "These?"

"Oh! I didn't hear you come in." She blushed, flustered, and pointed toward a stack of fancy red bowls. "Yes. They're the ones I use at the holidays. I normally grab my stepstool over there, but I thought maybe I could reach."

"Glad I came in when I did. That's one thing you don't need—a heavy stack of bowls toppling out on your head." Matt grabbed them with ease and handed them to her. "Did you think you'd gained an inch since last Christmas?"

"I never quit hoping."

Her laughter danced around the room, snatching his

heart and squeezing it. He tweaked her nose. "You're perfect the way you are."

"I have too many freckles."

"All gorgeous."

"I'm curvy."

"You're stunning."

"I have a mind of my own."

"I wouldn't have it any other way." This was fun. He could do it all night. "I noticed that right off the bat."

"Yeah. I'm sure you did." Her full lips parted as more laughter ensued. "Those really endeared me to you, huh?"

Flirting now, was she? He took the bowls from her hands and set them on the countertop next to the crock pot. "Yeah, they did. Your vivaciousness immediately won me over."

"Mmm-hmm. I remember."

Matt laughed and gathered her close. Their playful banter certainly beat the tense moments earlier. "As I recall, my suave deportment initially piqued your interest. Not to mention my charm, charisma, and good looks."

"Right. Might as well toss in humility—I found that utterly irresistible. Captivated me to the core."

Enough small talk. He bent down and covered her mouth with his, tasting her sweetness. Whatever tension existed earlier, dissipated. It began with the softest of kisses, a gentle expression of affection between two people of the same mindset. Then, within seconds, the kiss transitioned to a new level. Alarm bells pinged in Matt's head. *Whoa. Easy, buddy.* Slowly, he drew back, his mind racing. He. Loved. This. Woman.

"What is it?" Mel's face clouded, perhaps misunderstanding.

Could he even explain? "I know we've danced around the subject. Intimated it."

"The subject?"

Matt brushed her cheek with his fingertips. Lord have mercy, her skin was so soft, so flawless. She literally knocked the wind out of his sails, and he doubted she even knew. "I'm not sure when it happened. Maybe when you gave me that tongue-lashing about GIFTS at your parents' house. Maybe when you propelled yourself into my arms. When you passed out. All I know is...I'm in love with you, Mel. I love you. Yes. Yes, I do."

She blinked. Trembled. Teared up. Then, she wound her arms tightly around his neck, and hiking herself back up on her tiptoes, feathered a kiss on his jaw—the sweetest affirmation to acknowledge his sentiment. "I was afraid to say it first."

In that instant, Matt contemplated something crazy. Something completely insane that he wouldn't have considered before Edwin's encouragement.

He wasn't kidding. Matt did spicy well. Very well. Eating chili after that kiss reinforced it. Mel watched as he dabbed his mouth with a napkin, observing his every movement. His body language—the way he angled his shoulders and sloped forward, toward her—revealed what she already knew. He was as comfortable with her as she was with him. But not in a bored sense. "Comfortable" as in "I enjoy being with you. You put me at ease."

"You handled my chili like a pro. You didn't even add extra hot sauce," Mel teased.

"Honey, if I'd done that, I would have needed a fire extinguisher. I had all the heat I could handle." He grasped her palm in his and grinned. "Your chili was phenomenal. I wish I had room for thirds."

"If you like spicy, next time, I'll make enchiladas. Dad says mine are even better than Mom's."

"You're amazing. Is there anything you don't do?"

"Uh... Sew. Play sports. Watch horror movies. Quite a few things, actually." That he thought she was amazing delighted her, but she didn't want Matt placing her on a pedestal. The fall from such a place could leave one bruised and battered, either for a while or forever, and not without scars.

"Ahh, modesty. Such an alluring quality."

"You sure you don't have that confused with plain ol' honesty?"

"No, ma'am, not at all. I admire a great seamstress like my mom, but sewing isn't everyone's gift. I like sports and I enjoy watching 'em, but same thing. Not all of us are cut out to be rock-jock superstars. Horror movies? Some of the creepy, old flicks are good, but the gruesome, grisly stuff? Nah. I don't have much use for that. So, see? You're good."

"I don't have administrative experience." There. She'd said it. It must have entered Matt's mind, as well.

"Neither do I. But we have other qualifications. Unique gifts, if you will, that make each of us an excellent job candidate." He tipped his head ever so slightly, as if he were about to add something.

"What?"

"Mel, you bring experience and longevity to the table. You've proven your loyalty to The Meadows. You've learned to be flexible and adapt to change. Those are tremendous qualities in a team player. Plus, everyone at work adores you."

"Thank you. I appreciate that."

"Hey, it's true. I'm not patronizing you."

"I know." She loved him all the more for saying those things and meaning them. "You also offer a lot. You may be the new kid on the block, but you have an advanced degree. Maybe not in administration, but a Master's in social work is a great asset. You have the understanding and insight to address various situations that others may not."

"Now it's my turn. Thanks." He continued to clasp her hand, lightly running his thumb along her fingers. "Maybe we should interview in the other's place. We just made an outstanding case for each other."

"That's a terrific idea. And an innovative one." She giggled, knowing he'd get her drift. "I'm sure Foster and the hiring committee would love that."

Matt hiked an eyebrow, humor evident in his not-so-subtle reaction. "Ahh. The lady jests. Good to know we've come a long way since those early days."

"We have, haven't we?"

"I'm glad. You?" Matt's voice grew serious.

"You have to know the answer to that." Emotion lodged in her chest, warming every square inch of her. "I love you. On some level, it seems too soon. Yet, in other ways, I think we've grown into it over the past ten or so months."

"I know we joked about it, but I think for me, the connection was immediate. Yeah, we initially butted heads and it drove me crazy. I'd never had that happen before."

"Pricked your ego, did it?" She could tease now, but back then, he infuriated her.

"Some, I guess. Except not quite the way you think. I

wasn't used to locking horns with a woman. Not with anyone really. You challenged me in ways I wasn't used to. Caused me to think beyond my comfort zone and examine life through a new lens." Matt exhaled a weighty sigh. "You punched me in the gut with your bullheadedness...and your brilliance."

She remembered the bullheadedness part. All the buttons he seemed to push, and she pushed back. At the time, all she could see was his deliberate intent to reorder her world. The world she'd so carefully landscaped in an unopposed working terrain. *Wow.* How juvenile. Funny how time could add clarity to one's perspective.

"You echo everything I've thought about you. I don't think either of us intended to be bullheaded. Maybe, while we wanted what was best for The Meadows, our personal vibes derailed us for a bit. Sarah once asked me if the reason we clashed was because we had a thing for each other."

"Ha! What'd you say?"

"That she must be joking."

"You know swift denial is often a defense mechanism, right?"

"Sure. Like you know defense mechanisms protect us from imminent peril."

"Ooh. Good one." The edges of his mouth twitched. "You thought you were in peril? Really?"

"Yes. My heart was." Matt's delighted smirk upended her equilibrium. He was enjoying this way too much. "Blessedly, I didn't realize it at the time. Falling in love wasn't even on my radar then."

"Whew! What a relief. I would've hated to see you fall in love with Splinter—uh, Spencer. Digging him over me would've wreaked disaster."

Yeah. In more ways than she cared to imagine. But back to Matt. She bet falling in love hadn't been on his life agenda then either. Which made her want to know more. Had he ever been in love? Or was this a first for him, too?

"I see the wheels turning in that gorgeous head of yours. Care to share?"

"Joking aside, have you ever? Been in love?"

Matt held up the hand that wasn't holding hers, and slowly, began raising fingers. "Let's see. One. Two. Three. Or is it four—times?" Amusement amplified his attractive features and he paused for maybe ten seconds. Then, he lowered each finger, again, one by one. "No, Mel. I've never been in love. I thought I was once. A brief flame in college once captured my interest. Her penchant for self-absorption cured me of it. She appreciated my "humble roots," as she called them, but to be blunt, I wasn't good enough for her. My humble roots, and pursuits, didn't mesh with her future aspirations."

"Which were?"

"To marry wealth and advance her station in life. I count it a blessing that I saw how unequally yoked we were, and we ended things before it got messy. Oh, and for the record, I never introduced Elise to my parents. Other than a few sporadic dates prior to her, you're the only one. The one I wanted them to meet for longer than a simple introduction. And I told you that Mom and Pop called me again the day after Thanksgiving, didn't I?"

They did? She shook her head no.

"They wanted to tell me that you're the one. As if I didn't know." Matt lifted a palm to her cheek and caressed it. "They adore you. Like I do."

"I'm so happy your parents approve. You know how Mom and Daddy feel about you. I think Mom, especially, hoped for a love match all along."

"I'm a charmer. What can I say?" He stood, gently tugging her up along with him. "Seriously, your parents are incredible. I'll always appreciate how they and your brothers took me in—showed me hospitality and warmth when I was a newcomer here. I knew then I'd landed right where the Lord intended."

"I'm sorry it took me longer to warm up. Or at least show it."

"No apology necessary. I'm sorry I overstepped on work related matters."

"You didn't. I see that so clearly now. We each had our own reasons for acting and reacting the way we did, but let's put those days behind us, okay?"

"Agreed. But I have to tell you, I remember our earlier encounters with more fondness than I probably should."

A laugh escaped her lips. Right before he covered them with his.

The next morning, snow blanketed the Ozarks in a mantle of white. For a while, the flakes fell fast and furious, covering highways and byways, and hills and hollows, in silent, unsoiled beauty.

Matt rose early to shovel his driveway, then he headed over to Mel's and shoveled hers. Because of deteriorating weather conditions, Foster had sent out texts alerting staff that they were going to a skeleton crew today. This was a fast-moving storm, unlike the weather pattern meteorologists predicted for next week. Still, the roads were precarious enough for Matt to follow up Foster's text with one of his own.

Hi. Your chariot awaits.

The door jerked open and Mel stood there, mouth agape. Within seconds, she found her voice and tugged him inside. "What are you doing here?"

"Your VW isn't going to cut it this morning. I'm here to offer my services."

"You're nuts."

"For you."

The rise and fall of her mirth fell sweetly on his ears, taking the chill off this bitter cold December morn. She led him to the still warm embers of the fire. "Tell the truth. Did you and Daddy and the guys conspire?"

"Pardon?" Oh, man. Her obvious surprise pleased him. The way her hair crested her shoulders, falling in glorious waves across rosy cheeks, begged him to pull her closer.

"Yeah. The troops phoned at dawn, all offering their services."

"And?"

"And I turned them down. I'm a grown woman, Matt. I've been driving for almost twelve years, during a lot of Ozark winters. It isn't like I've never done it before."

"Well, Miss I'm-a-Grown Woman,' I can tell you that Volkswagen of yours—cute, though it may be—won't make it far in this. Trust me, please?"

She scrunched her eyebrows. "Come on. It isn't like you to be so melodramatic." Mel made her way over to the window and stared, open-mouthed. "All right. I suppose the snow has picked up a smidgen."

"You'll need to shed those pretty ballet flats for snow boots. Have some?"

"Of course, I have some." She tossed him an eye roll. "I'd already set them by the door. See?"

"Great. Put them on, please. And your heaviest coat. It's twenty-two degrees and the wind has quite a nip."

By the time they made it to The Meadows, the snow abruptly stopped, though The Meadows' parking lot was a mess. Matt pulled up close to the entrance, hopped out, and made his way around to the passenger side where Mel had already gathered her things. He opened the door and extended a hand to help her down.

Her gaze traveled to the surrounding snow-covered hills. "A precursor of more to come, I think. Exquisite, isn't it?"

"Dazzling." He sneaked a kiss as her feet touched the ground. "The snow is, too."

"Flirt."

"Only with you." He could hardly help himself. She emboldened him.

He opened the front door for her, ushering her in from the wind and cold, and went to park his truck. What a way to kick off the day! A brisk round of wintry weather and a woman who could make the December chill feel like a July heatwave. Good grief, he had it for her bad, and soon, he planned to do something about it.

Entering the building a few moments later, Matt spied Clinton ambling toward the dining room. A good sign. Lately, he was starting to venture out more, and not only at mealtime. When Clinton glanced back and saw Matt, he tarried.

"Made it, did you?"

"Yes, sir. I did. *We* did. A little tough going in spots, but the snow has stopped now, so I expect road crews will eventually be out. Looks like we'll be short staffed today. Can I do anything for you?"

"Nope, Wonder Boy. I'm heading for coffee. Nothing I can't handle." Grumpy Gus pivoted and tottered on his way. When he was almost out of sight, Clinton swiveled back around, raised his voice a hair, and said, "Good of you to bring Miss Melinda. Right gentlemanly of you."

A compliment? Clinton meandered on his way, leaving Matt to wonder if he'd indeed just paid him one or if he'd meant it as a dig. Praise, where Clinton Farley was concerned, though foreign and unexpected, was something Matt wanted to believe was growing on the man. Granted, as unbelievable as it was, Clinton's gradual metamorphosis couldn't be denied. *Thank you, Lord.* The changes might be small, but Matt noted them, and gratitude ballooned in his chest for these mini miracles. He yearned to know the rest of Clinton's story, and prayed, in time, Clinton would trust him with it.

Despite the fact winter wouldn't officially arrive for another two weeks, today's snow showers generated excitement among The Meadows' residents and townsfolk. The arrival of winter meant Christmas would follow only a few days later, and no one did Christmas better than Ruby.

For a town not much bigger than a postage stamp, the tiny Ozarks community stirred with colossal glee. Local businesses extended their shopping hours. Churches scheduled Christmas cantatas and fancy dinners. Vendors dressed their windows in grand displays with glimmering lights and elaborate backdrops. When snow fell in thick, fat flakes as it had this morning, anticipation of the approaching season only amped up the holiday cheer. Joy descended upon their resplendent, snow-clad corner of the world like butter on freshly baked bread still warm from the oven.

Mel immediately sensed the shift as she greeted staff and residents that morning. Grins and happy chatter made their way around the building, imparting a sense of camaraderie and merriment. Even with the limited skeleton crew, staff doted on retirees in the same conscientious and loving fashion as they always did. For Ruby to have such a place for their older citizens was nothing short of remarkable.

As Mel helped herself to coffee in the dining room, Clinton Farley shuffled in, cane in hand, but actually, with more of a bounce in his step than she'd seen in the past year. He bobbed his head in her direction and moseyed toward her.

"Glad to see you and Wonder Boy made it safely. How're the roads?"

She fought to keep a straight face at *Wonder Boy*. Every time Clinton used the term to reference Matt, she had to bite her cheek and fight the mental images of Matt in a cape and tights. "Dicey in places, but now that the snow's stopped, it won't take long to whip things into shape, I'm sure. How are you this morning, Clinton?"

"Bones are creakin' to beat the band. Weather, probably. You?"

Small talk again? Delight coursed through her. "I'm good, thank you. I'll amend that to 'great' after I finish this." Mel tapped the side of her insulated coffee mug.

"Say, would you care to sit and chat for a few moments?"

Clinton eyed her, as if contemplating a motive. "'Bout what?"

She should have expected that. *Remember, Mel. Baby steps.* "Your interests. What you enjoy. Whatever you want to talk about."

"Hmm. A fishing expedition then."

"No, sir. I hoped we might...get to know each other better. In the five years I've worked here, I don't believe we've really chatted all that much."

"Not for your lack of trying." He fiddled with the coffee carafe, the one labeled "Christmas Candy," and filled a cup half-full.

This wasn't going well. How could she convince him of her sincerity—that she cared for him and was truly interested in his life? "I'm sorry. I didn't mean to upset you. You matter to me, Clinton. I'd like to better understand you. How I can make things more enjoyable for you here."

"Yeah. Yeah." However, he inclined his head toward a table by the window. "That one all right?"

"You bet." She walked along beside him, careful not to outpace him. Clinton chose one of the tables with the prettiest views, not his usual one, where he often sat alone.

When Mel reached for a chair, Clinton surprised her by setting down his coffee cup in haste so he could pull out the chair for her.

"Thank you."

"You're welcome." He then seated himself opposite of Mel, giving a low groan as he stretched out his long, knobby legs. "You'd never know I was once a track star, huh?"

A track star? Naturally, like so many other details, his personal information didn't contain that tidbit. "No, sir, I didn't realize that. That's amazing. Did you run all through school?"

"Yes'm. All four years of high school. A couple other fellas and me. 'Course, we only competed against teeny area schools like ours. I was the fastest guy on Ruby's track team back in the day. Still have those medals tucked away somewhere."

"Wow. I'd like to see those." Mel sipped at her coffee, trying to imagine a very different Clinton Farley. He must have been extroverted then, and obviously, athletic. This snippet of his past thoroughly intrigued her. "I never played sports in school. My brothers did though. I cheered them on."

Clinton took a long, slow swig from his cup, set it down, fingering the rim. "You had quite the family. Three boys and a girl. Jake and Billie Gail did all right for themselves." He said it wistfully, not with malice. "You and those brothers of yours had a good raising. Decent stock, your folks."

Mel nodded. "Yes, I'm grateful for my parents. Mom and Daddy worked hard to instill respectable values and a superior work ethic in their children. I love them like mad, even if they are a smidge overprotective."

"Don't fault 'em too much. Any parent worth their salt would want to protect their children." The lines in Clinton's face deepened. His voice grew soft. Raspy. "I couldn't protect my son. He died in the womb. Still-born. No reason why. 'Bout killed my Marabel and me." For a moment, Clinton clamped his lips into a thin, straight line.

He gazed outside toward the snow-capped hills in the distance, and for a brief spell, went somewhere other than this room. "She handled it like the saint she was. I, on the other hand, couldn't get on board with God anymore. Not after that."

Mel took a risk. She touched Clinton's knuckles with her fingertips. When he didn't draw back, she covered his hand with hers. "I'm so sorry, Clinton. I don't understand why things happen sometimes the way they do. I've questioned God's rationale before. Asked him why a lot."

The elderly curmudgeon blinked. "You don't say. Really?"

"Absolutely. I'm human. Like everyone, there are matters I can't grasp. Circumstances I can't wrap my mind around." She searched for the right words. Something that would click with Clinton that wouldn't sound holier-than-thou. "I wonder why God allows things to unfold the way they do. Why sad or horrible trials befall us."

"That's the million-dollar question, isn't it? The one that religion can't answer." He said it with a smirk. Was he challenging her to dispute it?

"Well, I don't know about *religion*, but there's a passage in the Bible in First Corinthians, where Paul speaks about love. In chapter thirteen, he says that, because of our limited knowledge, we only know part of the story while here on earth. When perfection comes— meaning Jesus—the imperfect will pass away."

Clinton remained stoic. His face, granite. He didn't speak, so Mel continued. "Verses eleven and twelve in that chapter tell us *'When I was a child, I spake as a child, I understood as a child, I thought as a child: but when I became a man, I put away childish things. For now we see through a glass darkly; but then face to face: now I know in part; but then shall I know even as I am fully known.'"*

She'd memorized those scriptures by heart when Nana and Papa died. She couldn't fully grasp their meaning then, but even saying them now, brought fresh clarity. A renewed vision of God's promise for His people.

"Pardon my doubt, Miss Melinda. But that's the thing—doubt. I doubt the truth of things that don't have any rhyme or reason. Convince me. Convince me of this higher purpose."

Oh, dear. She wasn't a theologian. She couldn't explain it like Pastor Bill or the way a seasoned elder might. She was failing at this. She searched her memory for an analogy or an example she could use to explain it better. Something she'd heard a visiting pastor once say came to mind.

"We all have doubts. That's normal. We're fallible. It's okay to admit our doubt. To question situations and incidents we can't comprehend. Here's the simplest, and best, explanation I've ever heard." Mel paused and fixed her eyes on Clinton. "*Doubt* is something we don't understand. *Unbelief* is a conscious will of the mind."

Clinton's bushy eyebrows shot up. He swallowed. Toyed with his coffee cup handle. He opened his mouth to say something, then closed it.

Mel clasped his hand. He didn't pull away. "I used to be scared, and even embarrassed, to admit I had doubts. I thought that made me a terrible person. When I heard it explained this way, though, it brought so much relief. It normalized my feelings. Those feelings everyone has, yet we're afraid to talk about. I realized that just because we don't understand God's plan doesn't make it wrong.

Because we sometimes question God doesn't make Him untrue."

For the longest while, Clinton simply stared. At her. Out the window. Back to her. Had she gotten through to him at all?

"I...appreciate your thoughts, Miss Melinda." His labored sigh matched the gray sky outdoors, somber, and leaden with the unknown. "I believe it's too late for me."

"No. No, it isn't. Please don't say that." She couldn't bear to leave things like this. He'd given up and Mel didn't know what else she could say or do.

"I know you mean well. I thank you for that. But God and me? When He took my Marabel, I'm afraid that was the last straw. Didn't make sense then. Still doesn't now. Until she died, she was in good health. Not sick one bit. I just woke up one day...and she didn't. Died in her sleep."

Mel remembered. Edwin Ramsey had tried to console Clinton since he'd experienced a similar loss, but Clinton wouldn't have it. Eventually, Clinton sold his home and moved to The Meadows, where he'd become even more of a hermit, walling himself off from everyone and everything. Years of not joining in or taking part in any of the activities here had worn on Mel. She'd hoped she and Matt had made headway with the man, but at the moment, it didn't seem like their efforts mattered very much.

Yet, she refused to throw in the towel. She tried a different approach. "Clinton, I'm so sorry about Marabel. I know you loved her very much, and I know she loved you. What do you think Marabel would say, though, if she were here now?"

"Don't have the faintest idea."

"I think you do."

Clinton glared at her. Frowned. "You're pretty forward, young lady. Know that?"

"You didn't answer my question."

"Well, I don't rightly know what Marabel would say. Probably something like 'You ornery, ol' crabapple, snap out of it. Get movin', get doin', and quit your bellyaching.' She might toss in a word or two from the Good Book. That woman could wear me out with words. Hers *and* His."

"See?"

As if realizing what he'd admitted, Clinton's wrinkled face darkened. His Adam's apple bobbed. New lines etched their way into his forehead, aging him another five years. Mel halfway expected him to rise and leave or at least hurl a scathing retort. But he did neither. Gradually, his features relaxed, and softened.

"You remind me a lot of my Marabel."

"I'll take that as a compliment," Mel said softly.

"You should." Gently, he retracted his hand from hers and scootched around in his chair, reaching into the back-hip pocket of his faded blue jeans. He drew out a well-worn leather wallet. Opened it. "See for yourself."

It couldn't be. Inside the plastic photo insert was the colorized photo of a young woman—about mid to late twenties—with auburn, shoulder-length tresses, cornflower blue eyes, and a sprinkling of freckles. This woman was Mel's twin. *Marabel.*

Chapter Fourteen

"That explains a lot." Matt gave a low whistle. "No wonder Clinton's partial to you. You remind him of the person he loved the most."

"Yeah." Mel tugged at the tissue from the box he offered her. "It was like looking into a mirror. The physical resemblance between Marabel and me is uncanny. I think I also remind him of her in other ways. Maybe her mannerisms, the way she might lovingly challenge him to get on with life."

"That's a good thing, honey. Why the tears?" He couldn't bear the sight of her moisture-ladened lashes. It weakened his knees and made his heart race faster. If they'd been anywhere else but his office, he'd have taken her in his arms by now and kissed away every tear that fell.

"I don't know, Matt. I wish I'd known sooner. Maybe if I'd known, it would have given me some insight how to better handle the situation. I always sensed Clinton's affection toward me. Not in an immoral way. More like a fond, grandfatherly regard. But honestly, it seemed the more I tried to draw him out over the years, the more hermit-like he became. I can't believe the difference now. What's changed his mindset? I'm glad, but I'm sad, too, for the empty years he's spent here when his life could have been so much richer."

"I understand. I've never lost a spouse, but it has to

be one of the deepest heartaches there is. Still, he chose his path. He allowed his grief to corrupt his worldview. Bitterness, when left unchecked, is like that." Matt lowered his voice, so their conversation wouldn't float out into the hall. "Often, we don't get God's timing. I suspect God's been positioning Clinton's heart for a long while now. Maybe it's taken this length of time to get him to this place. Sometimes, the Lord allows us to be broken for a season to prepare us for a brand new *forever*."

"Matt, I hope you're right. I know you're right. But at Clinton's age, I can't imagine how God's going to turn this around. I mean, look at Clinton's life from his point of view. What does he really have to look forward to?"

"I don't have all the answers to that," Matt said honestly. "I'm aware that Edwin Ramsey experienced deep loss. First his wife of many years, then his daughter, who was only a young woman at the time she died. For a while, he and his former son-in-law were estranged. He hadn't seen his granddaughters in years. But look how that turned out. God brought about healing in a way no one expected. He mended that severed relationship with his son-in-law and restored a family unit in a miraculous way. Edwin currently enjoys a full and happy life, packed with purpose and bursting with promise. It can be the same for Clinton. I know it can."

Mel dabbed at her eyes and attempted a smile. "I think you just took me to church."

"Without the donuts and coffee, huh?" he joked.

"Yeah, but the preachin' was mighty fine."

"Why don't we go make rounds and check out the lay of the land before we head home for the evening?"

"You've got it." Mel jumped to her feet and strode

toward the doorway. "I haven't seen Clinton since we chatted this morning. Maybe you're right. Maybe things are on the uptick."

Matt could only hope.

Mel almost pinched herself. The day, indeed, got better. As it turned out, most residents had congregated for an early supper in the dining room, including Clinton. To Mel and Matt's delight, he sat with Edwin and some of the other folks, rather than isolated at his usual table. When Clinton spied them, he waved them over.

"Settle a conundrum for us. Why is it Tilly and the kitchen crew make the best dang vittles in these parts and we're not all fatter'n fritters?"

Clinton making a joke? Those at the table laughed. Clinton lightly jabbed Edwin's side with his elbow, and Edwin offered his two cents. "Guess they wave the piggy wand over the food and remove all the calories first before dishing it up. Sound about right, Matthew? Miss Melinda?"

Matt snorted. "No clue, Edwin. But that'd be my best guess."

"Hmm..." Mel rolled her shoulders. She had no clue either, but likely, it was because the delectable meals here were well-balanced and thoroughly planned by The Meadows' registered dietician. Though, meatloaf and mashed potatoes and gravy, offset with thick slabs of cherry pie, were hardly calorie-conscious fare, as her own waistline could attest to. Understandably, seniors processed and metabolized food differently, and maybe, the low impact aerobics classes and activities they offered here kept a few of the pounds at bay.

Minerva Walters, a seventy-something widow who also sat at the table, cackled like a hen. "Personally, I prefer folks to carry some extra meat on their bones. Adds character. That's why I'm not too worried about any ol' calories." She patted the swirly, silver curls that graced her earlobes, and flashed Clinton a one-hundred-watt smile. "Kind sir, could you please pass that basket of yeast rolls my way?"

Clinton's jaw dropped. His cheeks turned as red as the linen tablecloth. He gave a clipped nod, seized the bread basket with a trembling hand, which Mel doubted was solely due to his age, and passed it to Minerva.

"Thank you. I do so enjoy a good yeast roll, don't you Clinton? Oh, and I believe I'd like a little of that honey, as well. Nothing like a splash of honey to perk up a meal, am I right?"

Clinton gulped, even his ears now on fire, and stretched his hand out again, this time for the honey pot. To which Minerva gushed, "Why, Clinton. I do declare, you are artistry in motion. Anyone ever tell you that?"

Clinton's mouth moved, but whatever words he might have spoken were lost to his tablemates' chuckles.

Ahh. Minerva. So, it's Clinton, is it? In that instant, Mel watched an eighty-one-year-old gent transform into a blushing, tongue-tied teen. She didn't know who was more surprised. Her, Matt, or Clinton, but she could sure hazard a guess.

By Thursday of that week, most of the snow had melted, though more was predicted in a few days. Matt had learned that the mere mention of an impending weather event sent folks flying to the market like ducks on June bugs.

"I understand the need to prepare." Matt said as he and Mel entered the Come and Get It for supper that evening. "But how many loaves of bread and gallons of milk does one actually need?"

Mel giggled "Who knows? But remember the other day? That was a pre-show. Next week's the main event."

"Or so the weathermen claim." Ozarks weather, he knew, could be as unpredictable as Minerva Walters' hair color. Three days ago, matron silver. Today, ruby red.

Ida Mae Farrow, the diner proprietress, led them to one of her remaining booths, slapped down two menus, and with hands on hips, shot them a dazzling grin. "Well, hello, you two. Good to see you."

"Good to see you, Ida Mae." Mel reciprocated. "Looks like you have a full house tonight. But then again, you always do."

Matt noted only four empty tables and one spare booth. Patrons were plastered to every stool at the counter. "Looks like we arrived in the nick of time."

"Ahh, you know. Tonight's special is *Party Like a Piggy*. Brings 'em out in droves."

Yes, Matt knew that one. A hit with the regulars and visitors alike, *Party Like a Piggy* meant one thing. Grub. And lots of it. A ham steak the size of a football, thick mounds of fried potatoes with red-eye gravy, angel biscuits as light as a feather, and seasoned green beans, cinnamon apples, and spicy coleslaw in generous portions for the sides.

"Gosh, Ida Mae. I may need a minute to decide, unless you know what you want?" Mel directed her gaze toward him.

"I'm with you. I need to give this some serious thought."

"That's completely fine, sugars. I'll grab drinks while you make up your minds. The usual?"

The usual, as in sweet teas for both of them. "Mel?"

She gave a thumbs-up and Matt did the same.

Ida Mae waltzed away, giving pats on the backs to customers she left in her wake. The woman moved with the grace of a swan and the pace of a Thoroughbred. Her youthful countenance belied her forty years. Recently married to Chuck Farrow, her right-hand man here at the Come and Get It, Matt guessed a good measure of Ida Mae's glow had to do with being in love. No secret there. Love did that to a person.

He turned his attention toward Mel, barely containing the emotion that welled up inside. She had the glow, too. It made him want to move heaven and earth to make sure she never lost it. He'd do anything for her. *Anything.*

She caught him looking at her. "Do I have something on my face?"

"Besides those magnificent freckles, luscious lips, and gorgeous eyes?"

"*Goodness.* Thank you. Such high praise could go to a girl's head." Mel fanned herself with the menu in an exaggerated fashion. "What brought that on?"

He clasped the hand that wasn't holding the menu and circled her fingers with his. "Does a guy have to have a reason to compliment his sweetheart?"

"No. He doesn't. Except there's more to this, right?"

"I think people should never take each other for granted—especially couples. When we know we should say something important, we should. Too many opportune moments go by and things are left unsaid."

"True." She crinkled her eyebrows and set down the

menu. "What else would you like to say? I know you have more on your mind, and it doesn't have to do with my physical appearance either." Mel drew in a breath and released it. "Do you want to talk about next week's interview?"

"Yes. But I didn't compliment you to pave the way for that. I meant the things I said. In addition, I find your intellect extremely fetching—the ultimate turn-on beneath the surface stuff."

Ida Mae came back with their drinks. "Here we go. Two sweet teas for two sweet humans. Have you made up your minds yet?"

"No, ma'am. I'm sorry, Ida Mae. Could we have another minute, please?"

"Sure. You bet. Flag me down when you're ready." She sashayed away and Mel took a cursory glance at the menu.

"When she returns, I think I'll have the chef salad with ranch dressing and the soup of the day. I think it's homemade chicken noodle. Now, about the interview. Does it feel awkward to you?"

"A little, honestly."

"For me, too."

"To be completely up front, Mel, I've examined this new position from all angles. I want to be interested in the job for all the right reasons. As we've discussed, we're both great candidates with excellent qualifications."

"But?"

"No 'but.' I'm sure there are other applicants. Probably several with even better credentials and more experience than us. Except..."

"That sounds like a 'but' to me."

"Not really. I just think we should be prepared in case it comes down to you and me. You know as well as I do how these things usually work. Foster and the hiring committee will probably whittle down the candidates to the top five. Then, possibly, the top two. That could be both of us, one of us, or neither of us. If it happens that way, are you going to be okay with that?"

"I think so. You?"

"I think so, too. I wanted to double check because I'd take my name out of the mix in a heartbeat if I thought this would drive a wedge between us."

"You said something like that once before."

"I meant it."

"You'd really do that?"

"Yes. I would."

"I don't want you to, Matt. I appreciate your willingness to sacrifice what's important to you, but do you think either of us could live with something like that? First of all, removing your name from the candidate pool wouldn't be for the right reason." Mel took a sip of iced tea. Set down the glass and studied him. "Second, not moving forward with our goals because we're afraid we'll hurt the other's feelings doesn't really give us much credit. We're not children. We're mature adults who want the best for each other, as well as The Meadows."

"I couldn't agree more."

When Ida Mae returned, they ordered one soup and chef salad and one *Party Like a Piggy* special. Matt couldn't explain his unexpected appetite. Other than the fact trepidation over potential conflict, evaporated. Certain that he and Mel were of the same mindset now buoyed his spirit. Whatever the outcome of next week's interview, everything would be okay.

By Saturday, meteorologists continued to report an approaching snow storm, thought to hit Southwest Missouri and Northern Arkansas about mid-week. As was often the case, predicting the exact timing of said event called for finesse, and perhaps, a bit of guesswork. Nevertheless, locals flocked to town like ticks on a hound dog. Besides groceries, snow shovels, and cold weather supplies, folks happily plunked down their hard-earned dollars for Christmas presents and holiday fare. Nothing lit a fire under one's backside like a blizzard in December.

As Mel strode to her car with packages in tow, her brother Garrett pulled up alongside her and lowered his window. "Need some help unloading? I'm happy to follow you home."

"No thanks. I've got it. Besides, I have Christmas presents. One of them might be yours." She returned his grin, noting the mischievous sparkle in hazel-colored eyes that mirrored their father's. "Besides, I thought you had plans today. Aren't you and the guys helping Dad chop wood?"

"Check. Done and delivered."

"My goodness. You must have been up with the birds." Not that it should surprise her. Lazy-itis wasn't in her family's vocabulary. Besides chopping wood and delivering it to their own mutual homes, often the fellas would take care of others—senior citizens or the homebound—in their community. They viewed it as a ministry and refused to accept payment, though sometimes, recipients sent pies, cookies, or fresh eggs their way. "Where're you headed now?"

"The Come and Get It. Thought I'd pop in for an early lunch. Join me?"

"No, thanks. Actually, I'm meeting someone for lunch in a few minutes."

Garrett hiked an eyebrow. "Are his initials M-E?"

Naturally, he'd assume she spoke of Matt. Why wouldn't he? By now, the entire town buzzed about the newest courtship. It wasn't like they intended to keep their relationship a secret. Matt would shout it from the rooftop if she'd let him, but Mel preferred to keep some things private. People didn't need to know every aspect of their personal lives. Separating work from pleasure conveyed professionalism.

"I'll never tell. See you later." She waggled her fingers and continued her trek toward her car.

"Tell Matt I said hello!" Garrett called after her, his amused chuckles reaching her ears even as she hurried on.

Used to be, her brothers' teasing might've aggravated her. In recent weeks, she didn't mind it so much. Partly, because she knew they meant well, but being in love wasn't something to be embarrassed about. Gabe, Garrett, and Mike should try it sometime. Lord knew, some of the single ladies in town would volunteer to help them with that if given the slightest invitation.

On her way to Matt's, Mel flipped on the radio, and immediately, Christmas music filled her tiny VW. She hummed along, almost giddy, thinking of the holiday. Matt. Her upcoming interview. How neatly her life had started to fall into place. Even Clinton Farley, despite his crotchety, unpredictable self, had started to come around. Of late, he seemed to have more good days than bad, which was nothing short of miraculous. Though she didn't know the story he alluded to, she'd sensed a shift in Clinton. A willingness to communicate rather than disregard. A monumental change compared to how he used to be. No doubt, due to many a prayer. "Never minimize the size of a miracle," Pastor Bill once said. "A miracle is a miracle is a miracle."

Mel turned onto the graveled drive, leading up the short expanse to Matt's home. Her breath caught. *My goodness. You've been busy.* Christmas lights winked from the sloping rooftop, and wreaths trimmed in red bows adorned his front windows. Candy canes lined the path from the front door to his art studio where, even there, the season beckoned. In front of his studio, on the knoll, was an elaborate Nativity, complete with the entire cast of characters—Mary, Joseph, Baby Jesus, and the three wisemen—a donkey, a cow, and three lambs. A star, positioned above the intricately designed stable, illuminated the masterpiece. Had Matt built this? She'd never seen anything so beautiful.

Mel parked, and within minutes, Matt appeared at her car door, tugging it open. "What do you think?"

"Matt! It's spectacular! When did you do all this?"

"I worked on it in the evenings when I had time, but I finally assembled it late last night. You don't think it's too much?" He offered her a hand out.

"Of course not. It's incredible." But again, it made her wonder. Matt excelled at his current profession, but was it his true calling? The way he saw things, put things together, almost brought tears to her eyes. He had a gift for seeing objects in a unique light and bringing them to life.

"Come on. I want to show you something else. Then we'll have lunch."

Why did she have the feeling that whatever it was would blow her away? Maybe because Matt had continued to do that from day one. Just when she thought she had him figured out, he bowled her over with yet another revelation. The guy wowed her. Kept her on her toes. He'd be a shoo-in for the A-D position. Yet, that didn't worry her. It made her proud.

He led the way to his studio, and they went inside. He'd been painting again. On various easels rested new canvases—each a masterpiece in its own right. One of the canvases, he'd covered with dark fabric, its subject hidden.

"Matt..." She couldn't even find the words. Tears blurred her vision.

"When I need to figure out what God's teaching me, I paint. Crazy, I know, but it works. Helps me gain perspective every time."

"How? How do you do this? How do you capture reality so perfectly?"

"That's quite a compliment. I never think that way, I assure you." He gazed at his handiwork and shook his head. "The brushstrokes are God's. I simply paint. Whatever you see here—however this makes you feel—I owe to Him."

Three newer paintings were of local community high points. Grace Fellowship Church, with its soaring steeple that converged upon the heavens. The Come and Get It Diner hemmed in winter's white mantle. Hattie's Hair Care that boasted bright, cheery windows framed in red checked curtains. *Ahh.* Such homespun appeal!

Another canvas, apparently still a work in progress, revealed Deputy Sapp kneeling in prayer before morning patrol, a ritual Ruby's citizens knew well. Each canvas, remarkable, with startling attention to detail.

"These are amazing. I'm floored by how talented you are." Mel's gaze traveled to the other addition. The one that remained shrouded. "Why is this one covered?"

"It's a gift for someone."

A Christmas present? For her? Oh, she could hardly wait! "Okay. I won't press you about that one. Seriously, though, I've said it before. You should do something with this. Something with your talent. I'd be the last one to dissuade you from leaving The Meadows, especially if that's where you feel called. But...do you remember when I told you that we might be gifted in multiple areas, but generally, there's one that holds our heartstrings above all others? That it connects the dots for us in a way that another passion doesn't?"

Matt stuffed his hands in his pockets. Glanced around his studio. "I can't deny that I love this."

"There's no need to deny it. You're an integral part of The Meadows. You work hard. You're service oriented. You have a heart for people, and it shows. But...this... Matt, painting transcends your work there. I see a different side of you here than I do there. Painting transforms you. It's like you were made for this."

"I have a bachelor's degree. A master's. An LCSW. My degrees are in psychology and social work. It's what I trained for, what I went to school for. Six years, to be exact." He blew out a sigh. "I'm not a professionally trained artist. I know the basics, but much of what I do is second nature. The feel of a certain brush between my fingers.

The use of light. The blending of colors. All guesswork."

"Not guesswork." Mel lifted a palm to his cheek and let it remain there. "God-given talent."

"I agree I have talent, Mel. But right now, this particular talent doesn't pay the bills or provide benefits. Quite frankly, The Meadows pays me well. For a small facility, *very* well. With benefits and bonuses, I earn a tidy income, and I'm able to save for the future, and someday, provide for a family. If I add 'Assistant Director' to my job title, that's an additional salary increase."

Though they hadn't spoken about marriage, his inference was clear. How could she make him understand that it was all right to pursue another avenue, that they'd be okay whatever he decided? She made a great income. Had the same excellent benefits. A union was a partnership, not a one-way street. He needn't shoulder this decision alone.

Mel stood on her tiptoes, forcing him to look at her. "You don't need my permission. If you want to go for it, then do. You'll always regret it if you don't." She said what nagged at the back of her mind, and likely, his, too. "Having seen this again—your work here—I think adding a new job title to your list of responsibilities would be a detriment to your true calling. I can't believe I'm saying this, but this clinches something in my mind. I don't think you should interview Tuesday for the A-D position. Not anymore."

"I can't just up and quit my position at work. Not after less than a year. What if painting's only a pipe dream? What if I pursue it and flop? What then?"

Was this the Matt Enders she knew and loved? What happened to the confident, larger-than-life guy who wasn't afraid to try new things? The man who met challenges head-on?

"I'm not necessarily saying up and quit your job at The Meadows. I'm saying don't add another entrée to your plate when your plate's already full. Unless I'm way off base—filling more of your time with work tasks, when you're drawn to a higher calling, won't satisfy you. Not in the way God intended."

Matt let his head droop against hers. His breath was warm against her ear. His embrace, sweet and loving. "I think you're right."

Because when our dreams and goals align with the good Lord's, that's when miraculous things happen. Edwin's recent words played in Matt's mind like a broken record. Putting himself out there like this was, by far, the gutsiest thing he'd ever done.

Since the impending weather was still on track, Matt decided Monday would be the best day to go for it. He used an hour of vacation time and scheduled a long lunch break so he could accomplish his errand.

Mel called to him as he headed out of the building. "Everything all right?"

"Yes, ma'am. Just need to run an errand over lunch. Coffee later?"

"Sounds great. See you then."

He didn't have time to go into it at the moment, but he would eventually. It wasn't his intention to keep her in the dark, but since this was a spur of the moment decision, he hadn't thought beyond the initial phone call to Fryin' Pan and Into the Fire. When the owners expressed interest this morning in what he proposed, that was confirmation enough that maybe his crazy idea might not be so crazy after all. If it went over well there, maybe he'd see if smaller, more local establishments were interested, too.

Matt drove back to his studio and gathered a few select pieces, loaded them into the truck, and made the quick jaunt to Sapphire and back. When nerves threatened to get the best of him, he shifted his attention to the next order of business. The latest weather alert notification that chimed on his cell phone. A winter weather advisory had been upgraded to a winter storm warning, with accumulating snow amounts projected to hit the Ozarks tomorrow. The day of the interviews. *Hmm.* One more thing to prepare for. Hopefully, it wouldn't stress Mel out. Often, these predicted storms changed tracks from hour to hour, and possibly, they'd escape the brunt of it.

Sitting at his desk now, Matt checked his e-mail to see if the interviews had been rescheduled. Nope. Nothing along that line in his inbox. He updated charts, filed paperwork, and organized his desk. He made rounds to residents' apartments. About three 'o'clock, he popped by Mel's office, only to find it empty. Maybe she waited for him in the dining room. Sometimes, they met with residents there about this time.

As Matt trekked down the hallway, he encountered Clinton Farley just shy of the dining room entrance. "Didn't see you at lunch today, Wonder Boy. Not like you to miss a meal." Clinton's voice held the familiar crustiness, but the corners of his mouth tipped upward in what might be considered a smile. Possibly. Maybe. For Clinton anyway.

Matt extended his hand. "I ran an errand. Did you miss me?"

"*Humpf.* Dream on." Surprisingly, Clinton acknowledged Matt's gesture, reciprocating in kind. The greeting marked a milestone that reflected a deeper connection between the two men. Startling, but hard-won. *Respect.* "You up for coffee?"

"You bet. Lead the way." Matt couldn't quell the burgeoning hope that lit in his mind and traveled to the tips of his toes.

If someone had foretold this, this still fragile friendship between him and one of The Meadows' crankiest residents, Matt wouldn't have believed it. In fact, he might have snickered. The metamorphosis settled over him, renewing his confidence that God worked even in the grimmest situations where the outcome appeared nothing short of predictable.

He and Clinton poured their coffees and found a table of Clinton's choosing. Of late, that seemed to be one of those closest to the windows and nature. Mel wasn't in the dining room, but a few of the staff were, as well as other residents. Minerva Walters fluttered her fingers at them from three tables over. Today, still a redhead with traces of silver, she wore a red and green polka dot dress with a fringed hem, and red flats with green, powder puff pom-poms. Fire engine red lips dazzled beneath full, rosy cheeks and heavily mascaraed lashes.

"Look what the cat dragged in! What a handsome pair of gentlemen you are. Clinton, I believe blue is your color. Looks right sharp on you."

"Th...Thank you, Miss Minerva," Clinton stuttered. "You're too kind."

The only thing that prevented Matt from snorting was sheer will power. At the risk of offending Minerva, he reigned in his laughter and attempted a reply. "And aren't you quite fetching in your holiday...uh...attire. Ladies, you light up the room."

"Like lampshades on a circus floor," Clinton muttered under his breath. Anything else either of them might think to say was swallowed by the matrons' titters.

"Clinton, I think you've garnered a fan."

"Nah. She's friendly like that. Real pleasant gal, that Minerva Walters."

"I agree, that she is. I believe, though, Miss Minerva may think of you in an extra friendly manner."

A muscle twitched in the senior's jaw. "You don't say."

"I do."

"Well, what am I gonna do about that?"

"What do you want to do about it?"

Clinton scratched his head. "Jiminy. I've always been a one-woman man. There's never been anyone for me other than my Marabel."

"I understand what that's like."

"Yeah, I thought so. You love her, huh?"

They both knew the "her" he referred to.

"Yes, I love her."

"Try loving someone like that for sixty years. *Sixty*, bucko. That's a long time. Then, try to imagine having romantic notions for someone other than your life partner. The one who knew you better than you knew yourself. I daresay that would be an eye-opener. A real revelation for you."

"You're right, Clinton. I *can't* imagine being in your shoes. All I can offer is some perspective." Matt paused to take a swig of coffee. "I know Marabel was a good woman. Well-loved by all. A pillar of the community. From what I understand, others' happiness mattered a great deal to her. Including yours. Do you honestly think she'd deprive you or want *you* to deprive yourself of joy? Of fun, fellowship? Friendship?"

"No, 'course not. But since she's been gone, it's like my sail is busted. Her dying sucked the wind right out of it. I'll never get over it. Never. I miss her." Moisture formed in Clinton's eyes and he swiped at the tears with the back of his hand. "It's a persistent ache that never goes away."

"I'm so sorry, my friend." Clinton drew himself taller at the word. *Help me know what to say here, Lord.* Matt didn't want to opine textbooks and training. He wanted to identify on a deeper level. "I'd like to tell you that it gets better. I believe to a degree, especially, when we know Christ and we understand earthly death is only a temporary parting, the grief does ease. However, the reality is, in many cases, some of that grief may always be with us. Denial, anger, bargaining, depression, and acceptance are common ways we cope with loss. Grief isn't linear. Meaning, folks grieve differently, and they may experience some of these stages, but not all, and perhaps, even in a different order. Sometimes people get stuck. To work through these emotions, often it helps to talk to others."

"You mean 'professionals.' Like you."

Matt nodded. "Yes. Or someone with specialized training in the field."

Clinton tapped the table with his fingertips, as if giving it intense thought. "Counseling?"

Matt nodded. "That's an excellent option, yes."

"I thought that was for crazy people. Or cowards."

"Total misconception." Would stereotypes ever end?

"Counseling balances the scale when the weight of the world grows too heavy on our shoulders. It restores order in our minds as we seek to understand complex things that we don't normally deal with. Things like death, divorce, health crises. Stuff people from all walks of life face. Not 'crazy people' or 'cowards' as you put it. Ordinary folks who simply need an unbiased perspective."

"And then what?"

"And then we address positive coping mechanisms and healthy ways to improve our mindset." Matt went out on a limb. He took it a step further. "Tell me, Clinton. Is there anything—a hobby or an interest—that you were ever passionate about? A pursuit you enjoyed?"

"Besides being Marabel's husband?"

"Yes."

"There *is* something…"

Chapter Fifteen

Mel straightened against the comfy cushion. "You what?"

"I know Clinton's story. We had a good chat this afternoon. Actually, an extraordinary chat."

"Well, for heaven's sake. Don't keep me in suspense. Enlighten me, please."

Matt slid his arm around her as they cuddled on her sectional. They'd missed each other earlier today. Whenever she had a free moment, he hadn't. When he was free, she was busy. They kept missing each other, only seeing each other once as Matt left to run his errand, and another time, briefly, before leaving work. When she'd suggested supper at her place, he'd readily agreed. "I'll bring pizza. You have a big day tomorrow so no need to add cooking to the mix tonight."

Not *we. You. You have a big day tomorrow.* Matt had decided not to interview. Which meant he was going for his dream. His decision pleased her.

"Judging by that exaggerated pause, I'm guessing Clinton's story is a whopper."

Matt trailed a fingertip along her collarbone, down her shoulder, allowing his palm to rest on her upper arm. "Would you understand if I said Clinton's story is his? That I believe he'll share when he's ready?"

"Did you speak in a counselor-patient role?"

"Not formally, no. If we had, you would have access to some of that information, naturally. If it in any way affected his residency at The Meadows, that is. What we spoke about was more personal in nature. Friend to friend. Off the record, so to speak."

"I see." She admired that about Matt. His discretion. Yet, his reluctance to share Clinton's story aroused her curiosity. Was there some deep, dark secret that would help her better understand the man who'd, despite his best efforts to the contrary, endeared himself to them? "I'll admit, I can't wait to know what it is. It must be something big. I see that glint in your eye."

"Glint?" He grinned, leaning in to kiss her cheek.

"Yeah. The one you get when you're flirting. Or contriving. Or when something big is cooking."

"Ahh. The lady knows me so well." His lips moved lower, finding their way to her mouth in a gentle, unhurried way. His quest undid her in the most glorious fashion, yet his expression of affection maintained all the proprieties. Not that temptation was so easily dismissed. It wasn't. Yet, because they loved each other, restraint remained foremost in their minds. They well knew what could happen when physical desire went unchecked. Except that didn't make it easy. Not at all.

"I love the way you kiss me."

"I love the way you kiss me back."

Matt, again, pressed his lips to hers. He lingered over her mouth, communicating through silky, velvet caresses the depth of his feelings. Responding to his touch came naturally. All that he offered, she received. What she gave in kind, he treasured. As minutes ticked by, they held each other in the firelight's soft glow, contented in these beautiful, private moments where only the two of them existed.

"I probably should go. I *know* I should go." His voice, a whisper, wrought with emotion. "Tomorrow will be here before we know it."

Yes, it would. Matt's heartbeat vibrated beneath her hand, and his breathing quickened. Would he stay if she invited him to spend the night? Maybe simply hold her? *Why are you even toying with that notion, Mel? There's nothing simple about two unmarried adults holding each other all night.* Simply *holding* wouldn't last long.

Conscience and common sense railed against human desire. Why did this have to be so hard? They were adults. Consenting adults who envisioned a future together. Why overanalyze it? *You know why.* One could convince oneself of anything, given enough time and reason.

She could have said so many things, but at the moment, eloquence escaped her. "This is difficult, isn't it?"

Matt drew back, resting his forehead against hers. "Yes. That's why I'm heading home now. However, I want you to know something." He feathered one last kiss upon her brow before rising. "I love you, Mel Brewer. I'm so thankful God had you knock me for a loop."

"That's a fun way to put it." Mel stood and linked her arm through his as she walked him to the door. "It sums up those early days quite well."

"I kind of miss them, don't you—those days of light, playful banter?"

"Uh-huh. Light, playful banter, indeed."

"You have to admit, our gentle sparring led us to this point. I can't wait to see where we go from here." He tugged his jacket from the coat tree and poked his arms in the sleeves. Mel thought Matt might kiss her again, but he merely grinned, and stepped out into the cold, brisk night where he sauntered toward his pickup. He opened the driver's side door but wheeled back around before sliding inside. "See you in the morning. You'll crush the interview tomorrow. I know how much the job means to you."

She gave a final wave from the doorway and called to him. "Thanks! And thanks for the pizza tonight."

What about his comment bothered her? He'd encouraged her. Expressed confidence in her. Then she knew. *I know how much the job means to you.* Matt didn't think the A-D position meant more to her than he did?

She'd convinced him to focus on his painting and not interview for the job because of the additional time involvement that came with it. That was her sole motivation. More time away from his painting wouldn't further his dream. But would working more hours at The Meadows further hers?

Light, tiny snowflakes teased the breeze and tickled Mel's nose. She watched Matt's truck disappear down the street, the iridescent glow of his taillights fading into night's shadowy backdrop.

When daylight came, many Ozarks' towns had already reached their high temperature for the day. Ruby greeted her citizens with a brisk thirty-three degrees and snow-dusted streets. Matt's weather app continued to chime with alerts regarding the impending snowstorm and blizzardlike conditions. For now, dark, billowy clouds hovered above a silver-gray skyline. Hopefully, the rest of the snow would hold off until early evening, as predicted. Maybe they wouldn't even get the eight or so inches that were forecasted. However, Matt knew from the looks of the radar, they'd likely get something. Snow totals could vary.

They could get more—or they could get less. That's how the Ozarks rolled. As far he knew, interviews hadn't been canceled. If something changed, Foster would be sure to touch base with the job candidates.

Outside The Meadows' entryway, Matt stomped off the excess moisture from his boots and hurried inside the building, where scents of cinnamon rolls and freshly-brewed coffee teased his nostrils. *Mmm. Tilly and crew, you are a marvel.* Nothing like a blizzard to kick the kitchen and dining room staff into high gear. They'd prepared days ago for the possibility of inclement weather, and had probably been here well before daybreak, prepping entrées, stews, casseroles, and whatever could be frozen ahead of time and easily heated, in the event they were caught short-staffed.

Building maintenance, an assortment of smiling, talkative fellows, scurried about this morning, double-checking generators and reserve power. Additional staff started arriving, including Sarah Dawson who waved to him from the front office.

"How's it going, Matt? Ready for the big blizzard?"

"Yes, ma'am. Ready as I'll ever be. We'll see if the weather guys called it right. You?"

"Same. Andy says he has a feeling the weather team will nail it this time."

"Did he say that with a straight face?"

"Yep. The cornball."

"Tell him I said to let me know when he has a free minute and I'll treat him to breakfast some morning." At present, Matt bet Andy's hardware store We've Got Nails enjoyed a booming business. Especially near Christmastime, and especially, on days like this.

"Will do."

Sarah's face glowed. That's what love did to a couple, Matt guessed. Nearly five years of marriage and so in love that the mere mention of the other partner's name caused a blush to rise. That same glow ignited Mel's countenance when in his presence. He didn't let it go to his head—he became a complete goofball when the woman crossed *his* path. Not prone to blushing, his ardor manifested itself in other ways. Clammy hands. Racing heart. Wobbly belly. But in the same way she triggered those reactions, she tipped his world upright and centered it. He'd do everything in his power to make sure Mel knew it. He had a plan now. He'd begun executing it yesterday.

As Matt approached his office, Foster met him at his doorway. "Son, you and Mel should add 'miracle workers' to your resumés."

"Pardon?"

"Since when did Clinton Farley start eating and conversing with fellow residents? Not only that, but even joking, and actually smiling. Well, not a full-fledged one quite yet, but darn close. Word has it that you and our go-to girl sparked this wondrous conversion."

"Ahh. I see. Thanks, sir. I don't think we can take complete credit for that. I think Clinton's transformation is due to a whole lotta prayer more than anything else. Gotta admit, it's fantastic."

"Good to see the Lord using you two as instruments during this renovation. Honest to goodness, what we have here at The Meadows is rare. I'm proud of my staff. Of you two." Foster held his gaze. He extended his hand. "I best get moving. Tons going on today." As if on cue, his boss's cell phone chirped.

"I understand. See you later."

"You bet." Foster dashed away with a bounce in his step and a tune on his tongue.

"Jingle Bells." Never mind the guy had interviews all day or that a blizzard was on the way. Perpetually good-natured and not easily ruffled, Foster's chill vibe served them well. There couldn't be a better fellow at The Meadows' helm. Whoever the committee hired in the role of Assistant Director to work alongside him would have a terrific example.

That thought percolated in Matt's head and he grinned.

Mel peered into the hall from her doorway. She'd seen Matt's and Foster's brief exchange and hadn't wanted to interrupt, but now seemed a good moment to catch Matt. She tapped lightly on his opened door.

"Hi. Have a second?"

"*Wow.* I certainly do." His fingers dangled over the wall pegs where he finished hanging his coat. "You're gorgeous."

His compliment bolstered her confidence. She'd chosen a new ensemble weeks ago for her interview, but she hadn't anticipated the weather to shift so drastically. As an Ozarks native, she should have known better and selected a Plan B. "You don't think it's too flashy?"

"Cold, maybe. But not too flashy. Red's definitely your color. Did you bring something warmer to change into afterward?"

"Yeah. Jeans, a warm sweater, and boots. Already stuffed them in my office closet."

"Good deal. How are you feeling?"

"Excited. Nervous."

He reached for her hand and gently squeezed it. "You're sure this is what you want?"

"The interview or the job?"

"Both."

Hmm. An odd question. Well, of course she wanted to interview well. Five years ago, it'd come easy. But the position she'd interviewed for then, her current position, wasn't in the same league as Assistant Director. Added to her present job title, it was a much more important role. One which garnered more respect, as well as increased responsibilities. *Oh.* So that's what Matt meant. Back to the time thing. A schedule adjustment.

"Both. I want to do great at the interview, and I really hope the hiring committee views me as a standout candidate."

"Then I want that, too." He released her palm and gestured toward a chair. "Have a seat?"

"Okay, but only for a sec. I need to make a coffee run before I jump into my morning routine."

"Gotcha. I just wanted to say something quick."

"All right." Was she imagining it, or did Matt's tone change? A hint of seriousness belied the slight upturn of his mouth. He leaned against his desk, resting his backside partially against it, as she took a seat in the chair he offered.

"How should I say this?" He scratched his chin. Paused. "While I have some reservations about whether or not the A-D job would be a good fit for you, I want to make it clear that it has nothing to do with your abilities or how fantastic I think you'd be at it. What concerns me is that you're considering this for all the right reasons.

Because...if you're not, it's a lot to take on and risk burnout. Especially if the timing isn't quite right. Or if something else draws you. Maybe...your own dream?"

O-kay. First, he dished up a compliment. Then he served it with a side of doubt. Not only that, he was using the same rationale she'd used with him. Except his dream, his wish to do something more with his painting, seemed so obvious. Matt would be nuts if he didn't pursue his God-given gift. Why suddenly swing the focus back on her? Annoyance ballooned in Mel's chest.

"All this sounds vaguely familiar. Similar to my own words to *you.*"

"I'm sorry. I've upset you." The space between Matt's brows crinkled. "That's not my intention. I'm not trying to throw ice water on your aspirations. I'm wondering about other interests. Things you've mentioned you enjoy, and obviously, you're talented at. Maybe you don't even realize how animated your face gets when you talk about them. Where those would fit in if your duties here increase."

"I'm not following. What other interests?"

"Your cottage remodel. How you've lovingly restored and preserved a piece of history. Your knack for scouring flea markets and secondhand shops for the perfect, vintage treasures. You have a flair for putting it all together and creating warm, inviting spaces. It's a gift I think others would benefit from. If you wanted to pursue it, that is. Maybe by way of your own shop someday? A cozy niche along Main Street that fellow eclectics could enjoy?"

Mel swallowed. How had he honed in on her secret wish? A small vintage resale boutique. She'd never even talked about it. From the time she was ten and wished upon those three shooting stars so long ago, it often flitted around in her mind. Certainly, a creative outlet that, perhaps wouldn't pay the bills for a while, but one that spoke to her inner entrepreneur. The problem? She already had a job. A well-paying job and one she'd trained for. A job she liked and excelled at, and the job she planned to use as a springboard to advance her career here.

"I appreciate the vote of confidence, but what you're suggesting is purely a pipe dream. "

"Uh-huh. Like I said about my painting."

"Except the difference is your paintings are tangible. Concrete pieces of art that prove your talent. There's no way I could walk away from my job here to explore such a whim. Can you imagine what my parents would say? Or everyone else, for that matter?"

"You start small. Maybe rent a space first. Grow your business. And note, I didn't say to walk away from your job here. I only asked that you consider where you want to spend your time. To do what you really want to do for all the right reasons."

Mel gave a wry laugh. "A quandary for both of us. Guess it'll sort itself out." She stood to her feet and checked her Fitbit. "Gotta get going. If I don't run into you at lunch after a while, I'll pop in after my interview."

"Still going, huh?"

"Matt, I can't not go. How unprofessional would it be to cancel at the last minute?"

"I understand. I'm sure there will be a lot to weigh afterward."

"Well, they're not going to hire me on the spot. They'll probably narrow down the top candidates and go from there."

"Yes. I know how it works."

"Why so glum then? Placing a desire on hold while I examine a more sensible career path doesn't mean I'm forsaking a dream." She moved toward the door, adding, "*Temporary* doesn't define our forever. It only delays destiny. If it's meant to be, God will provide a work-around."

"I believe that."

"Great. We agree then." As she left Matt's office, Mel wondered what she'd read in his face.

Matt hadn't intended for it to happen this way. He figured there'd be ample time between interviews for him to make it back to his office. Sure, he'd known what time Mel's interview was, and sure, he probably should have shared that he planned to keep his interview, which happened to be scheduled an hour and a half before hers.

What he hadn't planned on was taking his full interview time, and he certainly hadn't planned on running into Mel as she stood in the waiting area outside of Foster's office. There wasn't time to explain. As Matt exited the room, Foster clapped him on the back with a final "Good to visit with you, Matt." Then, in the same jovial tone, he ushered Mel inside. "Come on in, Mel. We're ready for you."

We, as in The Meadows' hiring committee, which consisted of Foster Pearce and community locals Dander Evans, Sam Packard, Ida Mae Farrow, Hattie Sapp, and Pastor Bill from church. A fine sampling of honest, upstanding folks.

In that fraction of a second, Mel recovered quickly. She greeted Matt with a tip of her head, and then trained her eyes on Foster, masking the hurt and confusion with courtesy and professionalism. *Oh no.* He could only imagine what she must be thinking. How she must be jumping to conclusions. For good reason.

Foster closed the door behind Mel, leaving Matt no choice but to be on his way. He'd almost made it to his office when Clinton Farley trundled toward him. "Whoa there, Wonder Boy. What's got you in such a flap?"

"Hello, Clinton. That noticeable, huh?"

"Yep. I daresay it isn't the weather. Though, that wind is kickin' up a fuss now, and I wouldn't be surprised if the so-called experts called it wrong. I think snow'll start flying any second now. I have a feeling it won't wait and it's gonna be way more than they predicted." Clinton pointed to his knees. "That's what these tell me anyway. These, and living in the Ozarks way longer than those weather wizzes have."

Matt had silenced his phone when he went into the interview so he hadn't heard the recent alerts or the updated forecast. He scanned the window beyond Clinton's silver head and noted the swaying trees and darkening skies. In that instant, light, feathery snowflakes began to fall.

"Wow. You're right, Clinton. They should hire you for support."

"Darn tootin'. But you didn't answer my question. Whatcha in a stew over?"

Man, he was more astute than Matt gave him credit for. "Honestly, I think I may have mishandled something."

Instead of a dozen nasty comebacks Clinton might have returned, he merely stroked his chin and remained thoughtful. "Hmm. Happens occasionally. Have you apologized?"

"I haven't had the chance yet."

"I see. Well, when the opportunity presents itself, be honest. Explain your reasoning. Why you handled it the way you did. She'll come around."

Clearly, Clinton knew he referred to Mel. The irony of him giving relationship advice should have grated on Matt. But it didn't. Instead, it touched the deep pockets of his memory bank.

My, how far they'd come.

"Mel, of course you know everyone here." Foster gestured toward the small crowd assembled in his office. Not an especially large space, he'd brought in a couple extra chairs, and the group stood as she entered.

"I do. Hi, everyone." She shook their hands and walked toward the empty chair closest to Foster, the one obviously meant for the interviewees. When she'd interviewed five years ago for the Activity Director position, Mel had interviewed only with Foster. For the Assistant Director opening, a multifaceted job which involved many more duties, Foster had gathered the hiring committee, formally known as The Meadows' Board of Directors, to assist with the selection process.

She hadn't expected to feel so rattled. These were people she'd known all her life. Went to church with them. Knew them. Yet, where she'd been slightly nervous about the interview, now, Mel's hands grew moist and almost shook. A muscle twitched in her shoulder. Her stomach tilted. Full-blown jitters threatened to sidetrack her. *Great.* It started with Matt exiting Foster's office—from his own interview. The one he'd led her to believe he would cancel.

Get control, Mel. You don't know why Matt did what he did. Why he distorted his intentions. There's an explanation. There has to be. She took a deep breath. Released it. She envisioned a white, sandy beach with froth-tipped waves lapping at the shoreline. Slowly, the butterflies stilled.

Foster began handing folders to the committee members. "All right, friends, I know you've already seen this when I sent it to you a few weeks ago via e-mail, but take a moment and reacquaint yourselves with Mel's resumé." After he'd passed out the last folder, Foster turned to Mel. "Water? Coffee? Donut? Ida Mae brought some right fine ones. Boston Creams—best I've ever had."

"Donuts were for this morning. The Snickerdoodles are for now. But please have whatever you want, Mel." Ida Mae waved toward the serving cart over by the water dispenser. "Heavenly days, have both, honey."

Ah. Life in a small town. What was an interview without a combination of formality and fun? Mel tried to quell the snort that tickled her nose. "Thank you, Ida Mae, but I better not. I'm still full from lunch."

"All righty then. Let's get this party started." Foster seated himself at his desk, smoothing his tie with his fingers. "I'm not much of a tie man, as you probably know. Mind if I dispense with it?"

Was he asking her? Okay. Now she laughed. "I certainly don't, Mr. Pearce. Do whatever makes you comfortable."

Off came the tie, which he draped over the edge of his desk. "Ruthy picked that thing out. It's a mite too long and I'm not particularly fond of the Christmas bells and candy canes." The room erupted in titters. "Another thing. Mel, it's *Foster.* Don't stand on ceremony. Think of this as a friendly chat."

"I'll try," Mel replied.

"Good. Good." Foster inclined his head toward Sam Packard. "We'll begin with the president of the board. Sam, take it away."

Sam Packard—middle thirties, a family man, and highly regarded in Ruby—nodded. "Thank you, Foster. Welcome, Miss Melinda—Mel. As you know, the Assistant Director position is a newly created job here. One that will assist Foster with various administrative duties, as well as shouldering the work load and responsibilities when he's away from The Meadows. In other words, it's a multidimensional role. Would you mind sharing what interests you about the job?"

"Sure. In the five years I've been with The Meadows I've grown very familiar with the residents and staff. I know how things operate. What it takes to keep things running smoothly, despite various temperaments and unforeseen circumstances. I've also learned new skills and implemented new programs while ensuring The Meadows remains a cut above other retirement communities." Mel paused to take a breath.

Pastor Bill and Dander Evans scrawled a few notes.

"As Activity Director, I already wear many hats. As The Meadows' Assistant Director, I'd like to expand my skill set, focusing on resident satisfaction and community involvement. An administrative role would allow me more freedom to do this. I'd be instrumental in the decision-making process as we continue to grow our presence and our mission."

For the next thirty minutes, Mel fielded questions from

the board. They discussed internal policies. Schedule demands. How she viewed this new role meshing with her current duties. Then, Dander Evans asked the most basic question. "Tell us, Mel. Where do you see yourself five years from now?"

Five years from now. *Five years* from now? *Not here.* The answer slammed her in the chest. "I—"

She'd only uttered that one word when suddenly, an ear-splitting rumble pierced the room.

Chapter Sixteen

Thundersnow? Matt nearly jumped out of his skin at the deafening roar. Some who'd gathered for coffee in the dining room shrieked. Minerva Walters and friends clutched their sweater-clad bosoms and stared. Shock and surprise fell upon the mid-sized room as startled residents popped from their seats and beheld the scene unfolding before them.

"Holy cats!" Clinton barked. "Would ya look at that?!"

Surely not. Matt plunked down his insulated coffee mug and sprinted to the windows. Snow tumbled fast and furious from a milky-white sky as wind-whipped trees bowed low to the ground. As if dumped from a bucket, fat, powdery flakes poured forth, obscuring the hills in the distance, and within minutes, the facility grounds. *A whiteout.*

Folks' weather apps chirped, pinged, and chimed, including his. Warning notices lit up his cell phone screen, and in addition, new snow total predictions. *How in blazes did this hit so quickly?* To be fair, the weather guys had bantered the word *blizzard* around since last week. Some people had taken it to heart—the mega milk, egg, and bread grocery shoppers—and some hadn't. He'd laid in a few supplies but hadn't gone overboard. Honestly, from the looks of it, Matt didn't even know if staff would make it home.

"Friends," he grabbed a spoon from a nearby

silverware basket and tapped it against an empty glass. "Can I have your attention, please?" He waited as voices quieted and faces turned his way. "Looks like the timing of the bad weather was a tad off. I want to assure you that the building is secure and the generators are on standby in the event we lose power. I imagine Mr. Pearce will be making a statement shortly over the intercom system, but rest assured, you're safe and all's well." *Inside, anyway.* Outside was another story.

After the initial boom when everyone seated in Foster's office jumped, Foster immediately transitioned into Fearless Leader mode.

"Well, Mel, I think we'd all agree that this interview ended with a bang." He chuckled at his own joke. "We'll be in touch with the top candidates in a few days. Right now, there's the little matter of a blizzard that seems to be upon us."

Blessedly, they'd wound down Mel's interview without waiting for the answer to Dander's last question. Committee members filed out and took stock of the weather as Foster summoned the building maintenance crew to check the grounds and premises. Over the intercom system, he reassured residents of their safety since they were tucked indoors, but he also apprised staff of worsening road conditions.

"Use good judgment, team," he urged in a staff e-mail. "Don't venture home until the snow tapers off. We've planned for this and we have everything you need. Extra food, blankets, rest areas. You name it. I'm sure the road crews will be out as soon as they can, but that may be a while."

On her way to her office, Mel peeked at the parking lot—or where the parking lot would normally be. Snow was stacking up fast. She knew where her VW should be, but visibility was nil. It had been years since she'd seen the snow come down this hard and pile up this quickly. No way would she be heading home in this.

"Guess the weather guys are high-fiving each other about now." Sarah came up beside her, *tsk-tsk-tsking.* "The only thing they miscalculated was the timing of this actual event. It hit a few hours earlier than predicted."

"Yeah. Typical." Mel turned from the entryway doors and studied her friend. "How are you feeling?"

"Hungry," Sarah laughed. "But then, I always am these days."

"Will Andy try and come get you in that humongous jeep of his?"

"Not until the snow quits, probably. I promised him I wouldn't try anything silly. You know, like leaving on my own. And I won't. I'm safer here than I would be driving on the streets. How about you? Those crazy brothers of yours won't do something ridiculous, will they?"

"You mean like hitching a ride on a snow plow to come check on me?"

"Something like that."

"Even they aren't that crazy. I have a change of clothes in my office closet, and I always keep a spare toiletry bag in there in case of emergencies. Speaking of which, I guess I should shed this business suit and slip into more sensible attire."

"Wait a sec." Sarah glanced around, lowering her voice. "How did the interview go?"

Mel had known Sarah knew. How could she not? As

The Meadows' office manager, she was privy to a lot of sensitive information. She also used discretion and never shared anything private. In this instance, since Mel's interview was over, she probably assumed it was okay to ask.

"The interview went great. Until the last question, when one of the hiring committee members asked where I saw myself in five years."

"Oh. You mean you haven't thought about that, or do you mean you didn't answer the question adequately?"

Mel sighed. "Funny thing about that question. I started to answer but got cut off by that big thunderclap. It was spectacular timing."

"I see. Anything else noteworthy today?"

Sarah knew about that, too. That Matt had interviewed, as well. Mel didn't expect her to offer anything, but by volleying the ball back in Mel's court, that opened the door for conversation. "Yes. But I don't want to talk about it now, if you don't mind."

"Of course. Besides, I better get back to my hive. I'm sure the phone lines are going to get wild."

"Thanks for understanding."

"Sure thing."

They parted to go their respective ways, and when they did, Matt waved to Mel from the opposite end of the hall. She couldn't even look at him without the hurt pinching her heart. How could he act so nonchalant? As if nothing out of the ordinary had occurred. While he'd espoused dreams, gifts, and talents, he'd interviewed for the very job he knew Mel wanted. The one he'd admitted wasn't where he wanted to direct his attention. *Why?* Why had he done it? Was Matt's stupid sense of competitiveness worth risking their relationship over?

Mel immediately did a one-eighty, and tramped to her office, refusing to acknowledge him.

By seven that evening, the wind blew hard and snow continued to fall. News outlets reported six-inch accumulations around the area, which clocked in at about an inch per hour—something the Ozarks hadn't seen in many years. Meteorologists estimated snow would slack off during the wee hours of the morning although that could change. Thankfully, The Meadows hadn't lost power.

Matt figured he'd given Mel enough time. It'd been hours since their interviews. Hours since she'd marched to her office, refusing to speak to him. Hours without so much as a response when he'd tried to text her. At supper, she'd sat with Sarah and other staff, so that wasn't an option either.

Enough of this. Matt wanted to explain himself, and come heck or high water, she'd listen. Light trickled from beneath Mel's closed door and he gave three sharp raps. *Nothing.* He knocked again. Still nothing.

"Mel, I'd like to talk to you. May I come in, please?"

A minute passed. Maybe two. *Okay. If this is how you want to play it, fine.* He turned the knob and gave the door a shove. Mel stood with her back to him, facing the windows where Christmas lights and streetlamps illuminated puffy, fat snowflakes and tall, uneven snowdrifts.

"Ignoring me won't make me go away."

"I know." She didn't even turn around.

The pain in her voice made him want to kick

something. Make that *someone*. Himself. "I didn't cancel the interview because I had things to say. And it wasn't really an interview because I—"

"Matt, you didn't directly lie to me, but you led me to believe the A-D position wasn't right for you. That you were going to pursue your painting. And then, you caused me to question *my* true motivation."

"I'm sorry. I know that's how it seems, but that's not what I intended. I do think you should consider a business venture. You're gifted at interior design. The way you put colors and fabrics and pieces together—your sense of style—is unique. You also have an artist's eye. You're talented at what you do here, but there's a difference. I think you know that."

"What I *know* is that there's something horribly out of whack here. It isn't simply miscommunication. It's the intent. Saying one thing. Doing another. Spinning your version of truth and doctoring it with pretty niceties."

"You don't know the whole story." Matt crammed his hands in his pockets and waited. "Would you please turn around?"

"I can't look at you right now." Mel's words sounded all wobbly like she'd been crying.

Somehow, he knew there'd be no more explaining tonight. No matter what he said, she'd already tried and convicted him. "Will you bed down in here for the evening?"

"That's the plan."

"Can I get you anything? Extra blankets? A pillow?"

Mel shook her head. The backs of her shoulders drooped. "I know where the roll-a-way cots and blankets are. Don't worry about me."

"But I do, Mel. I do worry. I worry because I love you."

She grew very still, her breathing practically inaudible.

"Just one more thing. The errand I ran yesterday? I took some of my paintings to Sapphire to Fryin' Pan and Into the Fire. A spur of the moment, harebrained idea, I know. I asked the owners if they'd be willing to display the pieces on commission. I thought I'd gauge any local interest. Thought you might like to know."

Mel spun around. Her red-rimmed eyes blinked.

"Does that sound like I didn't take our conversations seriously?" Matt didn't try explaining the rest tonight, but gently shut the door behind him as he exited her office.

Sleep hadn't come easily, nor had Mel slept very soundly. The borrowed cot from the supply room didn't lend itself to a restful slumber. It provided basic relaxation. Very basic. The fact that other things distracted her—chiefly, the guy three offices down and that they were snowed in together at work—hadn't helped her sandman quest. Had Matt found sleep? Had he snoozed without nary a thought to the day's events?

Mel grunted against the onslaught of images that played in her head. *Him* leaving Foster's office…after he'd been found out. *Him* waving at her in the hall…as if he were her bestie. *Him* dropping by her office last night…with candor and confessions, but not the complete truth. If she didn't know the whole story as he claimed, he'd done a poor job of clarifying it. At this point, nothing he said would rectify what he'd done. Facts were facts. And the fact was he'd withheld information. Misled her. He couldn't pretend otherwise. Well, he could, but deluding himself or trying to convince her that other factors played into his reasoning only fueled speculation in her mind. If this were Matt's idea of love, she couldn't get on board with it.

Tears leaked from the corners of Mel's eyes, and she swiped at them with the back of her hand. *Traitor.* The word knocked around in her head like marbles in a can. They'd bared their hearts to each other. Shared their hopes and dreams. Fallen in love. How could he say all the right things and then do something so completely out of character? Only one answer came to mind. Matt had played her for a fool.

Mel stretched her legs as a glimmer of daylight eked its way through her office blinds. Did she even want to look? Not looking wouldn't make the snow go away. Since she hadn't heard the snow plows yet, she had a sinking feeling of what she would find. Might as well get up and face it. She'd either be snowed in for another day or she'd get to go home later to her own bed. Sleeping all night at The Meadows had been a first. While not terrible, she hoped it was her last time.

As she shook off the remaining vestiges of a rough night, she swung her feet over the side of the cot and grabbed her cell phone by the pillow. New weather alerts, all dire, streamed across the screen. *Wonderful.* There were additional updates from Foster reminding staff of emergency protocol, and on a more lighthearted note, a mass text to staff from Tilly Andrews informing them that the dining crew was ready, willing, and able to feed all the chicks in the henhouse. Bless her heart. Code for: *No worries. We have enough food and goodies in the kitchen freezer, fridges, and cupboards to feed an army.*

True to form, there were texts from her parents and brothers. Then, not surprisingly, Matt had texted, too.

Can we talk at some point today? I'd like to clear the air.

And another—

Doesn't look like we're going anywhere for a while. Meet for coffee this morning?

Nope. She wouldn't text him back yet. She didn't know what the day held, but talking to Matt or meeting him for coffee were last on her list for now. Honestly, whenever she thought about yesterday, the hurt resonated so deep, sobs clogged her throat. She'd probably see him soon enough anyway.

Mel rose to her feet and padded over to the windows. Maybe it wasn't that bad. But of course, it was. She didn't have to fully open the blinds to know what lay beyond. Mounds and mounds and mounds of snow…and more still falling. No longer a complete whiteout, though, poor visibility, with the parking lot, street, and grounds completely snow-packed and untouched, as yet, by road crews. *Super.* They were effectively socked in.

It would almost be kind of pretty, maybe thrilling, so near the holiday, if she weren't so emotionally spent. But at the moment, all Mel could think about was Matt's motivation. Why he'd intentionally deceived her about yesterday's interview. It seemed so atypical for him—the man she'd come to know…and love.

She ran her fingers through her hair and blew out the

breath she'd been holding. This wouldn't get her anywhere. In spite of everything, she had a job to do, and the first order of business after visiting the ladies lounge, was a bagel and coffee. By then, residents should be waking and moving about, no doubt, as awed by the extraordinary weather events as staff.

Perhaps she'd arrange a movie day in the rec room. Popcorn and snacks. Christmas card making. Creative, fun things to enhance the holiday spirit. Since many of the residents didn't drive anymore, inclement weather didn't affect their day-to-day routine too much, but she knew some would be concerned for loved ones' safety, and a few might worry, simply, given their age and nature. She could work with that. Redirecting that worry to something positive would brighten the day and improve folks' mindset.

Mel slid on her shoes, smoothed the wrinkles from her sweater as best she could, and made a beeline for the ladies' lounge. As expected, the four-stall, six-sink affair bustled with activity. In the separate alcove where there were additional mirrors, chairs, and make-up stations, friendly chatter temporarily took Mel's mind off Matt.

"Hey, you." Sarah edged up beside her to wash her hands. "Are we having fun yet?"

"Clearly."

"What's the matter? Don't you like an impromptu campout with cots and indoor plumbing?"

"Sure. When I get to pick the destination." Mel stifled a yawn. "My workplace isn't exactly that spot."

"Oh, come now. Where's your sense of adventure?"

Seriously? Mel cast her the side-eye. "It fizzled out somewhere between yesterday's snow dump and this morning's coffee run. Speaking of which, I'm heading there next. Join me?"

"Raincheck? I promised Andy I'd return his call after I finished here. He's determined to come get me when road conditions improve."

Mel could only imagine his concern. "I bet he's pacing the floors, huh?"

"Yeah. Usually, he isn't such a worrywart, but since this is one of the heaviest snows on record, he definitely doesn't want me driving." Sarah lowered her voice. "He's also convinced missing one prenatal vitamin will make me anemic or something. Silly guy."

"Nah, I think that's sweet. Go call him. We'll catch up later."

"You can count on it."

Sarah flitted away, leaving Mel to wonder if Matt worried about her like that. Though their circumstances were different, wasn't that what a truly committed couple did—fret when something unforeseen affected the other's wellbeing?

Never mind that Matt had so tenderly cared for her when she'd had the flu a few months back. Or that he'd handled the awkward situation with Spencer even before that. Sidestepping her feelings regarding the interview yesterday—deliberately trying to conceal his own interview—demonstrated deception and anything *but* concern. His actions did, however, prove one thing. You either rose to the occasion for your partner...or you didn't.

Finally, about two 'o'clock, almost twenty-four hours after the snow first started falling, it dwindled to mere flakes. By three that afternoon, it completely stopped, leaving a winter wonderland, albeit a precarious one, in its wake. Matt couldn't even hazard a guess how much snow lay on the ground. A foot, maybe? Judging by The Meadows' parking lot, snow drifts far exceeded that.

Mel's Volkswagen resembled a fat lump of frosting, the yellow exterior barely visible beneath winter's white blanket. Parked farther down the lot, his truck fared a tad better. At least he could make out where the windows were supposed to be.

As Matt strained to get a better view, somewhere in the distance, engines hummed. A far-off scraping sound followed and that meant one thing. *Hallelujah! Snow plows!* Hopefully, the contract crew would make their way over to The Meadows parking lot and there'd be no need to sleep over tonight. Even so, staff who drove smaller vehicles like Mel's wouldn't be leaving anytime soon. It would be far too dangerous. Those folks would have to hitch a ride with their four-wheel drive buddies or sleep at the center again tonight. *Hmm...* Possibly, he could help Mel out with a ride. If she'd let him.

Trouble was, she'd barely spoken to him since yesterday. Since he'd handled things badly. He realized how it looked. Him exiting Foster's office when she'd arrived for her own interview—except things weren't always what they seemed. If she'd only talk to him, he'd explain.

"I've been thinking..."

Matt whirled around to find Clinton ambling up beside him. The elderly fellow's eyes registered a new softness these days. His wrinkled face appeared gentler, somehow.

"Hi there, Clinton. Tell me, what have you been thinking?"

"All the God stuff. You really believe it?"

How like him not to mince words. Matt had come to expect it. "Yes, sir. I really do."

"It's just you and me here, Wonder Boy. No one else around at the moment, so you can answer truthfully, and I won't tell."

Matt didn't know where this was leading, but he had an idea. *God, give me the words. Your words.* "Clinton, I believe in God, Christ Jesus, His son, and the Holy Spirit. That's about as succinct as I can put it."

Clinton pursed his lips. Reached up to scratch his clean-shaven chin, where only a few weeks ago, stubble reigned. "I believed in Him once. Does that count? Do you reckon He still remembers me?"

Whoa. Matt's heart skipped. Were they really going to have this conversation? He'd prayed for God's timing. Prayed Clinton would be receptive to the subject. He'd not pressed or browbeat. Was today the day? Fresh hope ignited.

"Absolutely, He remembers you. In the Gospel of John, chapter ten, verses 28 and 29, we're told that Jesus grants us eternal life. Because of that we'll never perish. No one can pluck us out of His hand. God, the Father, who gave Christ to us and who is greater than all, also confirms this." Matt waited a moment so Clinton could ponder his words. "Naturally, Christ wants to have a relationship with us, and that relationship grows stronger when we allow Him access to our lives. But let me reassure you, Clinton— no matter what we do, what we say, how far we stray—if we've truly asked Jesus into our hearts, nothing can separate us from Him. Ever."

"Even if we haven't talked to Him in years? Decades?"

"Yes. Even then."

"Even if we spurned Him...but regret it?"

"Yep. Even then."

"Even if we still have doubts?"

"Yeah. Even then. Because, sometimes, everyone doubts. It's human nature to question stuff we don't understand. There's a big difference between doubt and denial. It's the blatant rejection of Christ and His free gift of salvation that separate us from Him—forever."

Clinton hung his silver head. "I'm mad at Him. After all these years, I'm still madder'n a hornet at God. That shames me...but it's the truth."

Ah, Clinton. "He understands, my friend." Matt clasped Clinton's shoulder. "He still loves you—wants a relationship with you."

"Think it's possible to rekindle that?"

"I do. When we're truly sorry for something, we only have to ask Him to forgive us, and then, we try to do better. We're not perfect. We're probably gonna fail again. But the cool thing is Christ understands and never runs out of love or forgiveness for His people."

"Kind of like our earthly relationships, huh? When folks really love each other?"

"Exactly. Except God's patience doesn't wax and wane. He's constant. Dependable."

Clinton studied Matt. Stared at him. His skinny shoulders quaked. A tear streaked down Clinton's cheek. He reached in his hip pocket and tugged out a frayed handkerchief. More tears slid down the craggy, timeworn face, and Matt took a gamble. Ever so gently, he drew the wounded soul into his arms and embraced him.

"I haven't had a hug since Marabel died. Never wanted 'em," Clinton said softly." Yet, he remained.

"Feels good, huh?"

"Yeah. Yeah, it does. But don't tell anyone."

"I won't, my friend." Matt's own eyes leaked with moisture, but he didn't care.

Mel watched from afar. Matt and Clinton *hugging*? Was it possible? From her vantage point where the hallway intersected, she observed the interplay between the two men. Seriousness, then smiles. Emotion, palpable and poignant, to the trained eye, or any eye that might be watching.

Too far away to hear what they were saying, she stood, transfixed, treasuring this moment. Clinton might hold a soft spot for her, but Matt had broken through. Broken through the elder man's armor-like exterior and self-imposed prison. Broken through years of isolation and anger. Broken through misery and heartbreak. *Matt, you did it.* Fragmented convictions—sidelined beliefs she'd held in reserve—reassembled themselves, restoring her faith in God's greater good.

Tears wet Mel's cheeks as she turned and retreated to her office. She wouldn't interfere with their private moment, but inwardly, she cheered. *Thank you, God.* This is what she and Matt had prayed for and worked so hard toward—a new beginning for Clinton. How could she stay mad at a guy who clearly had others' best interest at heart?

Again, she tried to analyze her upset. Maybe Matt simply changed his mind about the interview and didn't have the chance to tell her. Maybe he'd decided to place his painting on hold because he'd had second thoughts. *Maybe* it wasn't a competitive maneuver at all. Maybe.

In her office, Mel caught up on tasks she'd neglected since yesterday. With the snow, job interview, and unplanned sleepover, her normal routine had flown out the window along with any hope of getting home today. Snow plow crews had gone to work, but even if she could dig out her poor bug from its snowy camouflage, driving conditions were far too hazardous yet to venture out onto the roads.

Exhaustion settled in her bones, making it difficult to think. An exhaustion not entirely terrible, due in part to Clinton's transformation, but nevertheless, a mental and physical fatigue that craved a warm, comfy bed...and resolution to unanswered questions.

Mel rubbed at the cords in her neck. Deep down she knew Matt would never manipulate a situation to benefit himself. It wasn't who he was. He had too much integrity to risk wounding another or damaging his character. There had to be a logical explanation for him not mentioning his change of heart, his interview. Granted, he'd tried to explain yesterday, but she'd refused to listen. Partly because of her own ambivalence about the A-D position.

When Dander Evans had asked where she saw herself five years from now, Mel's immediate thought had been *not here*. But later, after she'd reflected, what she really meant was probably not in the assistant director slot. The extra responsibilities, the time involvement—while job advancement had always been on her radar, maybe it wasn't quite right for her now. To add the additional title to her list of present responsibilities no longer appealed as much. She didn't need to prove herself or earn others' respect. Staying true to her own self and embracing her calling were what mattered.

On the other hand, she couldn't see herself leaving her current position as Activity Director. She loved her job—loved serving the senior population here and making a difference in their lives. One day, she hoped to expand her talents and venture into the business world as Matt had encouraged. That might be next year, or it might be down the road. She didn't know. She only knew that twenty-four hours could sure add perspective. What seemed so clear yesterday, suddenly, didn't make as much sense today.

"May I come in?" The soft timbre of his voice washed over her, and Mel immediately glanced up.

"Yes."

"I gather you've seen the parking lot?"

She nodded.

"Then you know your car isn't going anywhere today. I'm wondering if I can give you a ride home in a while?"

"You're going to try it?"

"Yeah, my rig's rugged. The roads will be a mess, but I think I can get us home to our own beds tonight if you're game."

"Dad or one of the guys could come get me."

"I'm already here. No need to have them come if we can ride together." Matt planted himself in front of her desk. "Besides, we need to clear the air. Talk. I'd prefer to do that away from work."

"Me, too."

The sun, meager though it was, sunk lower in the western sky, and Foster encouraged those who'd been there over twenty-four hours to go home. With beefed up manpower, county road crews had done a better job at clearing than expected. Personnel who didn't want to risk driving, and folks with small or lightweight vehicles, contacted friends and family with sturdier transportation to come get them. Support staff would assist the work team over the next few days while everyone recouped from the excitement and added responsibilities. In spite of everything, The Meadows' community had rallied to the occasion and pitched in wherever needed.

Foster called an impromptu meeting before staff filtered out, and now he puffed out his chest and beamed. At some point, he'd changed clothes and donned a red flannel shirt and blue jeans. Normally, the reindeer antlers atop his head might seem too offbeat, given another work environment, but that's exactly what Matt loved about this place. The Meadows was unique in that way. Plus, "normal" was overrated. Levity balanced the more serious aspects of life.

"We haven't seen anything like this in quite a while, team." Foster cleared his throat. "Old Man Winter bit us in the backside, but we chomped down and bit him back. Thank you for your effort and sacrifice. Well done, everyone!" He raised his coffee mug to the crew. "We'll see most of you back here the day after tomorrow when you've had the opportunity to rest. Until then, we have support staff in place, so we have our bases covered. Now, go home and love on your families."

Love on your families. The words shored up Matt's confidence. Mel wasn't family yet, but he had plans to remedy that.

He caught her as they dispersed from the meeting room. "I already shoveled some of the snow away from my pickup, and I think we can negotiate the parking lot fine.

It may be slow going once we hit the road, but we'll make it."

"Sounds good. Let me slip on my snow boots and gather a few things."

Was that a smile? Matt decided it was. Maybe not a full-blown one, but the slight upturn of her mouth encouraged him.

Chapter Seventeen

The snow-packed streets remained slick and slow-going. Despite the road crews' efforts, there'd have to be a whole lot of melting before travel would be advisable.

"I'm thankful Foster gave us tomorrow off," Matt said as he negotiated the incline to Mel's cottage. "Good to know that relief personnel will pick up the slack for a while."

Mel gripped the edges of the seat with mittened fingers. No way would her poor VW have made it through this mess. "Yeah, until some of this melts, a lot of people will stay put."

They managed to dodge some of the heftier mounds of snow that the snowblades had missed, and Mel breathed a sigh of relief when they finally pulled up to the curb in front of her home. Where they guesstimated the curb to be anyway.

"Wait here," Matt told her. "I'll come around and lift you out."

"Are you worried a snowbank will swallow me?"

"I'd rather not find out. It'll be dark soon and it's too cold to play in the snow."

When he came around to the passenger side, Mel had flung the straps of her purse, garment bag, and laptop over her shoulders. She tugged the hood of her coat over her head as Matt opened the door and reached up to circle her waist with his hands. "Careful. It's crazy deep here.

The wind must have blown all the snow your direction."

"Naturally."

"I could carry you."

"You think? In this?"

Then of course, he had to prove it. As if she were a mere twig, he lifted her from the pickup and started for the door. "You forget I've done this before."

She remembered all too well. "Yes, but I'm not sick now. I'm not helpless either. Besides, trudging through the snow carting extra weight isn't easy."

"Piece of cake." His tone suggested he found this amusing. "Keep talking and I'm sure you'll come up with something."

Fleetingly, Mel wondered if any of her neighbors might be watching. It wasn't every day that a man tromped up to her front door with her in tow. No matter. If people wanted to know, they'd probably call.

Matt set her down and she whisked out her keys. She had to remove a mitten to insert the correct key into the lock. "My mittens are warmer than my gloves, but they're a pain."

"Here. Allow me."

Mel appreciated his politeness, and his chivalry so she didn't have to wade through the cold snow, but how long were they going to dance around whatever was going on? She wanted to discuss it.

"Would you like some hot chocolate? I could make grilled cheese sandwiches. I know you should probably go. The roads will get slicker after dark and—"

"I'll be fine. How about we talk over a cup of that hot chocolate? You don't have to worry about fixing supper."

"I never intended to interview for the Assistant Director

position, Mel. I *didn't* interview for it." Matt set down his cup of hot chocolate and stared into the fire he'd built earlier. "Also, I would never lie to you. I kept my time slot because I wanted to meet with the committee."

"That's where you lose me. If you didn't interview for the job, why meet with them?"

"To share my long-term vision for the GIFTS program. To offer something of myself apart from my current job." Matt knew he was talking in circles and he paused to collect his thoughts. "I officially removed my name from the candidate roster. One day, I do want to open my own studio, but I can't leave The Meadows yet. The timing isn't right. What I proposed is a specialized art program. Something that would benefit our residents, as well as generate an income stream for The Meadows. More income means more expansion, and ultimately, new and improved services we're able to offer our seniors."

Matt pointed to a painting that hung on Mel's living room wall. It was a magnificent meadow in springtime with a rainbow rising beyond a green, grassy knoll. "Doc Burnside left that behind in his things, didn't he? When he bequeathed you the cottage?"

"Ye—yes." Mel's brows furrowed. "How did you know that? Did I mention it?"

Matt shook his head. "No. Someone else did. They said it might still be here. Step over and look at it, Mel."

She rose from the sectional and walked over to the painting. "What am I supposed to see? Other than the fact, it's breathtaking. That's why I wanted to hang it again after I repainted the walls. I love it."

"Look at the bottom right-hand corner. There are some initials there."

Mel squinted and trailed the area with her fingertips.

"Found them!"

"What are they? What are the letters?"

"The initials are C-F. Hmm... I never noticed those before."

"Do you know whose initials those might be?"

"No. Should I?"

Matt came to stand beside her. "It's amazing how God orchestrates things. Brings like-minded creatives together even though they might be polar opposites in other areas. One, a cantankerous, old goat—make that a *reformed* cantankerous, old goat—and one, a guy with wild and crazy ideas and a desire to make a difference. *Wonder Boy*."

"Matt!" Mel's hands flew to her mouth. "Clinton? *Clinton Farley* painted this? He's an artist?"

He couldn't keep the grin at bay. "Don't tell him I told you. I'm only sharing so you have a better grasp of where my heart and head are. I went to Foster and the others on Tuesday to chat about The Meadows' future. I want to expand my gifts and pay it forward through GIFTS, *God's Incredible Free Treasure Supplied*. I'm going to continue painting, maybe try selling a few on commission, and then, see where that takes me. Meanwhile, Clinton has offered to help lay the groundwork for this new program. Apparently, he has some connections. Believe it or not, very influential ones."

"Why did I never know this story? This is incredible!"

"Clinton hasn't painted in a long time. He wasn't well known. Rarely showed his artwork or gave it away...except on rare occasions." Matt slid his arm around Mel's shoulders. "I realize how it looked. Me, coming out of Foster's office on Tuesday. For a lot of reasons, I didn't want to share Clinton's story before then."

"Oh, Matt." Tears trickled down Mel's cheeks. "I interviewed for the job, but guess what? I don't think it's right for me either. Not necessarily because of the business I hope to one day open, but because I really believe the timing isn't right on my end, as well. I'm happy in the job I have now."

"Aren't we a pair?" Matt gently wiped away her tears. "There is one thing I'd like to know. Or maybe ask. *Ask* is probably the more appropriate word."

He cupped her cheek within the palm of his hand, and Mel covered his hand with hers. His touch still had the power to undo her exactly as it had from the beginning. Now, she accepted why. It wasn't enough to simply recognize passion. When a couple fully appreciated God's design for their lives, their focus shifted. *Love*, fused with attraction, created a new tipping point. Mature love cherished the gift and used it wisely.

Mel stared up at Matt, keenly aware of what he wanted to say. She didn't rush him. She recalled past doubts. Days she wondered what God had planned. With Clinton. Her job. Matt. Admittedly, sometimes, she'd lost faith that God would reconcile situations and relationships. But that was the thing about God. He resurrected faith and restored from mere seeds. Seeds that produced something way better and far more beautiful than she could imagine.

"I love you, honey." Matt finally said. "Would you mind if I do this the old-fashioned way and speak to your dad first? I'd like to ask his blessing before asking you my question."

"I love you, too, Matt Enders. I think I like that idea very much."

In the firelight's crimson glow, he kissed her.

Epilogue

Christmas morning tiptoed upon the Eastern horizon in quiet grandeur. Pink, purple, and golden sky unfurled above the old Ozark Mountains, lighting the way for those in need of miracles and new beginnings.

For the first time in many years, Clinton Farley awakened with a heart full of hope. The emotion bebopped along the perimeters of his chest cavity and mushroomed throughout his entire body, lighting all the cracks and crevices where darkness once fell. What a glorious day!

Rising from bed, he reached for his cane and poked stockinged feet into red, corduroy house slippers—an early Christmas gift from Miss Melinda—and ambled over to the window where he shoved the drapes open wide. Immediately, orange-yellow sunshine washed his bedroom in bright, bold light. It had snowed again. This time, only a smattering, enough to coat naked tree limbs and cause the dormant grass to glisten, but nevertheless, a delightful perk on this joyful morn. *Merry Christmas, world. It's good to see you.*

Like a giddy schoolboy headed to prom, Clinton trekked toward the living room, to the modest corner Christmas tree that Wonder Boy had helped him erect and decorate. There, among a few other gaily wrapped gifts, the larger, rectangular one from W-B stood out. Clinton had promised to wait until today to unwrap it, but today had finally arrived and he could hardly contain his eagerness. What in candy canes was it? His old heart thumped with excitement. *Goodnight, it's almost too pretty to unwrap.*

Carefully, Clinton bent down and snatched up the red and white striped Christmas present with massive red bow. He ran his fingers along the outer edges of the present, noting the solid angles. A picture frame maybe? Other than the usual handkerchiefs, jigsaw puzzles, and word search books from The Meadows' staff, Clinton hadn't received additional Christmas presents since moving here. That Wonder Boy thought to even give him a gift brought tears to his eyes. *I don't deserve it, Lord.*

But something soft and gentle stirred in Clinton's heart. *Yes, you do, my child. And don't forget, this is the season we remember the greatest gift of all.* Clinton tottered backward.

God, is that you?

He'd never heard God speak. Couldn't say for sure that's who it was now. But something—a definite impression of love so pure, of peace so profound—lit in his soul and all but stopped him in his tracks.

Clinton sank into the comfy depths of the nearby sofa, mindful of the present he gripped in his hands. With deliberate precision, he poked a fingernail beneath a corner edge of the wrapping paper until, at last, he'd lifted away most of the tape. He shifted the item in his lap and repeated the process at the opposite end. He didn't know why he was being so meticulous. Maybe because he knew that whatever this was demanded his utmost care and attention.

With an inexplicable reverence, Clinton paused. Goosebumps raised on his arms. The rat-a-tat-tat of his own heartbeat thudded in his ears. When he could stand it no longer, he tore away the remaining vestiges of tape and giftwrap. A painting? He turned it over and sucked in his breath. *My goodness gracious.* A painting, indeed. It was a portrait of himself gazing toward the heavens—sheer delight written on his face—with hope-filled eyes and anticipation of better things to come. In the bottom right-hand corner, the artist's name stood out. *Wonder Boy.*

Across town, the Brewer clan gathered 'round the family Christmas tree. Gabe, Garrett, Mike, and their parents Jake and Billie Gail, watched as Mel tore open one final present.

"Oh, Matt! When did you...do this?" Mel held the gift at arm's length, taking in every nuance, every detail the painting depicted.

"Oh, I'll never tell. Do you like it?"

She swiped at sudden tears. "I l-love it. It's as if you were there."

"Gotta be honest." Matt slipped an arm around her shoulders. "I watched from afar. I could hardly wait to reach for my brushes."

In this painting, Mel clasped an octogenarian's hand as they sipped coffee, the two deeply engrossed in conversation and smiles. One would never guess this was the same Clinton Farley who'd previously spurned every attempt at kindness. In his eyes, a new light shone.

"It's perfect. You captured the new Clinton."

"Think so? I call this one 'Friendship Unbound.' Healing and restoration illustrated through a simple act of kindness." Matt hugged her close. "Friendship's an amazing gift, I've always said. When we're receptive—when the timing's right—it often leads to more."

Mel laughed softly. "That's true."

Then her eyes dipped to the bottom right-hand corner of the painting to Matt's name, and something more. Two tiny sentences. *Your dad said yes. Will you say it, too?*

In that instant, Matt dropped to one knee. Mom and Dad and the guys beamed as Matt reached in his pocket and drew out a red velvet box. No one said a word as he flipped open the lid, displaying the stunning princess cut diamond.

The man before her—Mel's forever friend—breathed life to the painting's words. "I love you, honey. Will you marry me?"

"Only if you'll catch me when I fall." This time, her nerves remained steady as Matt slid the engagement ring on her left hand, fourth finger.

"You bet I will. No fainting required."

"Wa-hoo!" Garrett cheered. "Welcome to the family, brother!"

The room erupted in happy chaos, and naturally, Mel's family clapped her fiancé on the back offering hearty congratulations.

"Oh, lamb!" Mom squealed. "Our baby girl's getting married!"

"She is, at that, Mama." Mel's dad kissed the top of her head, and swiped at his eyes. Such a softie, her father. *How I love you, Daddy.*

Later, after Christmas ham and all the trimmings, Matt caught Mel beneath the mistletoe and whispered, "Practice makes perfect."

If his kiss were any indication of practice, perfection was a fallacy. "I think you've already mastered the art, but then again...maybe we should keep trying."

To which Matt replied, "Happy to oblige."

Back at The Meadows, Minerva Walters sported a new hairdo and dress. She hoped Clinton liked Precious Pink. Today, she matched from head to toe. From the tips of her frosted pink curls to the soles of her pink sequined slippers, no one did the holiday quite like Minerva. *Hang on to your dinner buns, 'cause here I come, darlin'.*

When she glided into the dining room, all heads turned. But the one who mattered most, the gent who stirred her heart and made it sing—stood—and pulled out a chair. The indication was obvious. Clinton Farley wanted to marry her.

For now, The Meadows' Assistant Director opening had been tabled. The hiring committee aimed to revisit the issue after the holidays over coffee and deep-dish apple pie.

Meanwhile, Matt and Mel discussed future living arrangements. Where would they live as husband and wife—her house or his? Hmm... With Matt's on-site art studio, and the bigger square footage, his home made more sense. Especially if little ones came one day. But Mel's cottage held her heartstrings. Perhaps, the acreage could be rezoned as commercial? After all, it would make a darling resale boutique. Then again...the new vet in town—Erin Shaye—once expressed interest in the place. Living in the back room of her veterinary clinic was getting mighty old.

Certainly, quandaries and questions to consider another day. Today, however, rejoicing took precedence.

Like Christmases before, church bells pealed throughout Ruby's hills and hollows, ushering in a magnificent new season. To which, Deputy Horace Sapp shouted "Hallelujah!"

Author Note

If you're a member of my newsletter family or my Facebook Readers' Group, you know this past year challenged and changed me. It left me a little ragged around the edges.

As we continued to navigate a global pandemic, our family also faced loved ones' back-to-back deaths. Two of those due to COVID.

Here's the truth. The year left me battle worn.

We lost my dear mother-in-law in September 2020. In November, COVID claimed my precious Aunt Charlene. In December of the same year, another cruel blow—my beloved daddy. *Oh my.* I wondered if I'd make it through. At times, the grief overwhelmed me.

Honestly, on certain days—especially late at night when the house is quiet and the coyotes' cries carry on the wind—I still feel that way.

Grief is like that. Given enough leeway, when wave after wave of horrid events come, it washes over you like the tsunami it is and threatens to drown you.

There's no magic pill, no perfect potion, no fantastical daydream to make it go away.

The only way to navigate grief, is to put mental oars to water and row through it. As a former social worker, I know this.

It's uncomfortable. It makes others uncomfortable, too.

Because we're a live-in-the-moment society

accustomed to quick fixes and feel goods, grief is, understandably, an unpleasant topic.

Rather than allowing folks to mourn according to their own timetable, we expect hurt to instantaneously evaporate.

But—again—another truth.

Placing expectations on the grief-stricken is unrealistic.

For those who haven't treaded sorrow's dark waters, I understand.

Inexperience in such matters doesn't easily lend itself to empathy. It's human nature to shy away from life's chaos. It hurts.

Extending latitude and grace on both sides—to the unaffected and the hurting—is a delicate balance. We may not know what to say or how to react, but listening gives wings to healing.

We can't reclaim what was lost. We *can* seek hope in good things ahead. This is my daily mantra.

Still, this season sucker punched me. It made me a bit—dare I say it—jaded.

And oh, how I regret that. I miss the old Cindy. I pray that one day I'll find her again. New and improved, and healed to some degree, but always mindful of the beautiful souls here no more, the essence of their being forever imprinted on my spirit. I want to make them proud.

Let it be so, dear God.

It's been said that perspective is everything.

To give you some background, for nine months, due to COVID lockdown and restrictions in Daddy's care facility, I was unable to hold, touch, or kiss my father. For a brief time, staff allowed socially distanced, outdoor visits, but then, as COVID worsened, those eventually stopped. Window visits became the norm.

Those were happy days. Poignant days. Mediocre days. Days I railed against the travesty of it all.

In this author note, I won't visit the abyss that is our long-term care facility crisis. Suffice it to say, what our nation has witnessed in this arena is abhorrent. It should inspire a complete overhaul of a faulty, archaic system where accountability is at the forefront instead of mentioned as an afterthought.

But I digress.

Blessedly, despite Alzheimer's firm grasp, Daddy still recognized Mama, my sister, and me. Though window visits weren't ideal, for obvious reasons, we treasured each glimpse, each wave, and each conversation with Daddy—muted though it was because of the glass.

When we were notified by my father's care facility that Daddy had tested positive for COVID, my heart dropped.

I knew. I knew he'd weaken quickly. I knew he'd never be the same. I knew the probability of what would happen.

Fast forward about ten days.

The probability became reality.

My world collapsed.

Before my father died, a nurse held the phone to Daddy's ear so I could utter words that no child, no matter her age, can ever envision saying. I said a final goodbye.

"I love you, Daddy. I love you."

In a half-crazed haze, I repeated it dozens of times. Over and over and over. On a phone. With my heart in my throat. Without my arms around him.

This is my last memory spent with my father—the one who, other than God, was my first love. My biggest cheerleader. *My hero.*

And life meandered on.

I knew it must…because as a contracted author, I had a deadline to meet.

And so, during this whole, horrendous time, I wrote to deadline.

The day Daddy died (I still can hardly say the word), I think I cranked out one of my best chapters ever. I'm not sure how or why—but I have my suspicions.

Thank God, my editor extended my manuscript's due date, to which I'll always be grateful. When I hit SEND on book three in the Welcome to Ruby series, I literally curled up in a fetal position and bawled.

This book was the bane. So awful, in fact, I dreaded hearing from my editor.

As each day slid by, I imagined the worst.

One week. Two weeks. Three weeks. Almost four.

And then, *ping.* She e-mailed me.

My heart pounded.

"I seriously loved this book. I gave a happy sigh several times. I LOVED the parts about Clinton…"

My favorite part of my editor's e-mail though?

"You've nailed this one big time!!"

Huh?

This, my friends, is *the book.* The one I finished as my precious daddy lay dying from COVID.

It gutted me. It sapped my energy and depleted my emotional reserves.

Would you like to know the ultimate irony?

The *title* of this book? The one I had for well over a year? The *book* that was supposed to be book # 2 in my series, but in her divine wisdom, my editor suggested it as book # 3 because it worked best in that order? The *book* I started long before COVID and sickness and this gut-wrenching season?

Her Faith Restored.

Yep. Can you believe it?

I have to tell you, the joke's on me. Because somewhere in this labor-intensive process, I had to rely on the Holy Spirit to intercede for me. I couldn't even pray. *That's* what COVID stole from me. Thank God, He redeems beauty from ashes because about the middle of this book, that's all I had left.

When I shared the essence of my editor's e-mail with my mama, she cried.

Ohh, sweet Jesus!

The days are still tough, but I cling to this. Daddy's words, biased though they may be, bolster my deflated spirit. "Hey, Hollywood, I believe in you. You're going to hit."

Oh, Daddy. I'm not sure that'll happen, but without your encouragement, I would never have written this series, much less finished this book.

Somehow, I have to believe it's meant to be. Maybe someone, or lots of someones, will read it.

And maybe, just maybe, this heartwarming story will encourage others who've lost so much but found redemption in the ashes.

God bless you, dearheart.

About the Author

As an avid encourager and lover of the underdog, Cynthia writes Heartfelt, Homespun Fiction from the beautiful Ozark Mountains.

"Cindy" has a degree in psychology and a background in social work. She is a member of ACFW, ACFW MozArks, and RWA. She is a 2020 Selah Award Winner, a 2020 Selah Award Double-Finalist, a 2017 ACFW Genesis Finalist, a 2016 ACFW Genesis Double-Finalist, and a 2015 ACFW First Impressions Winner. Her work is represented by Sarah Freese @ WordServe Literary.

Besides writing, Cindy has a fondness for gingerbread men, miniature teapots, and all things apple. She also adores a great cup of coffee and she never met a sticky note she didn't like.

Cindy loves to connect with friends at the following places:

Her online home: authorcynthiaherron.com
Twitter: twitter.com/C_Herronauthor
Facebook: www.facebook.com/AuthorCynthiaHerron
Facebook Readers' Group:
www.facebook.com/groups/195462117765130
Instagram: www.instagram.com/authorcynthiaherron
Pinterest: www.pinterest.com/cynthia_herron
Sign up for her monthly e-NEWSLETTER at:
authorcynthiaherron.com

Welcome to the family!

If you enjoyed **Her Faith Restored**, please take a minute or two and post a review. A book review needn't be a long, drawn-out missive. Without revealing spoilers, simply sharing a few thoughts why you enjoyed the book and why you'd recommend it to others is such a blessing to authors *and* readers. Thank you so much for your support!

His Heart Renewed...coming in 2023!

CPSIA information can be obtained
at www.ICGtesting.com
Printed in the USA
BVHW070409161221
624023BV00011B/1062